A RELAXING STROLL—
AND A SHOCKING DISCOVERY . . .

He moved down the path a few feet and slid down the bank to the water, easing himself into its icy grip. He took a deep breath and walked slowly through the thigh-deep water. His heart hammered dangerously in his chest, just the sort of thing Doc warned him about. Stepping cautiously, he tested the rocky bottom with each foot before trusting his weight on it.

She lay facedown with a net of golden hair floating around her. Joan Cavanaugh, still in her evening clothes from last night's party.

Fred stepped back, horrified . . .

MORE MYSTERIES FROM THE
BERKLEY PUBLISHING GROUP . . .

DOG LOVERS' MYSTERIES STARRING HOLLY WINTER: With her Alaskan malamute Rowdy, Holly dogs the trails of dangerous criminals. "A gifted and original writer." —Carolyn G. Hart

by Susan Conant

A NEW LEASH ON DEATH
DEAD AND DOGGONE

A BITE OF DEATH
PAWS BEFORE DYING

DOG LOVERS' MYSTERIES STARRING JACKIE WALSH: She's starting a new life with her son and an ex–police dog named Jake . . . teaching film classes and solving crimes!

by Melissa Cleary

A TAIL OF TWO MURDERS
DOG COLLAR CRIME
HOUNDED TO DEATH
FIRST PEDIGREE MURDER

SKULL AND DOG BONES
DEAD AND BURIED
THE MALTESE PUPPY

CHARLOTTE GRAHAM MYSTERIES: She's an actress with a flair for dramatics— and an eye for detection. "You'll get hooked on Charlotte Graham!" —*Rave Reviews*

by Stefanie Matteson

MURDER AT THE SPA
MURDER AT TEATIME
MURDER ON THE CLIFF

MURDER ON THE SILK ROAD
MURDER AT THE FALLS
MURDER ON HIGH

BILL HAWLEY UNDERTAKINGS: Meet funeral director Bill Hawley—dead bodies are his business, and sleuthing is his passion . . .

by Leo Axler

FINAL VIEWING
GRAVE MATTERS

DOUBLE PLOT

PEACHES DANN MYSTERIES: Peaches has never had a very good memory. But she's learned to cope with it over the years . . . Fortunately, though, when it comes to murder, this absentminded amateur sleuth doesn't forgive and forget!

by Elizabeth Daniels Squire

WHO KILLED WHAT'S-HER-NAME?
MEMORY CAN BE MURDER

REMEMBER THE ALIBI

HEMLOCK FALLS MYSTERIES: The Quilliam sisters combine their culinary and business skills to run an inn in upstate New York. But when it comes to murder, their talent for detection takes over . . .

by Claudia Bishop

A TASTE FOR MURDER

A DASH OF DEATH

No Place
For Secrets

SHERRY LEWIS

BERKLEY PRIME CRIME, NEW YORK

NO PLACE FOR SECRETS

A Berkley Prime Crime Book / published by arrangement with
the author

PRINTING HISTORY
Berkley Prime Crime edition / July 1995

ISBN: 0-425-14835-1

Berkley Prime Crime Books are published
by The Berkley Publishing Group,
200 Madison Avenue, New York, NY 10016.
The name BERKLEY PRIME CRIME and the BERKLEY PRIME CRIME
design are trademarks belonging to Berkley Publishing Corporation.

PRINTED IN THE UNITED STATES OF AMERICA

10 9 8 7 6 5 4 3 2 1

To my father, Gene E. Lewis,
for all the sleep he's lost worrying about me

and in loving memory of my grandmother,
Edith Alma Casey Lewis

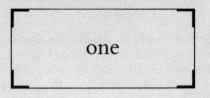

one

Fred Vickery took his morning constitutional at day-
break, just as he had every morning for the past twenty
years. Walking slowly, he admired the hillsides under their
amber canopy of autumn leaves. Fred loved mornings,
especially ones like this, when he couldn't see another
living soul anywhere and the lake seemed even more placid
than usual.

It seemed funny that the lake should be so quiet after the
goings-on at the Cavanaugh place last night. Though Cutler's
population increased every year, parties still weren't every-
day occurrences and there should have been some indication
that one had taken place. Fred thought that the day shouldn't
look so ordinary.

He watched his shadow waver across the ground between
the shade of the trees and tried to ignore the pain in his legs.
They hurt most of the time these days. Not long ago he'd
walked easily, his shadow straight and proud. Now he had
the silhouette of an old man.

Last month Doc Higgins told him he needed to slow
down. Heart trouble, he'd said. He told Fred to avoid
excitement, to eat right, and to cut down on cholesterol
and salt. Worst of all, he told Fred to give up caffeine. Fred
didn't want to listen to Doc. He hated to admit that age had
the jump on him.

He breathed deeply of the brisk mountain air. None of
Doc's remedies would ever make him feel any better than
watching the sun rise over the mountains. No change in his

diet would cure him of his ills like watching the sun paint the sky while he stood on the shores of Spirit Lake.

He followed the same path he took every morning—around the south end of the lake to Huggins's place, then back home. Four miles round-trip. If anybody needed to find him, they knew where to look for him.

He slid his hands into his pockets, seeking warmth, and fingered the house key there. Until a month ago he'd never had to carry one. But the day after Doc gave him the grim news about his heart, his daughter, Margaret, had come over while he was out and raided his cupboards. She threw out everything, even his half-gallon of almond toffee crunch ice cream. Of course, he'd bought another one at Lacey's the next morning. And, of course, that made Margaret angry. She called him stubborn. She claimed she had to do things behind his back because he wouldn't follow Doc's instructions.

Fred didn't like making Margaret angry. She'd been more than good to him in the two years since Phoebe died. His sons had all moved away to follow their careers, and only Margaret had stayed in Cutler with her family. She'd never complained when she helped care for Phoebe during the last stages of cancer. And if now she worried about Fred, it just proved what a good daughter she was.

Two or three times every week she came over to check on him. Most of the time she brought the kids, and having them around helped him ignore the real reason for her visits. She cooked a pot roast every Sunday, which gave him leftovers until Wednesday. And he appreciated it. Really. Even though he hated pot roast.

He rounded a bend in the trail, and Spirit Lake spread itself before him. It shimmered in the autumn sun, calm and empty. A gentle mist rose from the water in the half-light of sunrise.

The air felt cool and sassy, just the way he liked it. He'd

seen the lake through every season many times and he liked them all, but he loved autumn best.

He turned his face toward the rising sun and savored it in spite of its weakness. Not much heat burned through the pale sky this time of year, and the little that did lacked strength, a bit like Fred himself. Just a reminder of past days.

He followed the path north again, hurrying past the cabin where the crazy artist lived. Summer Dey. Probably not even her real name.

Just past the Huggins place he turned around and headed back. He caught a glimpse of Doc in the kitchen window, fresh from sleep, his hair in soft spikes around his head. Fred gave him a grudging wave and, with a twinge of jealousy, watched Doc pour his morning coffee.

He'd gone about halfway back home before he saw the body. He'd reached the spot between Huggins's and Summer Dey's properties where the path narrowed and the ground fell away sharply, straight into the water. A pair of small feet lay on the water's surface, exposing only the bare soles. A chokecherry bush, its heavy branches brushing the lake, obscured the rest.

He moved closer to the edge of the path and looked again. Had the feet moved? No, the motion of the water rocked them gently and gave the illusion of movement. He saw the skirt next, wrapped tight around her calves.

He moved down the path a few feet and slid down the bank to the water, easing himself into its icy grip. He took a deep breath and walked slowly through the thigh-deep water. His heart hammered dangerously in his chest, just the sort of thing Doc warned him about. Stepping cautiously, he tested the rocky bottom with each foot before trusting his weight on it.

She lay facedown with a net of golden hair floating around her. Her arms rocked gently in the waves he created while moving toward her, and her skirt, long and black and made of a soft-looking material like Phoebe's best dress, dragged at her legs and hips. Sheer and white, her blouse stuck to the skin on her back. Joan Cavanaugh, still in her evening clothes from last night's party.

He moved more quickly now, wondering if he could help her. Grasping her shoulders, he turned her out of the water. She stared with empty eyes at the sky, her face dark and contorted, her mouth open.

Fred stepped back, horrified. Losing his footing, he plunged into the icy water. He fought to the surface, gasping for breath and taking care not to look at her again.

Until that moment, death hadn't seemed possible, but now reality curled its fingers around his mind and terror clutched at his throat. He tried to cry out, but couldn't force any sound from his lips.

Fighting his way back to the shore, Fred scrambled to dry land and collapsed for a moment. Chilled and gasping for breath, he struggled to calm his breathing, pushing resolutely at the strange sensation in his left arm. Fear gripped him.

What if he died here, cold and wet and only a few feet from . . . her? What if he didn't last long enough to tell someone what he'd found?

With trembling fingers he reached into his front shirt pocket for the small prescription bottle Margaret made him carry. He fumbled with the cap, but his frozen fingers were unable to grasp it. He swore, counted to ten, and tried again. This time the cap budged, and at last he extracted a tablet and placed it under his tongue.

He'd be all right. He just needed another minute or two. As he lay in the dirt, his breathing slowed and his heart stopped hammering at his chest. Feeling stronger, he raised himself, rolled to his knees, and crawled into the bushes, where he was violently sick. He pulled himself to his feet and stumbled down the path toward home.

The air, suddenly frigid, bit at him through his waterlogged clothes. He needed to get home and change out of his clothes, get himself warm and dry before he caught pneumonia or something. Then he'd call Enos.

He got sick again on the way home, but didn't let himself take much time to recuperate. If possible, the air seemed even colder the farther he walked. He thought of the Hendricks boy who'd died last year. Fell asleep in his sleeping bag in wet clothes and was dead by morning. A tragic thing, and it could happen to him if he didn't get inside before his strength gave out.

Once home he fumbled with the key for a full two minutes before his frozen fingers could force it into the lock. Pushing open the kitchen door, he nearly fell over his feet as he rushed toward the wood-burning stove and its lifesaving warmth. Even the rustic smell of the fire seemed to make him stronger.

Stripping off his wet clothes, he dropped them to the floor. He inched closer to the stove, reluctant to leave it even long enough to go in search of warm, dry clothing. At last, warmed slightly, he turned away and padded through the house to his bedroom, where he found clean pants and a shirt. He stuffed his icy feet into thick socks and searched for his other pair of boots in the back of his closet.

Back in the kitchen he dialed the number to the sheriff's office. After eight rings Fred cursed and broke the connection. He couldn't remember the last time Enos had been on the job before ten o'clock. Enos believed that since the population of Cutler hovered right around three thousand, since there had never been a crime wave in the entire county, and since everyone in town knew where to find him any time of the day or night, he didn't need to break his neck getting to work in the morning. Nothing but an excuse for sleeping in if you asked Fred.

He punched the numbers harder when he dialed Enos's home number. Jessica answered on the second ring and had to shout to be heard over the television.

"It's Fred," he said loudly enough to be heard on her end, "where's Enos?"

"Fred? How are you?" Jessica shouted.

"Fine. Where's—"

"You feeling all right these days?"

"I'm feeling fine. Let me talk to Enos—"

"You're taking it easy, aren't you? Don't want you making things harder on Maggie. She has her hands full enough, if you know what I mean."

He knew what she meant. Everybody in town knew what she meant. Margaret's husband had been a bitter disappointment to Fred almost since the day she married him. "Jess, I called to talk to Enos," he said.

"I don't know if he's still here . . . hold on, his truck's in the driveway. Let me see if I can find him. When is Maggie going to Denver again, do you know? I want her to pick up—"

"I don't know. Will you *please* call Enos to the phone?" Fred insisted.

Jessica sniffed. "You got a bee in your bonnet this morning? Hold your horses, I'll get him." She dropped the telephone onto a hard surface somewhere near the television speaker.

After a very long time the receiver skittled across the surface again and Enos's voice boomed across the wire. "You all right, Fred?"

"I'm fine." Why did all his friends think he was having a heart attack every time they spoke to him? "You've got to come over right away."

"Should I bring Doc? What about Maggie?"

"Enos—Joan Cavanaugh's been murdered."

His voice must have dropped because Enos shouted, "What? What did you say? I can't hear you. Dad-blasted television anyway . . . Jess—turn that thing off a minute, will you? I can't hear a . . . Criminy! Now, what was it? What did you say?"

"Joan Cavanaugh's been murdered!" Fred shouted just as the background noise ceased. The words hung between them, echoing in the abrupt silence.

"Are you sure?" Enos demanded.

"Sure as I can be."

"Damn. Where is she?"

"In the lake."

"You sure she's dead?"

"I'm sure."

"What makes you think she was murdered?"

"Are you going to sit there asking me questions or are you going to come over here and let me show you?"

"Don't go getting all riled up. Take it easy and I'll be right there. You sure you're all right? You want me to call Maggie?"

Fred slammed the receiver down on its hook.

Though it seemed longer, it actually took Enos fewer than five minutes to arrive. But then he spent another minute or two digging around in his glove compartment for something before finally grabbing his old black cowboy hat and jamming it over his thinning hair.

Tired of waiting, Fred headed toward the path without a word. He knew Enos had followed by the noises he made as he crashed through the brush. Fred felt better now. His stomach had calmed a little and his heartbeat had just about returned to normal.

He and Enos walked for a few minutes in silence, broken only by the sound of their boots on the path and their jackets rubbing against the foliage. The sun played off the aspen trees, making their leaves look like shiny gold pieces tied to the ends of the branches. The forest whispered in the still air, sharing secrets mankind would never know. When they rounded the turn in the path, Enos stopped cold.

"There," Fred said, pointing with a shaky finger.

"Good billy hell," Enos said softly. He studied the path for several feet in each direction. "Here's where you went in?" he asked when he found Fred's footprints in the dirt. After scrambling down the bank, he inched into the water, then rejoined Fred on the bank after several minutes.

"She didn't slip in here. She must have fallen in somewhere farther up."

"She didn't fall in."

"She could have." Enos fished in his shirt pocket for a piece of gum. Last time Fred heard, it had been three weeks since Enos last had a cigarette. He claimed Jessica made him choose between quitting and sleeping on the hide-a-bed in the family room. He'd been buying a lot of Wrigley's ever since.

Enos folded the gum into his mouth and spoke around it as he led Fred a few feet away from the lake. "I'm going to go call the boys. And we're a lot closer to the road on this side than I thought we'd be when you called. You wait here and I'll bring my truck around so I can give you a lift back home." He gripped Fred's shoulder in a way Fred found reassuring.

Fred watched him walk away, his shoulders slightly hunched, his head bowed beneath his ragged old black hat. At almost fifty, Enos still looked enough like the lovesick young man who'd hung around Margaret for three solid years to warm Fred's heart. Fred still didn't completely understand what happened between those two young people, but since they'd both been married to other people for nearly thirty years, it probably didn't matter anymore. Still, other than his own three boys, Fred had never met a man he liked more than Enos Asay.

His eyes strayed to the lake, where Joan's body still floated on the surface. Looking away, he studied the tops of the pine trees towering above his head, trying to erase the picture of death from his mind. He fought down the bile that rose in his throat when his stomach threatened to revolt again, gasped hungrily at the fresh air, and turned his back on the scene, but he couldn't turn his back on the tragedy.

Enos returned after a few minutes, but half an hour passed before Ivan Neeley and Grady Hatch, Enos's deputies, reached the site, crashing through the brush like a couple of bull moose.

Enos motioned them to a spot on the path that was too far away from Fred for him to hear what they said. They put on solemn faces and glanced occasionally—uneasily—over their shoulders at the lake.

Enos left them to carry out his instructions and rejoined Fred. "You're as white as a sheet. Want me to call Maggie?"

"No. I'm fine."

He hadn't known Joan well. She associated with a different type of people, a flashier social group. Fred had always believed she would have been happier living a simple life—his kind of life—but her husband had other ideas.

Brandon Cavanaugh hadn't fit in since the day he and Joan arrived in Cutler ten years ago. He didn't like Cutler and Cutler didn't like him, and he'd stayed only because Joan insisted. His only interests were in money, power, and social position, and he'd married Joan to get them.

At the sound of footsteps Fred looked behind him, surprised to see Doc Higgins approaching, his old face grim. "Poor woman."

"You've seen her, then?" Fred asked. "How long do you think she's been dead?"

"Can't really say—a few hours, maybe."

"That long?"

"It's hard to tell in these conditions. The water is cold enough to lower the body temperature pretty fast. I'd say she's been in there a couple of hours at least—maybe longer."

Leaving the boys on their own, Enos climbed the bank. "Want to take a guess at the cause of death, Doc?"

"Not yet. Bring her on over to the office and let me run

a few tests. But I'll lay you odds we end up taking her to the county boys. I don't have the equipment they do."

Enos looked back at the lake. "She probably drowned."

With a covert glance at Fred, Doc pulled Enos a few steps away. But it didn't matter whether they spoke in front of him or not, Fred knew Joan hadn't died by drowning.

Suddenly weary, he longed to find a warm place with a comfortable chair and a steaming cup of hot coffee. If only he could find a way to ease the bitter ache in his hands and legs, he'd feel better.

The image of Joan's body kept drifting into his mind. For what must have been the hundredth time that day he fought nausea. Finding her had turned him to putty. Thinking about her kept him that way. And no matter what Enos said, his gut told him something terrible had happened at Spirit Lake.

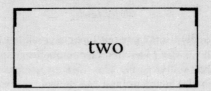

two

Fred climbed into the passenger seat of Enos's truck and took the weight off his tired legs. It felt so good to sit; he didn't mind waiting while Enos gave the boys their last-minute instructions.

He glanced at his watch. Nearly ten o'clock and his stomach ached. He'd finally stopped being sick, but now his stomach grumbled about missing breakfast.

The sun had climbed higher in the sky, but morning shadows still slanted across the road. He leaned his head against the seat back and let the air play across his face. He still felt weak and shaky, but other than that, he'd almost recovered.

Enos pulled himself into the cab of the truck and sighed deeply. He spent a couple of minutes shifting around behind the steering wheel, trying to get comfortable. "The last six months my biggest problem has been deciding where to have coffee in the morning or arguing with Doris Steadman about her barking dog," he said. "Now this."

Now this, as if this tragedy were nothing more than a pesky dog. Fred turned away and closed his eyes. "Who do you think did it?"

"Nobody did it." Enos adjusted his side mirror.

"What are you going to tell Brandon?"

"What is there to tell? Doc didn't determine the cause of death yet, and all I know for sure is that she's dead. I'll go tell him what I know."

Opening one eye, Fred squinted into the reflection of the

morning sunlight off the windshield. Everything he'd ever read about murder cases like this claimed the spouse was usually the guilty party. He tried to picture Brandon Cavanaugh as a murderer and had no trouble succeeding.

"Do you think he did it?" he asked. "The husband's usually the one, you know."

"You'd better not go around pointing fingers at people. There's nothing to say this is a murder."

"Of course it is."

Enos held the ignition switch on too long and the truck scraped as the engine turned over. Tugging at the gearshift, he looked over his shoulder and backed up in a wide semicircle. "I'm taking you to Maggie's so she can keep an eye on you. I don't want you to have any side effects from your excitement this morning."

Fred didn't need to be taken to Margaret's house—or anywhere. He scooted up in his seat a little. "She's not home."

"Where is she? I'll take you to her."

"I don't know. I think she and Webb went to Denver for the weekend."

Enos pulled onto the road too fast. Gravel spit backward from the rear tires. He mumbled something under his breath and sent Fred a harassed look before turning his attention back to the mud-splattered windshield.

They sped up Grand County Road to where it connected with the highway, and Enos made the turn, barely bothering to check for oncoming traffic. "If I take you home, I want you to promise me that you'll rest. I don't want you to do anything."

"I won't do any more than I have to."

"That's no promise." Enos frowned at him. "I want you to lie down and take it easy."

"Sure."

With that, Enos's face relaxed. The worry lines smoothed out, and he took on a more youthful appearance.

Fred almost hated to spoil it. "Cold today, isn't it?" Enos nodded and murmured his agreement. "Guess I'll just build the fire up a bit before I lie down. I got a little chill there in the lake this morning." Fred waited for a few seconds and stole a look at his companion to see his reaction. Nothing.

"I wonder if I have enough firewood in the house. Well, no matter. If I don't, I'll just bring in enough for a day—maybe two."

Enos shifted gears and settled in for the short drive back to town. "I'll bring in your firewood for you. You need your rest."

Fred waved away his suggestion. "I'm all right. Almost back to normal now. Besides, I've got my pills and you've got to get yourself up to Cavanaugh's. You can't be carrying firewood when Brandon probably has no idea his wife's dead." They rounded Kilburn's hill. The intersection with Highway 134 lay just four miles ahead. "I guess it would save you some time if I just rode on up to Cavanaugh's with you."

"I'm not taking you with me on official business, Fred. Especially this."

The intersection approached too rapidly. Enos must be speeding, Fred thought. "Well, you're probably right. Even if I just stayed in the truck, I guess it wouldn't do to have me along."

"No, it wouldn't."

"And I guess it *would* be best for me to go home and lie down. Quiet, that's what I need. Somebody can just look in on me tomorrow." He nodded solemnly. "Guess you don't think you need to have me there—since I found her and all."

"No, I don't think so."

Fred forced a deep sigh and leaned his head back against the seat. Enos spared him a worried glance that Fred pretended not to notice. Lifting his hand, he placed it on his chest. "Do you know Cavanaugh's number off the top of your head? In case I need to reach you or something? No, never mind. I'll be all right. It'll be much better for me to go home alone than to wait in the truck for you. . . ."

Enos took his eyes off the road for a second, long enough for Fred to see that he looked nervous. Inching his way up in the seat, Fred was careful not to look directly at the younger man. "I guess I could always call Jessica if I need to. She's home, isn't she?"

Enos licked his lips and shook his head. "Committee meeting in Granby. What about Maggie's kids? Aren't they home? Can't Sarah drive by now?"

"Sure. Sarah can drive, but I don't think they're home. No, I'm sure Margaret said they were taking the kids with them." Fred slowly rubbed his chest.

The truck lost speed. After a long silence Enos asked, "If I took you with me, you'd stay in the truck?"

"Of course."

"After that we'll take you to Doc's and have him look you over."

Fred had been looked over by Doc enough times in the last six months to last him the rest of his life. He pointed through the windshield to the intersection just a few feet ahead. "Turn left up here."

Enos shifted his eyes from the road, and Fred saw the question there. He looked away and Enos, apparently satisfied, turned left onto Highway 134.

After nearly fifteen minutes Enos turned off on the gravel drive that wound through the trees toward Cavanaugh's house. Pebbles popped under the tires as they wound through a thick stand of lodgepole pine. The house stood well back from the highway, hidden by the forest. The drive seemed to take forever, but at last the house stood before them, elegant in its simplicity. Too large for Fred's taste, but splendidly built. It grew out of the mountain as if it had been carved there. A full brace of windows running three stories high along the entire face of the house mirrored the forest, the lake, and the sky, giving the illusion that the house had been placed against the granite outcropping by Mother Nature herself.

Fred thought back to when the Cavanaughs first purchased the property and talked about building. Many of Cutler's residents had been worried that they would erect something inappropriate, something large and modern, built of brick or covered with aluminum siding. Members of the Cutler City Council had scurried about for weeks trying to pass zoning restrictions. At the eleventh hour Joan Cavanaugh arrived unannounced at a late-night meeting, blueprints under her arm and a sketch of the house in hand. Her gracious style and easygoing manner had broken the tension and earned her a place in the hearts of many Cutler residents.

Now she was dead and Fred wanted to know why.

The drive widened into a parking area large enough for several cars. Brandon Cavanaugh's silver BMW sat close to the house. Joan's Chevy 4x4 was nowhere to be seen. That seemed odd, since Fred didn't remember seeing it anywhere near the lake.

Enos pulled in next to the BMW. Reaching above his head, he flipped quickly through a stack of envelopes tucked into his sun visor, his face solemn.

Fred stretched his arm across the back of the seat. "Looking for something?"

Enos shook his head and pushed open the door. "Wait here," he said as he climbed out of the truck.

"You sure you don't want me to go in with you?"

With a glare, Enos jammed his hat farther down on his forehead. "No, I don't."

"All right, then. But if you need me . . ." Fred rolled down his window and stared at the BMW. Enos made a rude noise, which Fred chose to ignore. Nearly fifty years old and still acting like a kid. "I was just offering."

"Thanks." He sounded sarcastic. "Honk the horn if you

get to feeling bad." Walking away from the truck, Enos stuffed his shirttail back into his pants, readjusted his hat, and nudged his sunglasses up on the bridge of his nose. If he took any longer getting himself inside, Brandon would come out here to see what he needed.

Fred pulled down the sun visor and squinted into the sun. "Well, go on."

"Stay here."

Well, of course he'd stay here. He'd promised, hadn't he? Just because a fellow showed a little concern, he got treated like a criminal. He never once *said* he wanted to go inside, did he? But maybe if he could hear how Brandon reacted to the news, it would help him feel better. Goodness knows, he didn't want to suspect Brandon Cavanaugh of murdering his wife.

Settling deeper in the seat, he leaned his head back. From where he sat, he had a view of the front of the house looking out over the lake. Phoebe would have hated this house. Too much glass. Too many windows. And the kids—what did you do with kids in a house like that? There'd be finger-prints everywhere.

A curtain twitched slightly on the second story. Not the natural sort of movement you'd associate with an open window and a breeze, but more like someone watching and wanting to stay out of sight. But who would want to watch him sitting out here in this old truck?

Lowering his eyes, he pretended to rest, but he watched Enos cross the gravel and climb the three steps to the front deck. At the door Enos glanced back over his shoulder, checking on Fred to make sure he was behaving.

Fred turned away and let the cool breeze stream across his face. He savored the sensation of crisp air against warm skin and the almost vanilla smell of the pine forest. He loved this country.

Enos pounded on the front door until the sound of his fist against the wood reverberated through the air. After the second knock Fred turned back so he could see the house. Enos knocked a third time and waited.

He glanced over at Fred, still checking. Fred raised his hand in a reassuring wave. Enos walked a few steps away from the door and tried to see in one of the windows. From where Fred sat, it didn't look like anybody was home, except that curtain on the second floor. Something about this didn't feel quite right.

Enos walked back to the entrance and raised his fist to knock again when the heavy front door finally swung open. Fred couldn't see the door or inside the house, but the low rumble of voices carried across the still air. After a minute Enos removed his old black hat and stepped inside. The door closed behind him.

Even with the stillness of the air and the peaceful forest sounds surrounding him, Fred couldn't shake the funny feeling he had. He let three minutes pass—by his watch— before pushing open the truck door. Without moving his head, he shifted his eyes to the second floor of the house. The curtain didn't move. Whether or not he was being watched, now was the time to make his move.

After hopping out of the truck, he shifted from foot to foot impatiently, just in case he still had an audience. He hesitated for effect, then walked quickly toward the front door, hoping he looked anxious enough to be convincing.

He had to wait only a moment before a tall man in his late twenties opened the door. Tony Striker, Brandon Cavanaugh's cousin, stood in the open doorway. Though he didn't know Tony well, Fred liked him a little better than he liked Brandon.

"Mr. Vickery?" Tony's voice betrayed surprise.

Fred gave him his best smile. "Tony." He tried to look nervous and uncomfortable—even desperate. "I wonder whether I could use your facilities. I'm waiting for the sheriff." He gestured toward Enos's truck.

Tony glanced over Fred's shoulder with a little frown, but

he pushed the door open the rest of the way. "Sure. There's one down here. First door on your right."

As he walked past the stairway that rose out of the foyer to the second floor, Fred listened for the sound of voices. They must be downstairs somewhere—surely they hadn't gone upstairs. He wanted to hear the conversation between Enos and Brandon. Maybe he just wanted to satisfy his curiosity. Maybe he wanted to hear Brandon's reaction to the news. But in either case, he'd have to know where they were if he hoped to hear anything.

He passed an open doorway to a room on his left and heard the muffled sound of subdued voices. He'd found them. Smiling, he hurried on, trying to look preoccupied with his own needs.

Pausing outside the bathroom door, he looked back in the direction he'd come. Tony still stood by the front door, his arms crossed high on his chest. He hadn't moved since he'd let Fred in, and he didn't look as if he intended to move until Fred left again.

He'd hoped he wouldn't have to actually use the bathroom, but there didn't seem any way around it. He sent Tony a reassuring nod, and, surprisingly, the other man left his post.

Not willing to take any chances, Fred locked the bathroom door. He used the toilet and washed his hands. With the water running he pulled open the medicine cabinet above the sink. Empty. Obviously nothing more than a guest bathroom. Phoebe'd always said you could tell a lot about a person from the contents of his medicine cabinet, and it might be true—if you were lucky enough to get the right bathroom and if you knew what you were looking for.

He shut off the water and put his ear to the door for a moment before he unlocked it quietly and pulled it open. Carefully he eased into the still-unoccupied hallway.

He looked around, amazed as always at the size of the house. The entry hall was easily as big as Fred's own living room and his kitchen, large enough for several groupings of chairs and tables on either side. Evidence of the party they'd had last night remained scattered about. Full ashtrays lay on the tables, and several tall fluted glasses with varying levels of liquid had been abandoned in unlikely places.

The glasses bothered him. He lifted one and frowned at the ring it left on the wood. Joan must have left the house before the party was over, or surely she would have cleared away the mess.

He could hear the conversation in the next room clearly now. He moved closer to the door and held his breath. Enos was speaking.

". . . cause of death hasn't been determined at this time."

Glass clinked. Liquid splashed. Someone spoke. "I appreciate your concern, Enos. I can't tell you how horrible I feel. I think I'm in shock even though I knew it was just a matter of time." Fred recognized Brandon Cavanaugh's voice.

"What do you mean?"

"We were living on a tightrope up here. Nobody could possibly have guessed how it was the last few months—" The voice broke off, choked with sobs.

Tony interrupted. "Don't, Brandon. It's not your fault. You did everything you could."

A pause followed before Enos spoke again. "When was the last time you saw your wife?"

"Late last night—or I should say early this morning. We had . . . guests. You can probably tell just looking at the place."

"And what time would that have been?"

"Dinner was at seven. . . ."

"I meant what time did you see Joan last?"

A pause. A deep sigh. "One o'clock, maybe. I don't know. We came down to greet the guests together, and she seemed fine at first . . . happy and smiling. But even before dinner was served, she snapped. You never knew what was going to set her off. What was fine with her one day would send her over the edge the next. She moped around here for a while after dinner, and then she finally disappeared. I'm afraid I've become so used to her irrational behavior, it never dawned on me she'd actually do something this time."

Irrational behavior? Fred had never known Joan to act irrationally a day in her life.

"What do you mean 'this time'?" Enos asked.

Silence. Someone set a hard object on a table. "You might as well know. Joan threatened suicide several times over the past few years. We didn't talk about it outside the family. We tried to keep it quiet for her sake, especially since she always snapped out of it. I didn't think she was any worse than normal last night. And I *never* thought she'd actually kill herself."

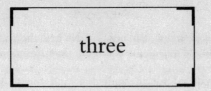

three

Fred bit back the protest that rose in his throat, but for a moment he feared he'd given himself away. Suicide? Ridiculous! You only had to take one look at Joan to know she hadn't done this to herself, even if she'd been the irrational sort of woman Brandon described.

After a moment of stunned silence inside the living room, Brandon's voice rose again. "I feel so guilty. I stopped listening to her, I'm afraid. But I'd heard it all so often. She struggled with a lot of things, I guess, and I finally decided a few months ago the whole suicide thing was a ploy for attention . . . sympathy." He paused, sniffled. Someone murmured something.

Well, if that didn't beat all. Surely Enos didn't believe this bunch of garbage. Fred inched his way closer to the door until he could see into the room with one eye.

Brandon, tall and dark and still wearing his trousers and shirt from the night before—they looked as if they'd been slept in—stood before a large plate-glass window, his head down. A dozen feet behind him Enos watched, hat in hand.

Against the far wall beside the fireplace, Tony rested one arm on the mantel. As Fred watched, Tony left his niche and walked toward Brandon. He put an arm around Brandon's shoulders and shook him ever so slightly, as if urging him to hold up under the strain.

Tony pulled a small brown bottle from his pants pocket and looked at it for a moment without speaking. "I guess there's no reason to hide this any longer. I didn't want to

worry you, Brandon. But now—" He held the bottle toward
Enos. "I found this on the bathroom floor this morning . . .
empty."

Enos reached for it, studied it, and finally looked up
again, a question written on his face.

"Her sleeping pills," Tony said quietly.

Brandon sagged visibly and murmured something under
his breath that Fred couldn't catch. Tony bolstered him
again. "This is very difficult for us, Sheriff. Would you mind
saving your questions until later?"

"Just one or two more for today. The rest can wait. What
was Joan upset about?"

Brandon shook his head. "She wouldn't talk to me about
it. I never knew if she was upset with me or with somebody
else."

Tony interrupted. "Like Brandon said, anything could set
her off."

"There must have been something. Money, health . . ."

"Not that I know of," Tony said quickly. He looked down
at Brandon and back at Enos. "I really think Brandon's had
enough, Sheriff. He's terribly upset already, and we still
have to tell Madison about her mother."

"I think that'll be it for now. If you think of anything, give
me a call." Enos took a step toward the door, then paused.
"I ought to let you know, Brandon, the county coroner will
insist on doing an autopsy."

Both heads jerked up, but Tony spoke first. "An autopsy?
Why?"

"It's routine in cases like this where there's no obvious
cause of death. That and your belief that she may have
committed suicide . . ."

"I don't think that's a good idea. Don't authorize it,
Brandon. This is going to be difficult enough on everybody
without adding an autopsy on top of it."

Enos settled his hat on his head. "You don't have a
choice, Tony. It's required in all cases of suspected suicide.

You may want to arrange for a memorial service to take place before the results come back, since they can take anywhere from ten days to two weeks."

Brandon looked surprised. "Two weeks?"

"But the pills . . ." Tony protested. "Surely—"

"Like I said, it's routine. And it can easily take that long to run all the tests, especially where there are no marks or . . . anything. An empty bottle doesn't prove she actually took the pills. But if she did and then wandered into the lake, it'll show up. Until then you ought to think about making arrangements for the memorial service. You won't want to wait for the—for her to be released before you hold the funeral."

Brandon shook his head and crossed to a small bar against the back wall. Fumbling with a decanter, he poured a heavy-handed shot of whiskey into a thick glass.

"Do you need help contacting her family?" Enos asked.

Brandon shook his head and lifted the glass to his lips. "She didn't have much family. Both her parents are dead." Brandon hesitated and Tony stepped in.

"Her sister's the only one we need to find, but I'll call her. No need for you to worry about that."

Sister? In ten years Fred had never heard anything about a sister. Wouldn't he have known if Joan had a sister? She'd never come to visit. In fact, now that he thought about it, Joan never had anyone to visit. If she had, he would have known about it.

He thought of his kids—so close, all of them. If one of them died, the others would be devastated. His insides twisted in sympathy for Joan's sister. With no other family to lean on, she would have a hard time.

Enos looked puzzled. "Can I . . . ?"

Tony adjusted his collar and smiled. He was a taller, darker, handsomer version of Brandon. Just now, the way he looked at Enos, the way he smiled, Fred saw a family resemblance he had never noticed before. They both had the same thick, black eyebrows set above narrow, dark eyes and the same wide, too-white smile. But where Tony's features were almost sharp, Brandon's had been softened around the edges.

Tony waved away Enos's words. "No problem. She's with some advertising firm in San Francisco. She and Joan lost touch years ago, but I'm sure we can find her. If we have any trouble, we'll let you know. Look, I've got to go check on the old man. Are you going to be all right, Brandon?"

Fred bit back an exclamation of dismay.

Brandon nodded and waved him away, but Enos turned, his face furrowed by a scowl. "Old man?"

As Fred backed quickly away from the door, Tony's voice grew louder. "Yeah. He came in to use the bathroom, and I haven't seen him come out. Didn't I hear he had a heart attack or something a little while ago? I wouldn't want him to keel over in there."

Fred turned and nearly ran back toward the bathroom, but only managed to reach the stairway as Tony rounded the corner. Immediately Fred strode forward trying to achieve a relieved look and steady breathing. "There you are! I wanted to thank you. You don't know how desperate things can get when you reach my age."

Enos appeared behind Tony, his face rigid with disapproval. Fred tried his best to look apologetic. "It was an emergency. Couldn't wait." He lowered his voice. "Prostate trouble."

Tony turned away, fighting a smile, and Fred, warming to his part, turned on him angrily. "Don't you laugh, young man. It'll happen to you one day. I read somewhere that every man will have trouble that way, if he lives long enough—"

Just as he got going, Enos stepped forward and grabbed him by the arm, a little too roughly, but Fred didn't mind. The end justified the means.

Keeping a firm grip on Fred's arm, Enos apologized to Tony. He didn't loosen it as he shook hands with Brandon, who lounged against the door of the living room, drink in hand, or as he ushered Fred outside.

He pulled Fred all the way to the truck and locked him in, then stormed around to the driver's side and settled himself behind the steering wheel. "What in the . . ." he began, then shook his head.

Pulling angrily at the gearshift, Enos jammed the truck into reverse and backed up too quickly. "Prostate trouble, Fred?"

"I'm an old man."

"You promised me you'd stay in the truck."

"I didn't have much choice. It got to be very uncomfortable. I don't have the control I used to have."

"I don't want to hear about it."

"Well, you don't think I went in there on purpose, do you? I used the bathroom—that's why I went in."

Enos stared at him as if trying to decide whether to believe him. Finally he shook his head and threw the truck into drive. "How much did you hear?"

"About what?"

"Come on—how much did you hear?"

Fred studied Enos for a moment, sizing up his options. He didn't want to actually *lie* to Enos, they'd been friends too long. "I heard enough. Too much. You don't believe him, do you?"

"I'll wait to see what the coroner has to say."

Fred snorted.

"The way I see it, there're two possibilities—accident or suicide."

"You're leaving one out."

Enos shot him a quick glance. "Don't you even *hint* at that to anybody but me."

"What are you going to do—ignore it?"

"No comment."

"You don't believe all that stuff about the sleeping pills, do you? Even if Lydel finds traces of the pills in her system, it doesn't mean she took them willingly. Somebody could have forced them on her."

Enos's voice took on a pained quality, an edge that Fred knew spelled exasperation. "That's exactly why I wanted you to stay in the truck. You heard one thing—that you weren't supposed to hear in the first place—and your imagination's getting away from you. Why can't you just admit that it's possible—no, it's probable—that Joan Cavanaugh died exactly the way her husband says she did."

"Because she didn't."

As they reached the highway, Enos brought the truck to a complete stop. He shifted into park and turned in his seat to face Fred.

"I don't like what you pulled up there. I just want you to know that. You're up to something and I don't like that, either. I'm warning you right now that you'd better leave this whole thing alone."

"Don't get all excited, Enos. All I did was go to the bathroom."

"I mean it! I'm not warning you as a friend. You keep your nose out of it."

Enos had become entirely too excitable since he stopped smoking. Fred only wanted to clear up a detail or two, get things straight in his own mind. After all, it wasn't his fault he'd been dragged into this business. He hadn't *asked* to stumble across a dead body when he set out on his walk this morning. But he had, and now he couldn't get the picture of Joan's lifeless body out of his head. So what did Enos expect him to do? Go home and watch the television and pretend it never happened?

Enos's stony face answered the question for him. He waited, tapping his fingers against the steering wheel.

Fred smiled. "I won't get in your way," he said in his most reassuring voice. But this time the lines on Enos's face didn't ease as he put the truck into gear and pulled onto the highway.

Leaning back against the headrest, Fred watched the trees blur. Enos worried him. He'd get old before his time if he didn't learn to relax.

He watched the lake in the distance, shimmering under the pale sun, and thought of Joan. He pictured her body floating on the lake's surface this morning, her face when he turned her body over. Suicide? A chill ran down his spine as if someone had dragged an icy finger along it. He'd never believe that poor woman killed herself. No matter what Enos said or what Brandon Cavanaugh tried to make them believe, there could be only one explanation.

Murder.

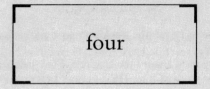

four

Fred dug through the plastic sacks, searching in vain for a few slices of bread. He probably ought to find something else for dinner, but nothing sounded as appetizing as bread and milk.

Since it was only a little past seven, he had plenty of time to walk to Lacey's before it closed. After shrugging into his coat, he pulled the door closed behind him and locked it.

He pulled the collar to his ears and crossed the street. Leaves propelled by the rising wind scuttled across the road, and all around him trees moved, their heavy branches sighing in protest. Somewhere in the distance a door slammed and a dog barked.

Fred crossed the street as quickly as he could, but the changing seasons always aggravated his arthritis, and his legs, still suffering from his plunge into the icy lake, complained against rapid movement. He hadn't slept well the last couple of nights. He'd dozed off for an hour or two and then suddenly found himself wide awake. So tonight he felt bone tired and gritty-eyed, but strangely exhilarated. He hadn't been able to rid himself of the strange feeling of apprehension that had plagued him since he'd found Joan, and it affected him in unexpected ways.

Even his neighborhood felt different to him—as if Cutler had lost its innocence. Someone had committed murder less than a mile away, and Fred wondered whether he'd ever feel the same again.

When rapid footsteps sounded behind him, Fred turned a

little too quickly for comfort, not certain just who he expected to see. Shadows, which grew out over the shoulder of the road, blocked his view. Stepping into the cover of darkness, he peered into the night. "Who's that?"

A muffled gasp sounded before the Kirkham boy stepped into the moonlight. "Just us, Mr. Vickery."

Not any older than about ten, he had his little sister by the hand, and she was still a baby in Fred's book. In the dark, with their wide eyes and round faces, they looked even younger than usual.

Feeling a little foolish for letting them startle him, Fred stepped out of the shadows. "What on earth are you doing out alone this time of night?"

"Mom had to work late, so we had dinner at the Jacksons'."

The Jacksons? Gracious sakes, they lived clear on the other side of town. "And they let you walk home alone?"

"It's okay. We do it all the time."

Maybe so, but not tonight. It was far too late for anyone's children to be wandering the streets on their own. Even in Cutler.

Pulling his coat tighter around his neck, Fred jerked his head toward the street. "I'm going right by your house. I'll walk up that way with you."

The little girl brightened considerably, and even the boy looked relieved in spite of himself. Giving the boy's shoulder a pat, Fred stepped onto the street and began to whistle. The Kirkhams lived just a few blocks away, and the detour wouldn't really take him far out of his way.

In fact, he'd be just around the corner from the sheriff's office. Twice lately he'd noticed the lights on and Enos's battered old Ford parked outside late at night—much later than Enos usually stayed. Usually Enos had eaten dinner and parked himself in his easy chair by this time of night.

Fred walked slowly, giving the little girl a chance to keep up, but when even the easy pace seemed too much for her,

Fred took her other hand in his. Maybe he ought to take a minute to look in on Enos after he got the kids safely home. If Enos had broken routine and stayed late, there could be only one reason: Joan Cavanaugh's death.

When they reached the Kirkhams' big, ugly cabin, Fred watched as the kids scampered up their drive and into the house. He waited until Loralee waved from the window before he headed toward Main Street.

But when he got there, he hesitated on the corner and studied the sheriff's office. Just as they had the last few nights, lights shone from the windows, and Enos's truck held its spot on the gravel on the street. But maybe Enos didn't want company. Maybe he wanted to be left alone, and if Fred disturbed him, he might get angry.

Fred took a few steps away. On the other hand, maybe Enos needed somebody to talk things over with. Maybe he needed somebody to help him clear his mind, somebody to run ideas past. Somebody already familiar with the crime. The least Fred could do was check.

As a matter of fact, while he lay awake last night, a thought had come to him. The perfect solution. And as he tossed and turned, wide-eyed, the idea had taken seed and grown until now it nearly consumed him. He'd thought of little else all day.

It seemed like the perfect plan. If Enos would just deputize him and allow him to work on the investigation, he'd find the proof they needed to investigate Joan's death as a murder. Fred knew everybody in town. He had plenty of time on his hands, and he'd already landed right in the middle of the case through no fault of his own.

And Enos couldn't possibly object. In fact, the pluses far outweighed the minuses. Given a few uninterrupted minutes, Fred knew he could bring Enos around.

Since he already intended to check on Enos, now seemed as good a time as any to bring it up. He'd mention it — that's all—and see how Enos reacted. And if Enos didn't like the idea, at least Fred would know he'd tried.

Climbing the two short steps up the boardwalk, Fred approached the lighted window. Enos hunched over his desk, his face wrinkled with concentration.

He looked up when Fred's boots sounded on the board-walk, smiled, and raised a hand to beckon him inside.

"What the devil are you doing out tonight?" Enos asked as Fred pushed the door closed against the wind. A coffeemaker gurgled as it finished brewing, spilling the earthy aroma into the air.

"Just on my way over to Lacey's. I saw the light and thought I'd see what you're doing here so late."

"Nothing. Thinking. Seems like that's all I've been doing the last couple of days."

"Me, too."

"You feeling any better today?"

"Fine," Fred said with enthusiasm. "Yep, just fine. It was more of a shock than anything." He pulled out one of the battered wooden chairs in front of Enos's desk and lowered himself into it, careful not to groan or do anything that might make Enos question how robust he felt. "I don't know about you, but I'm sure having trouble figuring out why somebody would want to kill her."

Enos closed the open file and placed a stack of papers on top of it. "You don't know that anybody did."

"Well, of course, I can't prove it yet, but I know." When Enos's face darkened, Fred waved away his protests. "Don't worry. I've kept my nose clean, but I can't help thinking—"

"Don't." Enos pushed himself to his feet and moved away from the desk.

Fred crossed one ankle across his knee casually. He craned his neck for a better view of the desk. "What are you working on, anyway?"

In two strides Enos came back to the desk and picked up the file folder. "Official business. Confidential." He shoved it into a desk drawer. "Let's talk about something else, can we?"

"I'm the wrong person for that. You know what I think."

Enos sighed and massaged his face with an open hand, then nodded toward the coffeepot. "Want some?"

"Coffee?"

"Don't act so surprised with me. I know you sneak over to the Bluebird and have a cup whenever you think Doc or Maggie won't notice. Besides, it's decaf."

"I guess so." He'd almost rather not have anything than drink decaf. It didn't seem natural, somehow.

Enos filled his mug and another one for Fred, then dug out two chocolate snack cakes in cellophane wrappers from a box and tossed one to Fred. "I just had an interesting phone call. Joan Cavanaugh's sister."

"Really? They found her, then?"

Enos tore at the wrapper with his teeth and grunted. "Apparently. She's working in San Francisco. She's arranging to get away from work for a few days."

Fred took out his pocketknife and cut a slit in his cellophane wrapper. He took a bite. The thing tasted like cardboard. He washed it down with coffee and set the uneaten remains on Enos's desk. "She's coming here?"

"Sounds like it. She wanted to know if there was a place in town she could get a room. She doesn't want to stay with Brandon. I told her I'd find her someplace, but I don't know where. I can't have her at our place, and Emma Brumbaugh's had the flu all week. There's a few places I *won't* let her stay." He paused, shook his head, and tried to smile. "Hell, I don't have the energy to figure it out tonight. I'll do it tomorrow."

"What did you think of her?"

Enos shrugged. "I don't know. She didn't sound particularly upset, you know?"

"Grief's a strange thing. Individual. Everybody handles it in different ways. I found that out when Phoebe died. All five of us reacted differently. Margaret cried every day for six months. Joseph never shed a tear, but Gail said he was a wreck at work. Nearly lost his job. Jeffrey and Douglas reacted in ways I guess you'd call typical."

"Yeah, well . . ." Enos crammed the rest of the snack cake into his mouth and worked on it thoughtfully. "Seems pretty strange we've never seen her around here, doesn't it?"

It did seem strange. Especially in a place like Cutler, where everyone knew his neighbors and even the neighbors' friends and families. Fred sipped at the coffee and wrapped his hands gratefully around the mug. The warmth soothed his stiff fingers. "I wonder why."

Enos leaned back in his chair and planted his feet on his desk, relaxing slightly. "Different lifestyle, maybe."

"Or trouble of some kind between them." Fred thought of his own children, as he often did. They were spread across the country now, from California to the East Coast. They still saw each other at least every other year, but it wasn't enough for him.

Enos drained his cup and placed it on the desk with a thud. "Don't read something into nothing, Fred."

After placing his own mug on the desk, Fred wiped his palms on his knees. "Listen, Enos, I've been thinking. What you need is someone who can help you out with this case. Full time. Someone whose interests aren't divided . . ."

"No."

". . . You're too busy. You got a whole town to run, and Ivan and Grady, well, they can only do so much. . . ."

"No, Fred."

". . . But if you had somebody who had been in on the case from the beginning, who'd already seen the scene of the crime, who knew his way around town . . ."

"Absolutely not."

". . . and who had contacts all over the county . . ."

"Forget it. There's nothing going on around here that me and two deputies can't handle."

". . . and you're going to need help shaking Cavanaugh's suicide story. Remember, I'm your only witness so far."

"I need somebody to shake you off your crazy murder idea."

Darned fool. He couldn't remember Enos ever being this stubborn before. "You saw her face."

"Yeah, I did," Enos conceded, "but that doesn't give me anything to go on, and you know it. If I had an autopsy report, it might be different, but I don't. Lydel's going to run every test in the book because Doc can't determine cause of death, and there isn't a blamed thing I can do to hurry him up. I'm looking·at ten days—minimum."

"So you're not going to do anything until somebody else gives you permission?"

"Dammit, Fred! What do you want me to do?"

"Conduct a preliminary investigation. Ask around, find out if anybody saw or heard anything. Find out if anybody knows what she was upset about or if anybody else in town thinks she was suicidal—which they won't, I guarantee you."

Enos pushed himself away from the desk and paced heavily. "I can't just run around town doing whatever I feel like. There are procedures, regulations."

"And in the meantime you're letting all your evidence be destroyed." Fred couldn't remember when he'd first noticed these signs of irrational behavior in Enos. Maybe he needed some time off. "You could be out there jogging people's memories."

"I'm doing everything I can right now."

"Then let me do it."

"No."

"I could help you."

"No."

"You could swear me in as a deputy."

Enos pushed his fingers through his sparse hair and turned away. "Absolutely not."

"I could save you a lot of time. I'd concentrate on this one case. You and the boys could just—"

"No!" Enos thundered, and the look on his face convinced Fred further argument would be futile. It must be the nicotine withdrawal that made him this way, Fred thought.

He watched Enos refill his mug and nodded his head when Enos held up the pot with a questioning look. It might not be real coffee, but it felt wonderful going down, and the warmth of the mug made his hands feel better.

They sat in silence, uneasy with each other for the first time in years. Fred felt cheated, empty, as if something had been taken away from him.

He had to find a way to make Enos change his mind. But how? He'd turned a blind eye to the glaring truth, refused to see what seemed so obvious to Fred, and unless he changed his mind, somebody would get away with murder.

If he could only find proof that Joan's death wasn't an accident—wasn't suicide—Enos would have to admit the truth. If only Fred had known Joan better, he'd have an excuse for poking around. If he'd been related to her, Enos wouldn't be able to say a thing.

With that thought he felt a smile tug at his lips. A member of the family—that's what he needed. "Say, Enos, I just had a thought."

Enos looked skeptical.

"I think I know where you can have the sister stay when she comes to town. Let me make a few phone calls. You don't mind if I do *that*, do you?"

"What do you have in mind?"

"I don't want to say anything definite until I've talked with everybody I need to, but I'm pretty sure it'll work out. I'll let you know."

"You're not trying to pull anything, are you?"

"For Pete's sake! I'm just trying to help out. You worry

about important things like catching Joan's murderer, and let me take care of the small stuff like finding her sister a nice, safe place to stay."

Enos looked suspicious.

Fred felt a tiny twinge of guilt, but he pushed it away. He shouldn't have to tell half-truths, and if Enos weren't so dad-blasted stubborn, he wouldn't. Besides, it didn't *really* count as a lie. He'd been up-front from the beginning. If Enos couldn't see the truth, Fred had an obligation as a member of the community to force him to see it. He'd be shirking his responsibility if he did anything less.

And Enos left him with no other choice.

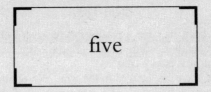

five

At twenty after six, just as Fred put his baked chicken breast in the oven to reheat, the telephone rang. He wiped the telltale evidence of garlic salt off the container labeled "salt substitute" and stuffed it back into the spice cabinet as if he feared Margaret would somehow be able to spot his subterfuge over the telephone.

Instead of Margaret's voice, Enos's boomed into his ear when he answered. "Joan Cavanaugh's sister got in a few minutes ago, and I can't reach Maggie. Do you know where she is?"

"Well, I—"

"I thought one of the boys could run her things over to Maggie's while I talk with her for a minute."

"I didn't exactly—"

"Or maybe I ought to see if Webb's at the Copper Penny. Maybe he could stop by on his way home."

But Fred hadn't made arrangements for Joan's sister to stay with Margaret and Webb. And Webb wouldn't be going home this early in the evening, even if he should. Fred hated anybody to mention Webb's tendency to spend his evenings at the Copper Penny, especially Enos.

He'd never actually *said* he was going to ask Margaret. He'd only said he'd make arrangements. And he had. "I'll be right there."

"No need for you to come out in weather like this. There's a storm coming up—"

"I've lived in Colorado all my life. It's not the first storm

I've ever been in." He replaced the receiver before Enos could say another word, turned off the oven, and zipped himself into his heavy coat.

Outside, the trees swayed in the wind. No doubt about it, a storm would hit soon. His legs never lied. When the barometer dropped, they stiffened and became conductors of the bone-deep pain that plagued him even in the best of times. He pushed his hands into his pockets, trying to cull some warmth from their depths.

Even in the rising storm he walked the two blocks to Main Street in less than five minutes and crossed with the wind at his back. He hurried up the rough wooden steps to the boardwalk and pushed open the door of the sheriff's office.

A woman, no older than thirty, perched uncomfortably on one of the chairs. She looked thin, the way they all wanted to be now, but too thin to Fred's eye.

She glanced up without any real interest when he entered. He'd have known her as Joan Cavanaugh's sister anywhere. Even with the difference in her coloring—as dark as Joan had been fair—and her style—she had her hair chopped off in a boyish cut—the resemblance startled him.

Enos lounged behind his desk, his chair tipped against the wall, his hands on his thighs. He nodded toward the only other chair in the room and Fred took it, grateful for the chance to get off his legs.

"This is Kate Talbot. Joan's sister." He turned to the woman. "Fred's found you a place to stay while you're here."

She refused to meet Fred's gaze. "I'm terribly sorry about your sister," he said, and at last she turned her eyes on him. Hard eyes.

Silence hung on the air for a moment, broken only by the rustling of dead leaves driven by the rising wind along the boardwalk. Given the slightest encouragement, Fred would have offered her comfort, maybe put an arm about her

shoulder. But she had an edge to her, something that held
him back, something that had been missing in Joan, but Joan
had been the better for it.

Enos's face scrunched into concerned creases. "Did
Brandon fill you in on . . . everything?"

"That Joan killed herself? Yes. Only Brandon didn't call
me, his partner did. Tony something, I think."

"Striker," Enos said. "Brandon's cousin."

The family tree could wait. Right now, right up front,
Fred wanted to know where she stood. "You don't believe
Joan killed herself, do you?"

"Fred!" Enos shouted.

She faced Fred almost insolently. "Excuse me?"

"You don't really think Joan killed herself, do you?"

"Shouldn't I?"

"*Should* you?"

Enos lowered his chair to the floor with a bang and
jumped up. "I apologize, Miss Talbot. Fred has an overac-
tive imagination."

"Horse feathers," Fred said. "What do you think? Do you
think Joan killed herself?"

This time Fred thought her eyes held a little less contempt
when she looked at him.

"I really couldn't say. I haven't spoken with her for some
time."

Or maybe he imagined the softening he thought he saw.
A sick feeling began to grow in the pit of his stomach.
Surely she couldn't believe it. He studied her face for some
sign that she at least questioned the suicide theory, but saw
nothing.

Enos pushed his chair back. "Maybe you ought to wait
outside, Fred."

Raising his hand in a gesture of surrender, Fred tried to
look contrite. He'd have to wait until he got her away from
Enos before he could make any progress.

With a little sniff of satisfaction, Enos sat back down and

started playing with his pencil. "How long has it been since you spoke with her?"

"About ten years."

"Why was that?"

"No particular reason. We just drifted apart. People do, you know."

People do. Friends might. Sisters don't. Fred couldn't keep his mouth shut. "You haven't spoken to Joan in ten years?"

She studied him with her hard eyes again, then turned back to Enos. "I don't think that matters."

"Of course it matters," Fred insisted.

Enos's face reddened again. Maybe Doc ought to check his blood pressure.

"It may have some bearing on her state of mind at the time of her death."

"I don't see how," she said coldly.

Fred snorted.

Enos shot him another warning glance. "Then you really don't know whether or not she was suicidal? Or whether she had been depressed or upset about anything recently?"

"No."

"Did she have any history of instability when she was younger?"

"Instability? No."

Fred sighed, nothing more, but Enos pointed at him and nearly spoke. Luckily, Miss Talbot interrupted, giving Fred a reprieve.

"Our family was not a typical one, Sheriff. Our mother died when we were both quite young. Our father was Russell Talbot—perhaps you've heard of him. The Talbot Group kept him extremely busy, both before and after my mother's death. We rarely saw him. Joan and I were quite close as children, but as we grew older things changed. We had different goals. After my father's death I worked in the Talbot Group for a year or two until it dissolved. After that,

I moved on to a profession I found more rewarding, and I've pursued my career with a great deal of success. Joan never wanted any part of that life. The only thing she ever wanted was to create the perfect family—her idea of the perfect family with a mother, father, and two-point-three children. Obviously we had nothing in common, and it should come as no surprise that we drifted apart."

Fred sensed a hint of something he didn't like. A note of disapproval for Joan's choice. A suggestion, unspoken but clear, that Joan's choice had been the lesser choice. That Joan had somehow failed a test with her decisions.

Enos looked a little taken aback by her words, too. "In your opinion, would Joan have been likely to commit suicide?"

She crossed her legs and adjusted her purse on her lap. "How can I answer that? I don't know what she was like before she died."

Enos made a note and looked back up at her, his eyes steady. "I think that's all for tonight, Miss Talbot. Thank you for your time. I would like to talk with you again before you leave town."

She nodded curtly and stood. Fred hadn't expected her to be so tall. Joan had been petite, but Kate stood nearly as tall as Fred himself.

Enos yawned hugely. He looked tired. His body sagged as if he carried a great weight, and dark rims had formed beneath his bloodshot eyes. He massaged his face with an open hand.

"Why don't you go home?" Fred urged.

Enos shook his head. "Can't. Too much to do. I feel better already now that I know she has a place to stay tonight. Maggie didn't have any problem finding the room?"

Fred hesitated, and in that instant Enos's eyes flew to his face.

"You did ask Maggie, didn't you?"

"Well, now, I got to thinking that she's got all those kids at home, and their place is so small . . ."

Enos brought his chair upright sharply. His eyes narrowed distrustfully, but he didn't speak.

". . . and there I am just rattling around in that old house with all that extra room."

Enos made a noise suspiciously like a growl.

"If there's any problem," Miss Talbot said quickly, "I'm sure I can find a room somewhere."

Fred answered her, but his eyes never left Enos's face. "No problem at all. You can stay with me as long as you want. I'll be glad to show you around town . . . take you anywhere you need to go while you're here."

"I don't want to put you out."

"Nonsense," Fred protested. "Got the room all made up for you. Used to be my daughter's. Plenty of privacy, and I'm a pretty good cook if I do say so myself. I'll fix you up a breakfast in the morning you'll never forget."

Enos sent her a weak smile. "Cutler's a small town, Miss Talbot. We don't have a hotel, and I didn't make any other arrangements after Fred said he'd work something out with Maggie." He turned a venomous look on Fred. "If you can put up with the arrangements for one night, I'll work something else out for tomorrow."

She shook her head. "I won't be staying. The only thing I need to do is speak with Joan's banker in the morning. I plan to leave after that."

"What about the funeral?" Fred asked.

"I'm sure Brandon will make adequate funeral arrangements, and I really need to get back to San Francisco. I'm in the middle of an important ad campaign."

More important than her sister's funeral? The more she talked, the less Fred liked her. But he didn't need to like her. He just needed to pull her around to his way of thinking— by tomorrow.

He pushed himself out of his chair, crossed to the door,

and pulled it open for her. She came toward him a little reluctantly. As she drew abreast of him, she looked at him with something like curiosity in her eyes. At least the blatant hostility had vanished for the moment. And even if it came back, he could put up with anything for the sake of the truth. For a while.

Enos watched as Fred led Kate down the steps. "Is that your car?"

She nodded, pointing toward a dark-colored Ford next to Enos's truck. Fred walked around it to the passenger side, but the door was locked, and at that moment Enos called her back.

Fred stood beside the car, chilled and impatient. He rubbed his hand across the back of his neck, but the action only brought more pain to his already inflamed fingers and did little to relieve the problem in his neck.

Enos leaned toward her, his voice low and covered by the wind, making it impossible for Fred to hear what they said. After a minute Enos touched his hand to his chest. Wonderful. He'd tell her about Fred's bad heart. And he'd tell her not to let Fred get excited, not to let him talk about Joan because it would get him riled up and his heart might give out.

Now Fred not only had to get her to talk with him about Joan's death, he had to convince her that she wouldn't kill him by discussing it. Though he didn't know whether or not she'd actually be concerned about that. She didn't seem overly endowed with compassion and warmth.

When the conversation ended, Kate hurried toward the car, her face tightened into a scowl. She gave Fred little more than a glance as she pulled open the door on the driver's side. "Where's your car? I'll follow you."

"I didn't drive."

She didn't look pleased, but she jerked her head at him; an invitation to ride with her.

Inside the car the air felt colder than outside. Their breath became frosted mist when it hit the air. She turned the key in the ignition, and as the engine caught, a blast of cold air from the heating system blew against Fred's legs, sending the dull ache even deeper.

"Which way?"

Fred pointed at the intersection of Main and Lake Front, just a few feet away. "Turn right up there. I'm two blocks down on the west side of the street—by the lake."

In less than two minutes they were home. She didn't look impressed, but Fred loved this house. He loved the rough log exterior, the wide front porch that ran the length of the house, and the deck in back that overlooked the lake.

Even now he could see the lake shimmering through the shadowy trees. It moved with the wind. Small silver waves pushed toward land with little force and ran out of energy as they moved ashore. Each wave melted upon the one before, merging with the sand and rocks in the night.

Fred led her into the house and down the narrow hallway to the bedroom where Margaret had spent her entire childhood and where some signs of her still remained: A Cutler High School bumper sticker on the vanity mirror and the place she'd scratched Webb's name into the wood of her dresser the night he proposed brought the young Margaret back to his memory. He liked this room. It felt good. He looked into it occasionally, when he needed a little something to help him through a long day.

He pushed open the door and stood back to let Kate enter. He expected some recognition of the room's goodness in her earthy brown eyes but received only scorn. Her mouth drooped and her eyes roamed without really touching anything.

"This was my daughter's room," he said, hoping to spark something kinder in her face, but she returned an empty stare and a sullen mouth where her smile should have been.

She looked at him expectantly, as if she wanted him to leave her alone. But that's not how he planned it. He hovered a minute, hoping she would change her mind and join him in the living room. She didn't give an inch.

"Since you're going to be staying here, it'll be easier if you call me Fred . . ."

She didn't respond.

". . . and, of course, I'll just call you Kate?"

She didn't even blink.

He gave up reluctantly. Maybe in the morning she'd be more approachable. She must be tired after her long trip. Maybe she just needed a good night's sleep.

He smiled at her. "Well—good night, Kate."

She turned away from him and closed the door behind her without a word. What a strange woman! he thought. And what an odd, unemotional, almost void reaction to her sister's death. Wouldn't most women weep? Wouldn't most people be angry or grief-stricken? But she showed absolutely no emotion. No matter what he'd said to Enos the other day, he couldn't find justification for her behavior. She showed no more emotion than if she'd heard about the untimely death of a stranger. It didn't seem . . . natural.

Turning away from the door, all at once he realized how tired he felt. The usual aches and pains had returned with force, and he recognized the need to give up the fight for the night. Limping down the hallway to his room, he closed his own door behind him.

He undressed quickly, crawling into the big old bed he'd shared with Phoebe for so many years. Even though she'd been gone two years, he still slept on his own side, and after nearly fifty years of it, he didn't suppose he'd ever change.

He wondered how Brandon Cavanaugh adjusted to sleeping alone. Did he feel as lonely, as inconsolable without his wife as Fred still did?

Stretching under the thick quilts, Fred hoped the warmth from his body would soon permeate the covers. He already knew he wouldn't sleep well in this cold.

He thought about phoning Margaret to see how she was,

just to hear her voice and reassure himself that all was right with her world. But after a glance at the clock he decided to wait until morning. She would call him tomorrow. She always did.

The wind moaned loudly and rustled the trees outside his window. Nature's sounds didn't bother him—he'd slept through everything imaginable in this valley—but beneath the storm another sound reached his ears; a softer sound, but one that didn't belong in his house.

Groaning a little, he threw back the covers and got to his feet. He'd never sleep for wondering what it was. Something he'd left unlatched, maybe, or something one of the grandkids left lying around outside.

Halfway down the hall, outside Margaret's door and bound for the kitchen, he pulled up short. The sound came again, slightly louder now. He stood for a moment, listening, then turned and crept quietly back toward his bedroom.

He fell into bed, pulling the quilt up under his chin. No doubt Phoebe would think him wicked, lying in bed smiling at the sound of another person's grief, but he liked Kate better for the tears, and in them he felt a certain sense of relief. She wasn't the heartless woman she pretended to be, and knowing this, he knew also that he could reach her. Success was within his grasp.

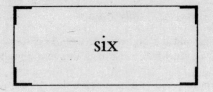

six

Under the pale morning light the lake shimmered. The wind had finally died in the early morning hours, but not before it pushed a cold front into the valley. The temperature must have dropped twenty degrees overnight, but even in this weather Fred loved the morning.

He took his usual path, not from habit this time, but with a definite goal in mind. The sun had tinted everything amber by the time he reached the curve in the path—light enough to see clearly. He looked around cautiously, but could see no sign of anyone else. Carefully he made his way down the embankment. A dozen different sets of footprints marred the earth. If Joan had walked to her death here, he'd never be able to tell.

He climbed back to the path and walked slowly toward Doc's place. Never once, from the moment he found Joan in the lake, had he suspected she'd entered it where he found her. Which meant that her killer must have put her in somewhere else along the shore. The Arkansas River flowed into the lake from the north; the current ran from northwest to southeast. For Joan's body to wash up where it had, she must have been placed in the water somewhere along the west shoreline.

A few houses dotted the shoreline here. Summer Dey owned the stretch farthest south, near the bottom of the lake, almost directly opposite Fred's place. Doc's extended a couple of miles to the north, and even farther north, the Kilburns owned nearly all of the lakefront property between

Doc's place and the highway. It would be slow going for him to cover the whole west bank this morning, but he had to do it.

He spent the next two hours climbing off the path every few dozen feet and inspecting the ground wherever the undergrowth permitted. In two places he found signs of recent activity, but all of the footprints looked much larger than Joan's should have, and none of them had been made by bare feet. It was just as he'd suspected.

A little south of Doc's property line, while still on Summer Dey's place, he scrambled down a gentler slope toward the lake. Expecting to find nothing, he scanned the ground listlessly. Maybe he'd been wrong after all. Or maybe he'd been right, but he'd never find the evidence to prove it.

Even when he actually found what he'd been looking for, it took him a minute to register. Beside the path the undergrowth had been crushed, and where the mud showed through the grass, an occasional footprint, deeper than Fred's own, had frozen into the soil.

He stopped, letting the implications seep into his consciousness for a moment. He walked back toward the path a few feet, scanning more intently than before, but here the undergrowth grew more thickly and the signs weren't as readily apparent to his untrained eye.

Near the lake, where the brush thinned and mud lay in a flat expanse near the shore, he found a clear set of footprints. Three prints close together, the last of which lay partially submerged in the cool blue water of the lake. Someone had moved through this clearing. Someone heavy— or someone with a heavy burden to carry. From the size of the prints, slightly larger than Fred's own, he guessed they'd been made by a man.

Excitement rocked him. He looked around for evidence of another set of prints, a woman's, but he knew they weren't there. Joan was already dead when her killer brought her to the lake, and he'd found the spot where the murderer had put her in the water.

He looked toward the south shore. From this spot he could see the stretch of shore where he'd found Joan's body. As he turned back toward the path, something just under the surface of the water caught his eye. A pen. Shiny and gold, it reflected the sunlight. Reaching into the water, he picked it up and turned it over in his hand. It looked new. Obviously it hadn't been in the water long.

He walked home rapidly, anxious to share this news with Kate. She would have to admit he was right. And so would Enos.

He found Kate awake and sipping a cup of hot coffee in the living room. She looked up with a start when he opened the door. She'd been looking at the pictures that covered the surface of the big old oak table that had belonged to Phoebe's mother. Every year he added new pictures to the clutter, but refused to remove any of the old ones. He just moved them all closer together. His favorites, the old ones where Phoebe was young and the kids were small, stood at the back of the table; a faded history of the people he loved most at various life stages, evidence of time's swift passage.

In the chill from the open door Kate shivered and crossed her arms across her chest.

He pushed the door closed behind him and wiped his feet while he studied her. She wore summer clothes—a flimsy blouse and pants that wouldn't even think of cutting the cold against her legs.

"You're going to need warmer clothes than those. Didn't you bring anything else?" When she shook her head, he added, "I'll find you a sweater to put on. Maybe that'll help."

"Don't bother," she said, but her voice didn't sound as challenging to him this morning.

Ignoring her, he moved stiffly down the hallway to his bedroom. It took only a moment to find Phoebe's sweater.

Kate shook her head when he handed it to her, but he shoved it at her again, and at last she relented and pulled it on over her blouse.

"Hungry?" Fred asked.

"No, not really."

"Well, you've got to eat. Got to keep up your strength."

He led the way into the kitchen, a little surprised that she actually followed him. He dug eggs and bacon from the refrigerator, got out a loaf of bread, and set to work. Scrambled eggs, bacon, fried potatoes, and toast with butter and jam—she'd feel better if she ate well.

He stirred the eggs in the pan and asked casually over his shoulder, "You're still planning to leave town this morning, are you?"

"Yes." The hostility had grown back into her voice.

"Don't you think you ought to stay—at least until the funeral?"

"Why does it concern you so much?"

Fred shrugged and looked back at the pan. What was that saying Sarah brought home from high school a while back? She needed an attitude adjustment.

As if trying to justify her behavior, Kate spoke again. "I have an important presentation at the end of next month. I can't afford to be away from the office for long."

"I see."

She shifted positions behind him. Hoping he'd unsettled her a little, he let her stew for a few minutes before he said, "Well, you're right, I guess. Whatever it is you do, it must be pretty important."

"There's no reason for me to stay."

He waved a spoon at her, dripping egg on the floor. "Other than the funeral, you mean."

"I won't be going to her funeral."

What kind of talk was that? She couldn't refuse to go to her sister's funeral.

He turned to face her again. "You must have a lot of questions about how she died. And why."

When Kate raised her eyes, he saw anger stirring in them. Well, good. He wanted to tap some emotion, and at this point, he didn't care which one. "I don't blame you for wanting to get the answers before you head back." He turned back toward the stove. "No, indeed. I suppose you'll want to look into things. Ask around. Can't blame you, really."

"I don't intend—"

"I guess if it was me, I'd want to understand why everybody thinks she killed herself. Unless you don't really believe Brandon's story about the suicide . . ." He stirred the eggs vigorously. "Can't blame you one bit for raising hell until he gives you the answers."

"Brandon?" Her voice held contempt.

"Sure. I got to thinking last night after you went to bed—maybe I'm just an old fool thinking there's more to the story than he's telling. I don't know why he'd hold anything back. And he's the one who'd know about Joan and what went on before she died—isn't he? If he says she'd threatened suicide before . . ."

"Mr. Vickery—"

"Fred. No, I understand. Absolutely. You're one-hundred percent satisfied Joan killed herself. And maybe you're right."

He risked a glance over his shoulder and caught her staring at him uncertainly.

"You don't believe Brandon's story," she said.

"Well, now, I didn't at first—" He tried not to smile as he turned back to breakfast.

"But you do now?"

"Well . . ."

"Just how well did you know Joan?"

"Fairly well, I guess. Nice lady, I always thought."

"But you don't believe she committed suicide."

He turned down the heat on the stove and crossed the room. "I just don't understand why. It's going to take some convincing to make me believe she had a reason for dying when she had such a good reason for living."

"And what's that?"

"Her daughter."

For one second she showed astonishment, but her mask slipped back into place so quickly Fred wondered if he'd seen her react at all.

She stared at the spatula in his hand as if the universe suddenly centered around it, but he knew she didn't really see it. She pushed her chair away from the table and tried to stand, and in that action she gave herself away.

Fred reached out a hand and placed it over hers on the table. "You didn't know about the child?"

"It doesn't matter."

"Of course it matters!"

"No. Joan had no reason to tell me about it. And anyway, what could I have done about it if I had known?"

"You could have come to be with her when the baby came. Spent holidays. Sent presents."

Rolling her eyes, Kate tried to move away from the table. "Please, spare me the lecture on family relations."

"The little girl is about four years old, I think. Not old enough for school, I know that much. Cute little thing— long blond hair and dark eyes. She looks a lot like her mother."

Kate's eyes flickered toward him uncertainly. Sensing an advantage, he pressed home his point. "She's a sweetheart. Once you see her, you'll—"

"I have no intention of seeing her."

Not see her? What kind of a woman would say a thing like that? "She's your niece. Her name's Madison and she's going to need you now."

Kate pushed away from the table and crossed to the door. "I don't want to see her."

"Sit back down," he grumbled. "Your breakfast's ready." This wasn't going at all well. He didn't even know what to say to her next to keep her from running away.

She ate little, but spent most of the time pushing her food around on her plate. Fred cleared his plate quickly and turned his attention to the table. He stacked dishes, scraped leftovers, and gathered silverware, all the while chafing at her stubbornness, her absolute refusal to budge.

Finally, unable to stand it any longer, he said, "I don't know why you like to pretend you're so heartless. I heard you crying last night, so don't tell me you're not upset. But for some reason you think you've got to sit here today and act like you don't care about either of them. Why do you do that?"

She didn't answer.

"Let me tell you something, young lady. Your sister didn't commit suicide, and I was counting on you to help me prove it. Don't you think you owe her that much?"

Her lip curled. "Tell me why you think I owe her anything at all."

"Because she was your sister. Period. I don't know what happened between you two and I don't care. Whatever it was, it's time for you to put it aside."

"What makes you think she didn't kill herself? Exactly. Tell me exactly and don't play games with me."

"Her face. There was fear in her eyes."

"She might have been afraid when she was too far out in the lake to save herself."

Fred shook his head. "No. This was different. Look, I was in the war, Second World War. I saw a lot of men die and I saw a lot of fear, but this was different. There was something out there I can't describe, a feeling that some-thing was terribly wrong. I went back out there this morning. There's not one place she could have gone into the lake on her own. Do you know what that means? Her footprints aren't anywhere by the lake."

Kate stared at him for a minute. "Are you saying—"

"Yes! It's what I've been trying to tell you all blasted morning!"

"—that you think she was murdered?"

"Yes!"

"That's insane!"

"Why? It's more insane to think she killed herself. Joan wasn't the type just to decide life was difficult this morning and trot off to the lake. I saw her with that little girl of hers many times. She was a good mother, always put her daughter first, and I know she'd never willingly leave her."

Kate dropped into her chair and stared at him. "I don't believe it."

"You can't possibly believe anything else. Let me come with you today. Let me introduce you to a few people in town. You ask *them* if they thought Joan could have done what Brandon says she did. Don't take *my* word for it." He grasped her hand tightly, as if by force of will he could make her agree.

At last, slowly, she nodded her head. "All right. I'll talk to a couple of people. I don't know why I'm even listening to you. I'm probably making a terrible mistake."

Fred lifted her hand to his cheek. It felt cool and soft against his face. "You're not," he assured her.

"One day." She jerked her hand away. "I'll stay one day. That should be long enough to talk to the bank about the provisions of my father's trust and do whatever it is you want me to do. But I'm leaving tomorrow, so don't ask me to stay any longer."

She left him standing alone in the kitchen, aware only that he had twenty-four hours—or less—to prove his case. The task loomed impossibly large before him. Maybe he'd bitten off more than he could chew. Maybe Enos had been right all along and he should stay out of the investigation. Maybe he should just admit right now that he couldn't do it and let Kate drive away after she went to the bank.

Maybe he should think of a contingency plan to keep her in town just in case he couldn't meet the deadline.

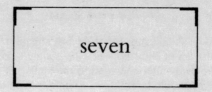

seven

In twenty minutes a relatively healthy person can walk from one end of Cutler's Main Street to the other. Most of the old-timers travel everywhere on foot. The younger generation, those in their thirties and forties, don't walk anywhere.

Fred had known Margaret to drive two blocks to Lacey's General Store for a gallon of milk. Ridiculous. Nothing wrong with her legs. Fred went very few places that required him to get the Buick out of the garage, but he started it three times a week just to keep it running. A visit to Silver City Bank was not one of the places he allowed himself to drive.

He led Kate by the elbow, steering her down Lake Front one block and across Main to the north side of the street. She shivered at his side wearing only Phoebe's old sweater under his fishing coat. Why she came to mountain country without a coat of her own, he couldn't understand. Even in the summer the nights could chill a person to the bone, and by this time of the year even the days turned frigid.

She'd wanted to go to the bank, but she acted put out that Fred made her walk the four blocks from his house. No matter. She'd get over it. After the discussions he'd had on the subject with Margaret, he wouldn't be seen driving no farther than to the bank from his house. Not for anybody.

He didn't look forward to this visit to the bank. He came along only because to stay behind would be unthinkable.

But Silver City Bank meant Logan Ramsey. And Fred didn't get along with Logan Ramsey.

Logan had been a stubborn, petty little boy who grew up to be a greedy, petty man, and Fred had never liked him. Logan had been president of the bank for only five years, and in that short amount of time he'd managed to drive the bank steadily downhill. More than once Fred had considered moving his account to the First National in Granby.

Ramsey hadn't been blessed with the sense God gave a goose. He didn't have one lick of common sense. He'd never shown an interest in anything except making money, and he hadn't even been successful at that. His wife, the spoiled daughter of a wealthy businessman from Denver, had the brains of a goat and the voice of a screech owl. But Ramsey adored her, a trait Fred used on occasion to prove his opinion of Ramsey's mental agility.

Main Street seemed unusually quiet for a Thursday morning. Two cars had been parked in front of Lacey's and three or four clustered around the Bluebird Café at the east end of town, but no one else appeared outside.

Fred glanced at his watch—going on eleven. Half the day wasted, and they were just now heading toward the bank. They could have left the house by nine-thirty if Kate hadn't decided she needed to call her office. Long distance. Then she'd asked him for another two cups of coffee and looked through the yellow pages for a place in town with a fax machine. Then, and only then, he got her out the door.

She pulled her arm out of Fred's grasp and moved slightly ahead. Slow as molasses all morning, and now all of a sudden she wanted to hurry. Fred increased his pace with some effort and caught her just as she reached the bank. He reached in front of her and held the door. It earned him nothing more than a scowl that ended in a look of disdain as she viewed the bank. Two teller windows, a tiny lobby, and a couple of offices at the back, one of which belonged to Logan Ramsey.

Fred waved to Pete Scott's new wife behind the first teller window—he never could remember her first name—and moved to the back of the building. The door to Ramsey's office gaped open, revealing the bank's president behind an ornate desk too large for the tiny room.

Ramsey glanced up as they approached and struggled to his feet. His pink striped shirt stretched tightly across his stomach as he extended a plump hand to Fred and then to Kate before dropping back into his seat. He studiously arranged a small stack of file folders, leaned his elbow on it, and faced them.

Funny that he looked so old. Fred still thought of him as a kid. A pudgy kid with a puffy face who'd turned into a swollen, corpulent man. Ramsey's head, shiny and glistening in the light that spilled over his shoulder from the window, was only saved from complete baldness by a wreath of graying hair and a vague memory there had once been more. He smelled spicy, of recently splashed aftershave so strong Fred's eyes watered.

Ramsey rocked back in his chair and laced thick pink fingers over his stomach. "Well, Fred, this is a surprise. What can I do for you?"

Fred settled himself in one of Ramsey's chairs and nodded to the other one for Kate. "This is Kate Talbot, Joan Cavanaugh's sister. She'd like to ask you a few questions."

Ramsey looked from Fred to Kate, his eyes narrowing slightly. "Oh? What kind of questions?"

Fred opened his mouth to speak, but Kate interrupted. "About my sister—mostly about the state of her affairs when she died."

"Well, I don't know whether—" Ramsey hesitated. "That is . . ." He reached across his stomach, picked up a pencil from the desktop, and placed it behind his ear in a deliberate movement. He spoke slowly. "I hope you'll understand, Miss Talbot, but the choice may not be up to me. There are certain rules I am required to follow. I can't give out information on Joan's financial condition to anyone."

Kate crossed her legs and lowered her purse to the floor beside her chair. She frowned at Ramsey. "I hope *you'll* understand. I'm not asking for specifics, but I am trying to figure out why Joan killed herself. If she was upset about money, I assume you would know that."

Ramsey began shaking his head after her first words and continued as she spoke. "That's not information I can divulge."

Kate's face didn't move, but her voice took on a steely tone. "Mr. Ramsey, my father left a substantial trust set up for Joan and me when he died. Her financial condition at the time of her death may have a direct impact—a substantial impact—on my own finances. If you'd rather, I can contact my attorneys and they can subpoena the information, but . . ." She shrugged almost lazily.

Ramsey settled himself more comfortably on the chair and smiled at Kate. "Well, now, I don't see any reason to go to all that trouble. I'm not trying to be difficult. I just don't want anyone to think I've done something indiscreet. I don't know how much I can tell you. I didn't handle Joan's money directly. She didn't bank with us except one small checking account and a couple of certificates of deposit. I believe she kept most of her money in a bank back East. Boston, maybe."

"Did she have any money trouble when she died?" Fred asked.

Ramsey ignored him, but the way he tightened his jaw slightly told Fred he'd heard the question. He kept his beady little eyes trained on Kate's face.

"Did she suffer any losses that you know of? Any financial trouble at all?"

Ramsey appeared to think. "No. To the best of my knowledge, she was in sound financial condition. In fact, I know that she had a couple of irons in the fire that would have guaranteed her a substantial profit within just a few years."

"What irons?" Fred asked.

Ramsey glared at him. "I beg your pardon?"

"You said she had irons in the fire. I asked you what irons. What fire?"

Ramsey rolled his eyes. "It was a figure of speech," he said as if Fred was a slow-witted child.

"Really?" Sarcasm dripped from the word, but Ramsey had lost interest in Fred and shifted his attention back to Kate.

"So you don't know of any reason why she might have killed herself?"

"None. But then, I didn't know her all that well."

"Well enough to know about her investments," Fred pointed out.

Ramsey shrugged. "Rumor. Hearsay. Whatever you want to call it. Look—Joan was a nice lady and I'm sorry she's dead, but I really don't know anything about her."

Kate looked resigned. "Thank you for your help, Mr. Ramsey. I suppose I'll have to contact her bank in Boston. Which one did you say it was?"

Ramsey supplied a name, and Kate jotted it down on the back of a business card. Replacing his pen in its stand, she said, "You have a very nice office."

Ramsey preened like a peacock behind his desk.

She ran a finger along the edge of the desk. "What kind of wood is this?"

"Cherry." Ramsey's chest puffed out until his buttons strained almost beyond the point of endurance.

Fred leaned back in his seat and waited for the inevitable story that went with the desk. Something about Logan's grandmother and a steam engine. He'd heard it a thousand times.

Kate leaned forward and practically caressed the wood. What on earth did she think she was doing? If he'd known she planned to discuss interior decorating, he could have stayed home.

Just as he decided he ought to ask the questions himself, Kate settled back. "Has Brandon given you any indication why Joan killed herself?"

Fred would have said something, but Kate shot him a thunderous look intended, he supposed, to keep him silent. She turned back to Ramsey with a buttery smile.

Ramsey smiled grimly and pulled the pencil from behind his ear, studying it silently for a moment. "He would hardly confide in me. I don't know him that well."

Fred grunted. "But do you believe that cockamamy suicide story?"

Ramsey frowned. "Cockamamy?" He snorted a laugh. "Why shouldn't I? If Brandon says she was upset about something, that's good enough for me. I mean, he's the one who ought to know, right? And I didn't know her well enough to—"

Enough was enough. Fred couldn't stand it any longer. He shot out of his chair. "What are you talking about? This is Cutler, not Denver."

"Even in Cutler, some families are better acquainted than others. For instance, I am probably better acquainted with the Cavanaughs than I would be with, say, someone in a lower social bracket. Small towns aren't really so different in that respect." Ramsey's thick lips twisted into a smile.

"When was the last time you saw her?" Fred challenged.

Kate arched her eyebrows at him and shook her head almost imperceptibly, but Fred ignored her magnificently. He kept his eyes riveted on Ramsey's face so that Kate couldn't catch his eye and send him another signal. He had more important things to do than argue with her.

Ramsey's back stiffened and his face darkened. He laughed shortly. "What is this, Fred? You trying to be Dick Tracy?"

"I'm just helping the lady out."

Ramsey pushed himself to his feet and turned to stare out the window behind his desk. "Well, I suppose there's no harm in telling you—if I can remember. Like you said, Cutler is a small town. I might have seen her any time." He paused to watch a truck drive slowly down the alley behind the bank. "I guess the last time I saw her was one day last week when she came in to cash a check—Wednesday or Thursday, maybe. I don't remember which."

"Not since Wednesday or Thursday?" Fred asked. "You didn't go to their party Sunday night?"

Even at this angle Fred could see the color creep into Ramsey's face. "How did you know about that?"

"Everybody who shops at Lacey's knew about it."

"It wasn't a party," Ramsey said defensively, "just a few people for drinks and dinner."

Kate looked interested. "But you were one of the guests?"

"Yes. That is, I was invited, but I couldn't stay. I had to go to Denver that evening. I did stop in for a few minutes, so I guess I did see her that night. I'd forgotten."

Death, by whatever means, was always a major event in Cutler. The last death they'd had, Mabel Shelby's passing just two weeks after her eighty-fourth birthday, had kept the town buzzing for weeks. If Ramsey said he couldn't remember seeing Joan the night before she died, he was lying.

As if she'd reached the same conclusion, Kate's face turned to stone. "You *forgot*?"

"I'm a busy man. It certainly wasn't the only thing on my calendar last week."

Kate spoke again. "If you can remember, how did she seem that night? Was anything bothering her?"

Ramsey turned away from the window quickly and faced them, his face agitated. "Of course not. What could there have been?"

Fred answered quickly. "She's asking you."

Kate's eyes remained locked on Ramsey's red face. "Did she seem upset to you? Suicidal?"

Ramsey shook his head noncommittally. "I don't know."

Kate stood and placed both hands on his desk, leaning toward him slightly for emphasis. "Then let me rephrase the question, Mr. Ramsey. Were you surprised to hear that she'd committed suicide the next morning?"

Ramsey gripped the back of his chair unsteadily. "I didn't hear about it the next morning. I told you I left early and drove to Denver. I didn't get back until yesterday morning."

Kate persisted. "Then were you surprised to hear about it *yesterday*?"

Ramsey didn't answer, his face reddened, and he broke out in a sweat. He was obviously upset.

Grasping at straws, Fred asked, "Did she argue with anyone at the party?"

Ramsey's shoulders tensed. With visible effort he smiled, but his eyes stayed hard. "I don't know what you're doing here, Fred, but I think I've been wrong to encourage you." He moved around his chair and lowered himself into it.

"Just tell me whether she argued with anybody at the dinner party Saturday night. And tell me who else was there—unless you have some reason you don't want to talk about that night."

Ramsey smiled and shrugged broadly as if trying to look relaxed. "Just a few people." He tilted his head as if searching his memory. "There were a couple of people from Denver. Winona was there and Tony Striker. I don't remember anyone else."

"What people from Denver? Can you give me names?"

"I don't think I'd remember them. I was only there for a minute or two."

Fred didn't believe him. "You weren't introduced?"

"I don't know. If I was, I don't remember who they were. Ask Brandon—it was his party. Look," he said shakily, "if you're looking for answers, you won't find them here."

"Where will we find them?"

"You're asking the wrong man. Joan and I weren't that close. I didn't know her well enough even to begin to speculate about what was going on in her life. Nobody knows what happened."

"Except the person who killed her," Fred mumbled.

Ramsey turned toward Fred, his face puckered into a frown. "Why do you say that? I understood it was a suicide."

Fred pushed himself to his feet and faced Ramsey squarely. "It's pretty hard for me to believe she committed suicide when nobody can tell me a blasted thing she was upset about."

Ramsey busied himself with a stack of papers, but Fred refused to be dismissed. "What was she upset about, Ramsey?"

"How the hell would I know, Fred? It was probably her marriage or maybe that art store of hers."

Kate's face took on a funny expression. "Her marriage?"

As if aware that he'd said something he shouldn't, Ramsey flushed and shifted his glance from Fred to Kate. "Rumor is that there's been some trouble lately. Brandon wasn't always the *best* husband, if you know what I mean."

"Probably," Kate said coldly, "but why don't you tell me anyway."

Ramsey hesitated. "He . . . that is, I'd heard that he was seeing—"

"He was seeing someone else?" Kate demanded. "Brandon was cheating on Joan—is that it?"

"Well," Ramsey began and stopped again, flustered. He swallowed deeply and said quickly, "I guess I thought she must have heard the rumors and that was why she committed suicide."

"Why did you assume that?" Fred asked, genuinely curious about the last part.

"Because when I got to their house on Sunday night, they were arguing. I felt uncomfortable, so I left right away."

Finally something he could hang his hat on. Anxious, Fred leaned forward. "What were they arguing about?"

"I don't think—" Ramsey stopped and looked pointedly at Kate.

"Don't worry," she said. "You can say it in front of me."

"It's not that," Ramsey protested feebly. "I just don't want to stir up any trouble. I have to live in this town, and I don't want to be responsible."

Now, there was a lie if Fred had ever heard one. Ramsey might not want to do a lot of things, but stirring up trouble or controversy had never been one of them.

When he obviously thought he'd made them wait long enough, and just as Kate began to gather her purse as if she intended to walk away, Ramsey raised his eyes and gave a fair impression of a man in torment. "I shouldn't say anything about this to anybody, but"—he lowered his eyes again— "they were having a terrible argument about Winona Fox."

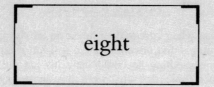

eight

Fred and Kate stood outside the bank facing into the wind. Logan Ramsey had darted out of his office just moments ago, claiming he suddenly remembered an important appointment.

Color suffused Kate's face—whether from the cold or anger, Fred couldn't tell. She spoke softly, her words nearly carried away by the wind. "Who is Winona Fox?"

"Joan's partner. They owned this little shop just down the street. Sold art stuff, some original paintings, I think. Phoebe used to go in there from time to time."

"If we talk to anyone else, I'd appreciate it if you'd let me ask the questions."

Fred leaned down to rub the ache out of his left knee. "If I'd left it to you, we'd still be sitting there admiring his desk."

"I wasn't admiring his desk, I was taking a look at the files he had on the top of it. What's Shadow Mountain?"

"Piece of property about six miles outside town. Nothing much on it. Why?"

"There was a file on Ramsey's desk with Joan's name on it labeled 'Shadow Mountain,' and another one marked 'Reclamation.'"

"Reclamation at Shadow Mountain? Now? I don't think so. There's nothing there but an abandoned surface mine that's needed cleaning up for years. The state did a little with it right after the mining company pulled out, but as I understand it, the owners have primary responsibility for the reclamation, and it's not a pretty sight. It's going to take a fortune to get it back in condition to be used for anything."

"Who are the owners?"

"I don't know." He hadn't heard anything about Shadow Mountain for years. There had been a scandal when the mining company first pulled out and left the land degraded. The fizzle had died over the years, and most people were used to the scarred face of the land now. "I haven't heard anything about that property in years. Last time I heard, some company headquartered in Colorado Springs owned it."

"It might be worth going to the county recorder's office to verify the current owners," Kate mused. "You haven't heard any talk about Joan and that piece of property?"

"No, and I think I would have unless she was trying to hide it for some reason. You don't suppose *she* owned it?"

"It would be easy to find out." The wind blew another icy blast around them, and Kate shivered. "Did you know about that? What he said in there about Brandon?"

Fred looked away, reluctant to admit it. "I'd heard rumors."

"And you didn't bother to tell me?"

"I didn't think you'd believe me. You needed to hear it from someone else."

"Thank you." Kate's voice dripped sarcasm. "I can't tell you how much I enjoyed hearing it from that odious little man." Turning away, she walked a few steps up the boardwalk, then returned to him, jabbing her finger at his chest. "You probably thought you had good reason not to tell me about Brandon, but as far as I'm concerned, this proves what Joan's frame of mind was the night she died."

"What do you mean? It proves that Brandon had a strong motive for killing her!"

She cocked her head to one side and stared at him as if he'd grown another head. "You're not serious?"

"Absolutely."

Taking advantage of her momentary silence, Fred pressed on. "It's pretty obvious to me. Joan finds out he's cheating on her, and she decides to divorce him. He panics—after all, she has all the money—and he kills her."

"Interesting," Kate mused, "but I'm afraid I can't agree with you. Joan would never have kicked Brandon out. She wasn't that type of woman. If you didn't know that about her, you didn't know her very well at all. She was absolutely desperate to be loved. Always. And even if she'd changed, even if she'd found the strength to stand on her own, Brandon wouldn't be stupid enough to kill her. She was his meal ticket."

"If she knew he was seeing someone else . . ."

Kate shook her head vehemently. "Never. I know how she felt about divorce—under any circumstances."

"So you still believe she committed suicide?"

"Yes."

Why did she refuse to recognize the truth? What more did she need to make her see? What could he do to convince her? He suspected she would not be an easy woman to convince of anything. If he said the sky was blue, she'd argue that it looked green. Mention the cold, and she'd say it felt unseasonably warm.

He grabbed her arm. "Come with me."

"Now what?" Kate twisted away. "I've got my answers. I just want to leave here and go back home and get on with my life."

"I want to know who killed Joan."

"*Why* are you so convinced somebody killed her? I still don't get it."

"I saw her. I found her—remember? And besides, I knew her. She wasn't the kind of person who would have done what you're suggesting."

"I didn't suggest it, I just believe it."

Fred smiled tightly and stepped off the boardwalk into the

street. "I think we ought to go to her art store. It's only a little ways down the street."

"Look, Fred . . . I think I made a mistake agreeing to come with you today. I think it would be best if I went back to your place and got my things and went home."

"Sorry. You promised me a day and I'm going to hold you to it. If you don't want to go to the art store, we ought to drive up so you can see Brandon—and your niece."

"No!"

"So we'll go to the art store."

"No."

Fred stopped and faced her again. "Just what are you doing here, Kate? Did you really just come to find out about the money? Don't you care what happened to your sister? Your *sister*, Kate! You don't plan to stay for her funeral. You don't want to see her husband. You don't want to see your niece. I don't understand you, and I don't understand why you came in the first place."

She met his gaze unflinchingly. "I needed to find out about my father's trust fund."

Fred's lungs labored for breath and his knees ached. "You could have asked Logan Ramsey anything you wanted to know over the telephone. Why did you come to Cutler?"

She stared at him without even the grace to blush or look away. Well, he'd had just about all he could take of her. Maybe he'd been wrong to include her in his plans in the first place. She had no softness, no flexibility, no feelings for anyone else.

But he remembered hearing her cry last night while locked in her room. There *was* something soft there. If only he could reach it. If only he could touch the trigger to her emotions, he could make her care about Joan—about Madison.

To his surprise, tears suddenly filled her eyes. She turned away quickly, but one spilled over and left a silver trail on her cheek. He released her arms, and she dashed the tears away using the back of her hand. "I'm sorry," she said, her voice husky.

"For what? For being human? Take all the time you want." He handed his handkerchief to her, but as he touched her, she jerked away. When she met his eyes again, the steel had returned and her moment of vulnerability had passed.

"All right," she said coldly. "You want me to go to the damned art store? Fine. Let's go."

"I think you ought to buy a coat first. It's going to get colder throughout the day. Probably snow tonight."

Kate sighed deeply. "I don't need one. I won't be here that long."

"You're going to catch your death of cold."

"Don't push it, Fred!"

He considered his odds of winning, stuffed his hands in his pocket, and turned on his heel. "I've got to stop at the store anyway for a minute before we go. All right?"

Kate threw her hands up in the air and looked exasperated. "Fine. Let's just get this over with. I don't have all day—literally."

Quickly Fred led her toward Lacey's General Store. Their breath painted the cold air as they walked. Half a block away Enos stepped out of his office, stopped to watch them, and raised his hand in greeting. Fred waved back cheerfully. Kate growled.

Lacey's store was puny by city standards, but Bill and Janice Lacey kept it stocked with everything a person could want in a town this size; cold remedies and cowboy boots, bread, bologna, and buttons. Kate would turn her nose up at it, but it suited Fred just fine.

It felt almost too warm inside to Fred, but Kate let out a sigh of relief as they entered. The air carried a fragrant, spicy scent, as always; like warm cookies or Phoebe's pumpkin pie.

Fred led the way, barely nodding at Janice Lacey, who stood behind the front counter. He'd hoped Janice wouldn't be working this morning. She liked to talk and when she opened her mouth, there was no telling what might come out. Anything you didn't want the rest of the town to know, you didn't tell Janice Lacey.

He stopped in the headache remedy section and nodded toward the back of the store behind the paper towels and aluminum foil where the clothes hung on racks. "You could just check out the coats while I look around here for a minute."

Kate frowned at him. "I don't need a coat."

He shrugged and concentrated on the boxes in front of him. "It's going to snow before the end of the week."

"I won't be here."

George Newman came into the store and lumbered toward the heartburn remedies, nodding a greeting. Bill Lacey called out to Fred from behind the pharmacy counter.

Janice waited for them behind the front counter, giving every appearance of being completely engrossed in the morning newspaper. Fred gave up. Let Kate freeze, if that's what she wanted. He'd never met such a stubborn woman in his life.

As they approached the counter, Janice put aside the newspaper with a great show of reluctance and dimpled at them again. "How are you, Fred? Feeling better today?"

Fred hated it when people treated him like an invalid. They'd only started acting this way since Doc announced he had heart trouble. Wasn't there some rule about doctors keeping their big mouths shut about their patients? "I'm just fine. Couldn't be better."

Janice smiled sweetly and turned to Kate. "This must be that niece of yours from Michigan I've heard you mention." Her voice dripped honey, but her eyes blazed with curiosity.

Kate returned the smile. "No, I'm not."

"Oh? Really," Janice said. She began to scribble on an invoice. "Are you just passing through our little town?"

"Yes."

Janice studied Fred's box of aspirin. "What brings you to Cutler? Family?"

Kate bristled and smiled stiffly. "I guess you could say that."

"Oh? Who are your people?"

Kate's eyes flicked over Janice. Fred watched the two square off and take each other's measure. Kate might be made of stone, but Janice Lacey always got her way when she set her mind to something, and she'd obviously decided she wanted to know all about Kate.

In the back of the store George Newman had found the Pepto-Bismol, an industrial-sized bottle, and joined them at the counter. He eyed Kate curiously and waited.

Kate looked away, dismissing Janice effectively. "I'm staying with Fred for a few days."

Janice turned to Fred, her eyes round. "At your place? Really." Disapproval brushed her voice. "By the way, Maggie was in here a little bit ago." She turned a vicious smile on Kate. "His daughter."

Fred picked up a *Field & Stream*. "She generally comes in every day, doesn't she?"

"She stopped by to get some things for the kids. Said she was going up to Cavanaugh's." Janice's head bobbed in affirmation of something only she knew. "She's going to help out with that poor little girl for a few days. What will happen to her now that her mother's gone, I'm sure I don't know. It's a tragic situation—just tragic."

She shook her head and leaned toward Kate, who stiffened perceptibly at Fred's side. "One of our local young women, a young *mother* of all things, killed herself here two days ago." Her voice dropped to a whisper. "Absolutely tragic is what I say. Left that poor little girl up there with those two men, and neither of them knows the first thing about raising a child. One of them's the child's father, but I don't think he's much of one."

Janice looked at George, as if inviting him to agree.

George cleared his throat and obliged her. "Terrible."

"You just can't imagine!" Janice abandoned all pretense of writing up the sale. "Maggie's going to have her hands full up there, that's for sure. He'll take advantage of her. Expect her to be up there all the time . . . You'd better warn Webb to watch her."

"Margaret can watch herself," Fred snapped. "She's not likely to be caught off guard by Brandon Cavanaugh."

George harrumphed his agreement in the background and held out his Pepto-Bismol to Janice, who ignored him and turned back to Kate.

Before she could say anything further, the front door flew open and a tall young man blew in, all legs and arms with a stick body. The boy stomped his feet and then looked up into the faces of the adults clustered around the counter. "Hey, Grandpa!"

Benjamin. Fred rarely admitted, even to himself, that the boy was his favorite of all his grandchildren. He loved them all, sometimes overwhelmingly, but this boy touched a chord somewhere deep within him. He reminded Fred of himself at that age.

Fred felt his smile widen at the boy. He was full of energy, high spirits, and enthusiasm, and Fred's own spirits rose just looking at him. "What are you doing out of school?"

"Got out early. I promised Summer Dey I'd help her out around her place this afternoon, and I wanted to get started before it gets dark." He removed his hat and revealed a sheaf of thin blond hair.

Janice Lacey leaned toward Kate and whispered, "That's Ben—his *grandson*. Bright boy. Good kid."

Fred scowled. Benjamin always had some new plan he was excited about, but he didn't like this one. He didn't want Benjamin working for Summer Dey. She lived on her own out there at the lake and spent all her time painting. She looked like a throwback to the 1960s. A flower child. He didn't like her. He didn't trust her.

Benjamin loped across the floor and threw an arm across Fred's shoulders. "I know you don't like her, Grandpa, but she needs me. Says she's scared!" He danced away from Fred and wailed eerily.

George chuckled.

Benjamin moved close to Fred again and said, softly this time, "She said she saw somebody hanging out around the lake the night Mrs. Cavanaugh died. She thinks somebody's going to kill her next!"

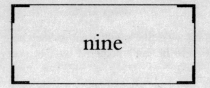

nine

Dead silence filled the room. Benjamin's eyes rounded out, and he sent Fred a silent plea for help. Though he wished Benjamin had chosen some other spot besides Lacey's to make his announcement, at least the boy knew he'd made a mistake. But of all the people in town to feed gossip to, Janice had to be the worst. At Fred's signal Benjamin beat a hasty retreat.

Janice puffed up like a peahen, full of self-importance. "Well. Can you imagine that? I always said she was a strange one—didn't I always say that, Bill?"

Bill didn't even look up from his clipboard. "That's what you always said."

"Can you imagine that?" she repeated. "She's probably told half a dozen people that story by now, and no telling what that'll do to folks. Can you imagine what Emma Brumbaugh will do if she hears that? She'll be on the phone to Enos half the night. She'll be imagining she hears something next. I declare—"

"It's a shame." Fred took his wallet out of his pocket. "How much do I owe you?"

Janice figured the total quickly. "Of all the irresponsible things to do. It's a good thing Ben's the one out there working for her—at least he has a level head on his shoulders. Can you imagine what would have happened if she'd told the Johnson boy? I shudder to think . . ."

Fred handed her the money and waited for his change.

"You don't suppose we ought to let Maggie know what's

going on, do you? She might want to keep an eye on Ben and make sure he isn't bothered by that crazy woman's notions. . . ."

Fred pocketed his change and led Kate by the elbow to the door.

"Someone ought to let Enos know what she's saying. At least that way he can be prepared. There's bound to be a commotion when this gets out. You know, George, some people just can't keep their mouths shut. . . ."

The door closed behind them. Kate's lips twitched.

Fred folded his sack into the pocket of his jacket and pointed Kate in the direction of the Frame-Up. "I'm going to have to explain a few things to that boy."

This time he could have sworn Kate almost smiled.

Ten minutes later they stood in front of the small building that housed the Frame-Up, wedged between the barbershop and Alan Lombard's insurance office. The only indication of the store's existence came from a simple hand-painted sign on a wooden shingle above the door.

Though two large display windows fronted on Main Street, Fred had never paid much attention to the place. He knew of it simply because Phoebe bought two paintings from Joan when the store first opened.

He pushed the door open for Kate, and above their heads a bell tinkled merrily. From inside the pungent odors of turpentine and oil-based paint hit him. Kate hesitated for a moment on the threshold, almost unwilling to cross it.

Winona Fox emerged from a room at the back carrying a box of supplies. She gave a brief nod to acknowledge their presence, then placed the box carefully on the floor and started toward them, a thin smile stretching her carefully painted lips.

Tall and slim with a headful of unruly red hair, she dressed in expensive clothes in strange combinations of vivid colors. Today she wore green slacks that fell in soft folds against her slim legs as she walked, a simple white blouse of a soft-looking material and a purple jacket.

Her face reminded Fred of a cat, mysterious and slightly foreign. It was the eyes, clear golden-brown and tilted upward on the outside edges, that made her look like a hungry animal.

It took her a minute to reach them across the long, narrow room. Elegant and graceful, the store surprised Fred, and he wondered briefly whether it would be acceptable to speak aloud.

Near the front an ornate, antique-looking table acted as a natural stopping point for customers, but papers, magazines, catalogs, invoices, and an open can of Diet Coke littered its surface.

Winona stopped behind the table. "Won't you come in? I wasn't expecting much business, and I must say you're a welcome break." She turned her smile on Fred. "How are you feeling, Mr. Vickery?"

Ignoring the reference to his health, Fred introduced Kate. Winona turned her cat eyes on Kate, studied her for a heartbeat, then smiled brilliantly. "Well! Kate Talbot. Is it really you?"

"Have we met?"

"Met? No, I don't think so. But I've heard Joan speak of you so often I feel as if I know you."

"Kate has a few questions she wants to ask, if you have a minute."

Winona smiled pleasantly. "Of course. Please, won't you both come into the back? I have some chairs, and we could be much more comfortable."

Without waiting for an answer, she led them behind the curtain to a small storage room. A number of old chairs scattered around the room held boxes and clutter, leaving no place to sit, but Winona swept three of them clear and lowered herself onto the one nearest the door. "I hope you don't mind if we stay down here. The office upstairs is much more comfortable, but I ought to stay here in case any customers wander in."

Kate perched gingerly on the edge of a chair. "To tell you the truth, I'm a little surprised you're open today."

Winona lowered her eyes. "I know it's probably not in the best of taste, but if I don't keep busy, I'll go crazy."

"Yes. Well. Tell me, who authorized you to open the store today?"

"Authorized? I don't know what you mean."

"I mean Joan's dead, but her estate isn't settled, and I'm wondering who authorized you to open her store today. Who gave you the authority to transact business? To alter the estate prior to probate?"

"Alter the estate? I think you must be confused. The store has nothing to do with Joan's estate."

"I understood you and my sister were partners."

"Well, we were up until about six months ago. But Joan decided to move on, I guess. She decided to dissolve the partnership."

"So you bought her out?" Fred asked.

Winona smiled. "Not exactly. She signed her share over to me in settlement."

"Why did she do that?"

Trailing one finger along the edge of a box, Winona tilted her head and eyed Fred coyly. He felt himself blushing as he met her cat eyes.

"It was a personal matter."

Determined not to let her keep the upper hand, Fred pulled himself together. "You two were pretty close?"

"Very."

By this time Kate had regained a little of her self-control. "And that's why she gave you this business?"

Winona's eyes narrowed, and when she spoke, her voice sounded venomous. "You misunderstood me. Joan didn't *give* me the store; she signed over her half of it as part of the dissolution of the partnership."

"I'm confused," Fred admitted. "When did you become partners?"

"Joan made me a partner about six months after I came. When she decided to get out and I didn't have the money to buy her share, she realized my contribution was significant enough to be worth her half of the business."

Kate looked suspicious. "Just what was your contribution?"

"Contacts across the country and an insider's knowledge of the industry. I also helped turn the place into a store with class and distinction, instead of the quaint little country store Joan started out with. The only reason this place made any money at all was because of me."

"You're telling me that you were so close to Joan, that you added so much to the business, that Joan just signed it over to you?"

Winona smiled softly in response.

Fred shook his head, trying to sort the pieces of the puzzle. "Tell me why Joan and Brandon were arguing about you the night she died."

If he hadn't been watching closely, Fred might have missed Winona's reaction, the slight pulling back, the almost imperceptible narrowing of her eyes. A blink and she'd recovered.

"Were they? Where did you hear that?"

"One of their guests."

"Who? I was the first to arrive and the last to leave, and I never heard an argument between them—especially not one that concerned me. In fact, the only person who was upset all night was Logan Ramsey, and he was only there for a few minutes."

Fred tried to keep his tone casual. "What was he upset about?"

"Logan? Who knows. He came down the stairs just before dinner, mad as hell at Brandon about something, and then out the door he went. He never came back."

"He was shouting at Brandon? Are you sure? Could he have been shouting at Joan?"

Winona looked thoughtful, then shook her head decisively. "No, I'm sure he was shouting at Brandon. He didn't start shouting until he came downstairs. Joan might have made him angry, but it was Brandon he argued with. He said it was all Brandon's fault—whatever 'it' was. He told Brandon to find a way to fix it or Logan would."

Kate interrupted. "But you don't know what he was upset about?"

"I was busy with some of the other guests, so I didn't hear the whole thing, and it all happened so quickly . . . I was just glad he left when he did. Brandon had some very influential people there, and I was afraid Logan would just be an embarrassment if he stayed."

"Why were you concerned about Brandon's dinner guests?" Kate demanded.

Winona's pretty face clouded, but Fred suspected it took concentration to bring the pout to her lips. "Joan hadn't been herself lately, and Brandon asked me if I would be there to help him. He thought it might be too demanding for Joan."

The bell tinkled over the front door again. Winona excused herself, leaving the two of them together. Kate looked at him, a question burning in her eyes, but he didn't know the answer she sought. Did she want him to reassure her that Joan hadn't been in such bad shape that Brandon chose another hostess for his dinner party? Or did she want him to acknowledge this as proof of Joan's frame of mind?

He didn't do either. Instead, he crossed to one side of the room where several unframed canvases leaned against the wall. He flipped through them idly. Some were pretty good; he found two landscapes he liked. Interspersed between the work that showed talent, three atrocious canvases caught his eye. They were the ugliest paintings he'd ever seen. No form. Nothing but heavy splotches of browns and blacks with occasional bright colors flicked across the darker paint.

He would never understand that kind of "art" if he lived to be one hundred. How odd that of all the paintings here, and there must have been a dozen in that stack and two dozen more in the showroom, only three looked like that. And they weren't on display. He studied them again. On second thought, maybe it wasn't so odd after all.

Leaning the stack against the wall again, he returned to his seat just as Winona pulled aside the curtain. "I'm sorry. I'm the only one here now so I'm afraid I'll have to keep an eye on the store while we talk. I hope I've been able to answer your questions, Kate. It's a terrible situation. I wish I could help."

"You were saying that Ramsey might be an embarrassment to Brandon," Kate prompted. "How?"

Again Winona gave them that pouty look, but Fred sensed tension beneath her well-cultivated exterior. "Some of Brandon's guests were very important people. Powerful. Logan suffers from delusions of grandeur. He thinks he's one of them, but he doesn't know enough about investments or real estate even to carry on a decent conversation. I was afraid he would try to act like an insider, get in on the money talk, and that would make Brandon—and Joan, of course—look foolish."

"Then why did they invite Ramsey in the first place?" Fred asked.

A funny look twisted across Winona's delicate features. She waved one hand at him and then lifted it to her brow. "Enough about that night. The whole subject is morbid."

But Fred wasn't willing to drop the subject so easily. "Do you believe she killed herself?"

Winona's eyebrows arched. "Of course."

"Then maybe you can tell me why," Kate said.

Winona stood and folded her arms across her chest. "Why does anybody ever do it? She was so odd at the end. So distracted. She could hardly carry on a conversation. Brandon finally asked me to stick by her—to make sure she was all right. Not that he had any idea she'd actually kill herself, but because he didn't want her to ruin anything for him."

"Ruin what?" Kate asked.

"I don't know, just . . . things. Impressions people might have gotten, that sort of thing."

Kate stood and faced Winona, the look on her face faintly challenging. "Why did Brandon have the dinner party in the first place? He must have had something definite in mind."

Considering that question an open door for his next one, Fred pushed himself to his feet. "Did it have something to do with Shadow Mountain?"

Winona's eyes flickered. They'd caught her off guard, but she hid it well. "Shadow Mountain? That old abandoned mine north of town? Why would Brandon's dinner party have anything to do with that?"

"Why don't you tell us?" Kate demanded.

"I can't imagine what you're talking about."

She looked convincing, but Fred didn't believe her. "I think you know what's going on with Shadow Mountain, and I think Brandon is somehow involved in it. I think he's trying to keep it quiet, but word is getting out. You might as well just tell us what's going on."

But Winona's eyes looked blank. "I don't have any idea what you're talking about. And I'm afraid I've spent far too long chatting with you anyway. I've got a big shipment of paintings going to a gallery in Dallas at the end of the week." She crossed to the doorway and pulled back the connecting curtain.

Kate didn't move. "Local artists? Is that where you get your artwork?"

"For the most part. We have a number of talented people around the area whose work we exhibit regularly in larger galleries around the country."

"Is Summer Dey one of them?" Fred asked.

Winona's lips pursed slightly. "She's brought us one or two things, but I think she works mostly with a gallery in

Granby. She's not one of our big sellers, anyway. Are you interested in her work? I could probably arrange a showing."

"No." He held up a hand to stop her. "I don't know anything about art."

"You know what you like, don't you? I ought to show you one or two things you'd probably like. A good painting in the home can do wonders with the atmosphere."

He shouldn't have asked, but he hadn't wanted to let her get away so easily. He'd bet his bottom dollar she knew about Shadow Mountain; he'd seen it in her eyes a minute ago. But she was good. She showed no sign of it now.

Fred stepped through the door into the showroom, but Kate refused to budge. Her face was set in those stubborn lines Fred already recognized. "One more thing, if you don't mind," she said. "I'd like to see the documents in which Joan assigned her interest in the store to you."

A tiny flicker of a smile passed over Winona's lips. "But I do mind, Kate. I mind very much. I don't believe my business arrangements could possibly be of interest to you."

"Anything connected to Joan is of interest to me."

Winona smirked. "Obviously."

Though tension filled the air, Kate held her ground, barely reacting. But Winona clearly had no intention of telling them anything more. And until they had information about Shadow Mountain and about Winona's relationship with Brandon and Joan Cavanaugh, they would accomplish nothing else here.

At last Kate followed Fred to the front of the store, stopping at the desk and looking over the clutter once again. She fingered the elaborate carving on one leg almost reverently. "This table was my grandmother's. It's been in the family for as long as I can remember. Joan and I had to wax it twice a week when we were small so we'd learn to appreciate fine things. We were *never* allowed to put anything on it. Now look at it." She shook her head in disgust. "I don't believe Joan left this table here."

If it took a table to make Kate see reason, so be it. Fred didn't care what it took, if she realized the truth in the end.

Kate raised her eyes and faced Winona squarely. "I hope you have a good attorney," she said coldly.

Winona did not look apprehensive. Instead, she looked almost triumphant as she claimed the seat behind the table. "You want to take me to court over this table? Let me save you the trouble. It belongs to me—every inch of it."

"I never had any sentimental attachment to the damn thing, but Joan did. I don't want the table, I want answers."

"That's rich. After all these years I'm supposed to believe you cared about Joan? That now you're suddenly burning with concern? *I* cared more about her than you ever did."

Kate turned away.

"It's kind of funny, really," Winona called after her. "You don't recognize me, do you? Not my name, my face— nothing. Think about it a minute, Kate. Winona Fox. Or does Winona Sullivan sound more familiar? Or Dierdre Sullivan?"

Kate's step faltered. She looked back, her face white, her fingers trembling as she touched them to her mouth. Her lips moved, but made no sound. "Dierdre?"

Winona nodded. "My mother."

Without warning, Kate fled. After only a moment's hesitation Fred scrambled after her. She'd already passed Lombard's insurance office before he made it out of the art store.

He called to her, but she didn't slow down. Muttering under his breath, he kicked himself into high gear. When she had to wait at the corner while Grandpa Jones drove past in his dilapidated Ford truck, Fred finally caught her. Determined not to let her escape him again, he took her arm.

"Kate? What happened? Who's Dierdre Sullivan?"

Kate turned toward him, her eyes opaque. She stared for

a moment, almost as if she didn't see him, then gave a small shudder and relaxed slightly.

"Tell me! What was that all about?" Fred demanded. "Who's Dierdre Sullivan?"

She buried her face in her hands. "I can't believe I didn't make the connection. You'd think I would have realized it immediately!" She tried to pull her arm out of Fred's grasp, but he held on.

He shook her slightly and asked one last time. "Who is Dierdre Sullivan? What happened?"

Kate raised her eyes to his. Fred recoiled at the level of pain he saw there. She smiled weakly. "You wanted to know all the skeletons? Well, here's one for you. Dierdre Sullivan. I've hated her since I was eight years old." She paused and looked down at her feet. When she spoke again, her voice shook. "Dierdre Sullivan was my father's mistress."

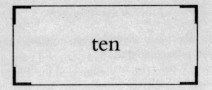

ten

Fred took Kate's arm, intending to lead her across the street toward the Bluebird Café. The wind gusted, chilling him to the bone. Like an omen. A portent of something evil coming his way.

Shivering, Kate huddled into his old fishing coat. The encounter with Winona Fox had left her visibly shaken, and Fred felt the need for a little pick-me-up. He wanted a hot cup of strong coffee, and as long as Doc wasn't at the counter, he intended to have one.

He wanted to get the answers to a few questions at the same time. To his surprise, Kate didn't argue with him, didn't ask where they were going, didn't say a word.

They walked to the Bluebird in less than five minutes. Though not yet noon, several cars took up space in the parking lot. He hoped they'd be able to find a table far enough away from the counter to have a private conversation.

What the Bluebird lacked in privacy, it made up for in friendly atmosphere. Lizzie Hatch ran the place with a soft hand. Fred often saw customers nurse one cup of coffee, refilled endlessly, for hours. Lizzie liked having people around, but she rarely spoke to anyone.

Every stool at the counter had someone perched on it when Fred and Kate entered. Every head in the place turned to see who'd just arrived. Fred called out greetings and passed around vague answers to questions about his health while Kate stood silently beside him.

Lizzie spotted them and waved a coffeepot in their direction, a clear sign that Doc had been and gone and Fred could have a cup. Fred chose a booth near the window as far away from the rest rooms as he could get. Kate lowered herself onto one Naugahyde bench while Fred slid in across from her.

The Bluebird had been here as long as Fred could remember, but when Lizzie took it over, she'd changed the decor. She'd ripped down the wallpaper covered with the twining green vines, bluebirds, and giant morning-glory blossoms Fred remembered from his youth and replaced it with wood paneling and posters of Elvis Presley in various stages of his career. Faded now and peeling in spots, the King looked out over a clientele grown so used to his image they scarcely gave him a glance these days.

Someone put money in the jukebox, and the opening bars of "Jailhouse Rock" blared into the large room. Fred had been listening to these same songs for twenty years and knew every one by heart. In all these years Lizzie had never allowed anyone to remove an Elvis record from the jukebox. In fact, other than the five records she allowed the teenagers, every selection must have been at least thirty years old. Patsy Cline, Frank Sinatra, Doris Day, the Beatles . . . but Elvis would always be King in the Bluebird as long as Lizzie Hatch wrote the checks.

Lizzie gave them a few seconds to adjust before arriving with the coffeepot. She arched an eyebrow at them, and Fred nodded, turning over their cups and setting them on the cracked saucers. Lizzie poured silently, then stepped back and looked at them expectantly.

"Hungry?" Fred asked.

Kate shook her head.

"You ought to eat. Keep your strength up."

"I'm fine. The coffee's a good idea, but I couldn't eat a bite."

"Lizzie's got a good little salad bar here. Peas, corn, mushrooms most of the time . . ."

"I'm not hungry."

Fred glanced up at Lizzie, then leaned toward Kate and whispered, "If you don't eat, she'll be insulted. Just order something."

Kate sighed elaborately. "All right. I'll have the salad bar."

Fred smiled up at Lizzie. "Two."

Satisfied, Lizzie nodded and walked away.

Now that they were alone, Fred hesitated, unsure how to broach the subject he wanted to discuss with Kate. They needed to talk about Winona and about Brandon, but he didn't know how to bring up either without upsetting her further. If he upset her, she might leave. If she left, he'd lose the inside track into the case. If he lost that, Joan's death might go down on the record as a suicide, and somebody would get away with murder.

A burst of laughter floated toward them from the counter. Kate spooned sugar into her coffee and stirred, her eyes riveted on her cup. The front door opened to admit Enos. He stomped his feet on the mat by the door and looked around. Nodding at Fred, he paused for a moment to greet the crowd at the counter, then crossed the room to their booth.

After dragging a chair from a nearby table, he straddled it and leaned his chest against the chair back. "I just had a visitor you might be interested in. Brandon Cavanaugh."

Fred added sugar to his coffee and stirred vigorously. "Oh?"

"Yeah. He wanted to file a complaint against you two."

Fred slopped a little of his coffee over the side, scalding his fingers.

Kate sipped delicately, her brow furrowed. "A complaint? I'm afraid I don't understand—"

Neither did Fred.

Enos motioned to Lizzie to bring him coffee. "He says

you're going around town asking all sorts of questions and that you're sticking your noses where they don't belong. Now, I don't know about you, Miss Talbot, but I know Fred, and I know how he can be when he decides he wants something."

Fred scowled. "Didn't know it was against the law to have conversations with friends and neighbors."

Enos shook his head and dug a piece of Juicy Fruit from the pack in his pocket. "Conversation is one thing, but you know as well as I do that you're not having conversations. You want to tell me what you think you're doing?"

"Nothing." Fred nodded toward Kate. "I'm just helping the lady find answers to a few questions."

Folding the gum into his mouth, Enos asked, "What kinds of questions?"

Kate smiled sweetly, her earlier distress hidden. "Nothing important, really. I needed to clear up a few things about my father's trust fund, so I needed to ask a few questions."

Enos narrowed his eyes suspiciously, but she met his gaze without blinking. He hesitated for a moment, then turned to Fred. "Where else did you go?"

"I took her over to the Frame-Up, you know—the art store Joan and Winona Fox owned?"

"That's right," Kate interrupted. "I wanted to see whether I could be of assistance in disposing of Joan's personal property. Apparently there's no problem on that end, either."

"That's it?"

Fred smiled. "That's it. So how'd Cavanaugh know what we were doing?"

Enos rocked forward on the chair and shook his head. "He didn't say. Somebody you talked to must have told him."

George Newman came in, holding his Pepto-Bismol. He waved in their direction and bellied up to the counter.

Enos lowered the chair to all four legs while Lizzie placed a cup and saucer before him and filled it. She'd provided free coffee to the members of the sheriff's department ever since her son Grady became a deputy. She refilled Fred's cup, looked at Kate's nearly full one, and left. Enos filled his mouth as if he were gargling and swallowed loudly. "Did you find out anything interesting?"

Fred couldn't stop the grin that spread across his face. "Some." He took another swallow of too-hot coffee, grimaced, and replaced his cup on the saucer. Across the table Kate looked displeased, but he ignored her and gave Enos a brief sketch of the stories they'd heard that morning.

He'd expected a reaction from Enos, but he didn't get it. Enos lifted his shoulders and smiled without enthusiasm. "Listen, Fred, Cavanaugh's pretty upset. He wants me to keep you—both of you—on a short leash. He asked me—no, *told* me to order you to stop snooping around."

Kate made a choking noise in her throat. Enos glanced at her, but didn't stop speaking. "The way I see it, as long as you're not interfering in an official investigation, I can't keep you from talking to people. Just be careful—okay?"

"Of course," Fred agreed. "But tell me, *is* there an official investigation to interfere with?"

"Not yet."

"Then I guess we're all right."

"No, you're not all right. You're pushing a little too far here, Fred. There isn't anyone else in town I'd let go as far as you have, but you've got to back off now. All right?"

What did Enos expect him to do, promise he wouldn't ask any more questions? Swear he'd stop trying to bring the truth to light? If so, he wouldn't get it. Until Enos admitted that Joan had been murdered, Fred had a moral obligation to continue his own investigation. He could not—*would* not allow her killer to get away with murder.

Kate sat across the table and watched them, a smile tugging at her lips.

Enos sighed heavily, patiently, the way he sighed when he spoke with Emma Brumbaugh on the telephone about

Loralee Kirkham's chickens. "Listen, if it'll keep you happy, I'll tell you as much as I know right now—okay? Ivan found a pair of women's shoes by the path on the west shore early this morning. I haven't asked Cavanaugh to identify them yet, but chances are real good they're Joan's."

Having secured both Fred's and Kate's complete attention, he looked satisfied and tipped back on his chair again. "The real interesting thing is that one of 'em's missing a heel. It's broken right off."

"Did he find the heel?" Kate asked.

Enos shook his head. "No sign of it yet. It could be anywhere. She could have tried to walk without it for a ways. . . ."

Fred leaned forward eagerly. "Or somebody could have dropped the shoes there as a decoy."

"Far as I'm concerned, Fred, this sort of backs up Cavanaugh's theory. The shoes were right there. She could have gone into the lake anywhere along that shore."

"But she didn't. I walked every inch of that shoreline this morning. There's not one place she could have walked to the lake. Not one place where there's a bare footprint along the west shore, and that's the only place she could have gone into the lake and ended up where she did."

"You went out there again this morning?"

Fred shrugged. "For my morning constitutional. I just happened to notice while I was there—"

"What's the matter with you, Fred? What am I going to have to do, lock you up?"

Kate placed her cup on the table carefully, laced her fingers under her chin, and looked at Enos. "Why do you say that, Sheriff? Do *you* believe Joan was murdered?"

"I didn't say that."

"No, but you might as well have. What do you know about Joan's death you're not telling me?"

Enos scowled and pushed himself to his feet. "All I know right now is that I've got a dead woman who may or may not have committed suicide, and I'm waiting for the autopsy to tell me what happened. Beyond that I haven't got a blamed thing, and I don't want either of you to start digging things up and getting folks riled up if there's nothing to it. Now, Fred, I'm warning you to keep your nose out of it."

Fred nodded. "I hear you."

Enos tossed back the rest of his coffee and, with a last warning look, left them alone. Before Fred could speak, Lizzie appeared with plates and pointed toward the salad bar at the back of the room.

He picked up his plate and slid to the edge of the bench, but Kate reached across the table and placed her hand on his arm. "So what are you going to do now?"

In spite of himself Fred smiled. "We've either got to talk to Brandon or try to find the heel to Joan's shoe."

Kate nodded and looked out the window. "You're right." She paused. "I don't want to see Brandon yet."

She'd have to get over that before they could accomplish anything, Fred thought. But he wouldn't push her now. Just then it had sounded as if she planned to stay, and he didn't want her to change her mind. If he played his cards right, he'd get her to Brandon's later. "Then it's the shoe?"

"There's one other possibility," Kate suggested. "What about the woman your grandson mentioned?"

"Summer?"

Kate nodded. "The one who's afraid she'll be the next to die?"

Fred shook his head. "She's a strange one. Probably decided she heard something *after* she heard about Joan."

Kate slid out of the booth and looked down at Fred. "I think we ought to talk to her. I want to know what she heard that night. I want to know what kind of contact she had with Joan through the store. I'd like to hear what she has to say."

Fred fought to keep his face impassive, but inside he exulted. He didn't care who she wanted to talk to. He'd talk to Emma Brumbaugh's dog if that's what it took to get Kate to stay in town.

Sooner or later Kate would tell him the whole story about Winona Fox and her mother. Until then his theory would have to do. But he felt so certain he'd reached the right solution, patience was very easy to come by.

Kate crossed toward the door with long, purposeful strides, and Fred followed. Halfway there she turned and faced him. "So tell me, how are you really? Is your heart as bad as the sheriff tells me?"

"No."

"You're not about to keel over with heart failure? Honestly?"

"Honestly."

She nodded and moved on. Fred stopped at the counter and paid for the lunch they hadn't eaten. He dropped four quarters into the jukebox and selected B-271. As he opened the door for Kate, Elvis came to life again singing his version of "My Way," and Fred hummed along as he strolled back out into the cold.

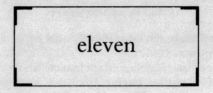

eleven

Fred drove the Buick carefully up Lake Front, past the bank on Main, and then north on Porter to the highway. Not yet five o'clock and already the trees pooled lengthening shadows across the countryside as the sun shot weak rays of gold over their tops.

The temperature always dropped quickly when the sun went down, and he'd agreed to take the car to Summer Dey's, but only because of Kate. As the crow flies, Summer lived only about two miles from Fred; traveling the highway made it closer to ten.

Once he'd pulled onto the highway, Fred brought the speedometer up to fifty, then pressed on the brakes.

"What are you doing?" Kate glared at him.

"Checking my brakes." He accelerated again and repeated the process twice more.

"Will you stop that?"

"Something's wrong with the brakes. I nearly rear-ended somebody a month ago."

"Why don't you take it to a garage?"

He checked the brakes again. "I did. Twice. The jokers claim there's nothing wrong."

"But you don't believe them? Wonderful." Kate turned away.

"I know something's wrong with them. I've been driving nearly sixty years, and I've never rear-ended anybody."

"Tell me something. Don't you *ever* believe what somebody else tells you?"

Fred pressed the brake pedal again. "Nope."

Conversation lagged a bit after that. In fact, neither of them spoke again until they reached the turnoff to Summer Dey's. Her property fronted on Grand County Road and backed on the southwest shore of the lake. The house, a sturdy A-frame cabin, nestled in a stand of lodgepole pine, Engelmann spruce, and white fir. With its long, narrow deck that stretched for several feet on either side of the door, the house looked snug and comfortable. Near as Fred could remember, Summer had lived here about fifteen years, and it still looked like a summer cabin.

A handful of hummingbird feeders swayed from bent nails along the deck. Two rusted lawn chairs looked out over the front drive, and at the far end, a wooden table shrugged on uneven legs. A chipmunk looked up from its perch on the railing and scurried for safety, chattering angrily.

Kate climbed out of the car slowly and stood in silence as her eyes swept the landscape. Trees sighed overhead, and in the distance an owl hooted. She shivered, taking in the surroundings with barely repressed distaste. A far cry from her sister, Fred thought. Joan had loved it here. Kate hated it.

He led the way up the gravel drive, past a long row of trees whose shadows stretched eerily in the half-light. As he placed his foot on the bottom step, the door squeaked open on its hinges to reveal Summer Dey.

She was a short, sturdy woman. Blond hair hung into her face, nearly obscuring her eyes and falling almost to her waist in the back, straight as a yardstick. She dressed, always, in black. Severe. Today she wore a long skirt made of some sort of gauzy material, a faded T-shirt, and a heavy denim vest that looked like she'd bleached it herself to remove any hint of color. Her face glowed pale in the light that spilled over her shoulder from the interior of the house.

"What do you want?"

Fred worked a smile to his lips. "You remember me? Fred Vickery? My grandson Benjamin is helping out around here in the afternoons."

Summer nodded warily.

Fred gestured behind him, motioning Kate to his side. "This is Kate Talbot. Joan Cavanaugh's sister."

Kate stepped forward and extended her hand. "I'd like to ask you a few questions if you don't mind."

"What about?"

"Could we come in for a minute? It's awfully cold out here."

Summer looked hard at Kate, then turned to Fred and shrugged. She didn't look pleased. "I guess." She pushed open the screen with a paint-stained hand and stepped back to allow them to enter.

Fred had never been inside before, and he looked around eagerly. They entered into a living room that she'd converted into an artist's studio. From one end to the other canvas, frames, paint supplies, boxes, and easels littered the floor and every imaginable surface. Two large paintings hung on the inside wall; two very ugly paintings. A third stood in the center of the room on a large easel. It looked as if someone had thrown a bucket of dark brown paint at it and then tossed a little bloodred on for good measure. Ugly.

So ugly, they looked like the paintings he'd seen earlier in the Frame-Up. Odd, especially since Winona claimed Summer wasn't a client. But surely there couldn't be two people painting such hideous pictures.

He grimaced and looked away, hoping to find a place to sit. But Summer led them through the studio to a small kitchen area.

Here, dishes formed piles on the countertops and on the table, a bowl of cat food held a place of prominence in the middle of the floor, and the whole room smelled of rancid food. Fred looked wistfully over his shoulder toward the studio, which looked clean and comfortable in comparison.

If Phoebe's kitchen had ever looked like this, she certainly would not have let guests into it. Summer looked unconcerned. Fred watched Kate, surprised at her control as she gingerly accepted a chair at the cluttered table. She maintained eye contact with Summer the entire time. "I understand you may know something about my sister's death."

Summer shook her head. "Where'd you hear that? I don't know anything."

Fred took a seat and pushed at the dishes nearest him to make room for his arms. He leaned an elbow into a sticky substance on the surface and removed his elbow at once. "Benjamin said you heard something the night Joan was killed."

Summer pushed a lock of limp hair behind her ear. "I thought so at first, but it must have been the wind. There wasn't anything out there."

Kate's disappointment showed. "Are you sure?" While she'd obviously been banking on Summer to have all the answers, Fred hadn't expected a thing.

Crossing to the refrigerator, Summer pulled on the door, and a fresh wave of stale air wafted across the room. "Yes, I'm sure. You guys want a beer?"

"No, we don't." Fred ignored the irate look Kate tossed at him. She didn't need to start drinking beer when there were so many important things that needed to be done. "Tell us what the wind sounded like that night. Benjamin got the impression it made you nervous."

Summer pulled a beer from the refrigerator, popped the top, and took a long drink. "Is that what this is all about? Look, Ben's a sweet kid, but he's mixed up. I don't know why it matters anyway. They say she killed herself, so what's the big deal?"

"Maybe it's no big deal to you, but it is to me and I'd appreciate your help." Kate paused, but Summer didn't respond. "I understand you were a client of hers at her store."

Looking at her skirt, Summer flicked at some dried paint. "Yes. Or at least I used to be."

"How long ago did you stop?" Fred looked in vain for some place to lean his elbows.

"A few months."

"Why?"

"Difference of opinion, I guess you could say."

"With Joan? Or Winona?"

"I never dealt with Winona. Didn't like her. She wasn't like Joan, but maybe I made the wrong choice after all. Joan turned out to be the one who cheated me. She took three of my paintings and shipped them off to some art gallery in Dallas. They never came back, and she never paid me for them. When I asked her about them, she tried to tell me she didn't know anything about them. She tried to claim she'd given them back to me months ago."

This didn't sound like the Joan he knew. "Are you sure it was Joan?"

Summer looked at him over the top of her beer can. She took another drink and wiped her mouth on the back of her hand. "She's the one I took my paintings to. She's the one who said she didn't know anything about them when I confronted her." She pretended to think for a minute. "Yeah, I guess you could say I'm sure."

"Who told you the paintings were being shipped to Dallas?" Kate interrupted.

Summer's face settled into a frown. "Joan. I told you I never dealt with the other one." She sat the beer can on the counter and leaned against the cupboard. "Maybe I should have worked with—what's her name? Winona? But I'd worked with Joan for so long. You know how it is when you work with somebody for a long time. I never had any problem with her until right near the end."

"What other kinds of problems did you have?" Kate asked.

"I don't know. Nothing, really, it's just that a few months ago she just sort of wigged out. She started acting real strange and forgetful, you know? I finally had to pull my stuff out of the store. Not that I wanted to, but I couldn't afford not to. I've been having a hell of a time since then. Do you have any idea how hard it is to find a decent market?"

Fred glanced over his shoulder into the studio at the hideous paintings and said, "I can imagine."

Summer relaxed a little, evidently somewhat pacified by the sympathy she thought he offered her. "Don't get me wrong, I liked Joan—I really did." Her voice lowered confidentially. "I tried to warn her about the energies I saw around her. Until a couple of months ago her aura was pure. Then suddenly everything around her became dark. That's when she started to change."

Fred pulled his eyes away from Summer's with some effort and caught a glimpse of Kate trying to get his attention from across the room. He didn't look at her. No way was he going to take responsibility for Summer's screwball ideas. He studied the kitchen walls, the dirt around the light switch, and the cobwebs stretching across the corners and tried not to let either woman catch his gaze.

"What happened around that time—the time her . . . aura turned dark?" Kate asked. "Is there anything you can think of that might have brought about the change?"

In spite of himself Fred turned toward Summer again. As he did so, a wall calendar hanging off center beside the refrigerator caught his attention. Last Sunday's date had been circled in red. Interesting.

Brushing her hand across her skirt, Summer smoothed the wrinkled fabric. He thought she would speak, but at that moment a plaintive yowl sounded behind her. Her face registering concern, she ran from the room and returned a second later holding a large gray cat whose thick fur totally obscured its face.

Summer buried her face in the animal's side and spoke to it with tiny mewling noises.

Kate's impatience began to show. "Ms. Dey?"

Summer's head jerked up and her face held an expression of surprise, almost as if she had forgotten them. "Yes?"

"Can you think of anything that might have happened about the time Joan started acting differently? About the time her aura changed?"

"Well, let me think." Summer scratched the cat absently and stared at the ceiling, as if hoping she would find the answer there. "No," she said at last, "nothing."

Fred signaled Kate with a wave of his hand. Maybe if he asked the questions they'd get somewhere. "I've got to tell you, Summer, I don't believe Joan killed herself, and I'm going to prove that she didn't. If you know something—anything at all—tell us right now." He held up a hand to stop her from interrupting. "Keep this in mind: If her death is made to look like a suicide, her killer will still be around, probably living and working right here in Cutler."

Summer's hand moved more rapidly across the cat's back. The gray fur rose in protest, but she appeared not to notice. "Why can't you just accept the fact that she killed herself? Everyone else believes it!"

By now Fred had heard that attitude expressed one too many times. His face burned, his throat constricted, and when he spoke, his voice came out much too loud. "Who's everyone?"

"Why does it matter? What's done is done, no matter the reason behind it. No tears can undo it. No regrets can call it back. . . ." She stopped and bit her bottom lip. She looked up at Fred for a second, then closed her eyes and began to sway. "Her marriage."

"What about her marriage?"

"It was doomed from the beginning. Doomed. She should

have seen it. She should never have married him. Something . . . something was wrong." Her voice sounded faraway. Fred felt a chill creep up his spine as he watched her. Starting tomorrow, Benjamin would have to find another place to work. Suddenly Summer's eyes opened wide. "I mean, look at them," she said matter-of-factly. "Besides all their other problems—she was a Virgo, right? And he's a Gemini—totally wrong for each other. If you want, I could do their numbers; that might help you focus on what was really wrong between them."

Kate stood and pulled the strap from her bag over her shoulder. "I really don't think that's necessary."

"I tried to warn her," Summer went on as if Kate hadn't spoken. "I wanted to give her some idea how to protect herself, but she wouldn't listen. It was there, though. All around her. I guess she finally couldn't take it anymore." Her hand moved roughly across the cat's back. The cat arched and growled low in its throat.

Kate took a step toward Summer. "If you know anything concrete, please tell us. If all you're going to do is rattle on about this kind of stuff, skip it. I want to know what you heard the night Joan died."

The cat yowled, broke free of Summer's grasp, and disappeared. Summer's eyes, as wild as the cat's, flicked around the room as if seeking an avenue of escape. She took two steps backward, ran into the wall, and cried out. She threw her hands over her head in a protective move and, with her back to the wall, slid to the floor.

Fred pulled himself to his feet and stared at her. If that didn't beat all. Maybe Doc ought to come over and have a look at her. Take her to some hospital or something where they could straighten her out.

"I've been so afraid," Summer said softly. "I did hear something that night, but I've been trying to tell myself it's all in my imagination. I mean, it doesn't make sense."

Kate crossed to where Summer sat and crouched beside

her. In a gesture almost too tender to be Kate's, she touched Summer's arm. "Tell us anyway."

Summer cringed, pulling away from Kate a little. But something in Kate's face must have convinced her she faced no danger, because all at once she began talking rapidly, as if she couldn't tell her story fast enough. "I was working on this new painting—an impression of the free-election process—and I lost track of time. I was really depressed, which is good because that's the only time I can really paint well. That's why I wear black all the time—to help create the proper mood.

"Anyway, I thought I heard a car turn in here about nine o'clock or so, but when I went to look, I couldn't see anybody. It didn't bother me until I heard it leave a little while later—fifteen minutes or so, I guess. I looked out the window. I didn't think anything was there—there weren't any headlights or anything. I went to turn around again, and all of a sudden I saw a flash of red by the road, like someone stepping on the brake for a minute, and then it was gone."

Again, she pushed the hair out of her face and looked at Fred, testing his reaction. He forced a smile and nodded at her to go on.

"It bothered me, you know, living out here alone and all. I have contacts in the other world who help protect me, but they must not have been here that night, because I felt totally alone. Sometimes it's necessary to order them away when I'm working, but—" She broke off and shuddered.

Kate met Fred's eyes and raised her eyebrows in disbelief. Well, he'd warned her, hadn't he? But she'd insisted on coming out here anyway. Whatever she heard now, she'd asked for it.

"I worked a while longer," Summer went on, oblivious to them. "I didn't really pay attention to how long because the work was going so well. But then I heard it again—the sound of a car or something being driven past the house. Not on the highway, you know, but right here on my drive.

When I looked at my watch, it was one-thirty. It spooked me, so I stopped working and turned out the lights and waited. After a few minutes I went to the door and looked out. I saw Joan's truck in the moonlight over by the lake."

She stopped. Fred felt himself leaning forward, anticipating her next words. "Then what?"

"Then? Nothing. That's all."

"Wait a minute," Kate said. "You saw Joan's truck? That's all? Something must have happened after that to make you so nervous."

"That was all."

"Did you go outside? Did you check on the truck? Did you see anybody get in or out of it? Did you hear them leave?" Fred shot questions at her like ammunition.

"I never did see anybody, and I didn't hear a thing after that."

Kate looked confused. "Then why did you feel so afraid?"

"I heard about Joan the next day. At first I worried that somebody might think I had killed her, then I realized how crazy that sounded."

"Why were you worried about that if you believed she committed suicide?" Fred demanded.

"Because we'd had that argument just a couple of days before she died."

"What argument?"

"The one when she threatened to sue me for slander or something if I didn't stop telling people what she did."

Fred met Kate's gaze and shook his head, denying any prior knowledge of the argument. "But Joan hadn't been involved in anything at the store for months."

"I didn't care about the store. I just wanted her to take responsibility for what she'd done. *She's* the one who stole from me, *she's* the one who should have been in jail, but she threatened me."

"And she wouldn't admit what she'd done?"

A note of derisive laughter burst from Summer's lips. "No, she wouldn't."

"I still don't understand," Fred said. "If you believed she killed herself, why were you afraid you'd be suspected of murdering her?"

When Summer shook her head and refused to answer, Kate reached toward her again. "Surely you had some reason."

Summer rolled her eyes at Kate and looked exasperated. "I already told you—the paintings. The money she owed me. The way she was trying to cheat me. She got mad when I pulled my work out of the store, but what else was I supposed to do? I couldn't let her get away with that, could I? So maybe I got a little carried away trying to make sure she didn't cheat somebody else. I got scared. She couldn't have sued me, but it still scared me at first."

Kate rubbed her forehead. She looked exhausted. "And her truck? Was it still parked by the lake the next morning?" Kate brought the conversation back on track.

"No. It disappeared some time during the night."

"How could her truck disappear after she committed suicide?"

"Someone else drove the truck down here," Fred suggested.

Kate patted Summer's arm and got to her feet, crossing toward Fred. "Where does this leave us?"

Summer watched them both suspiciously. "You don't really believe she was murdered?"

To Fred's surprise, Kate said soberly, "I'm beginning to wonder."

As they crossed the drive to the car, Fred noticed the ache had nearly gone from his knees and his step felt unnaturally light. In fact, he felt a little giddy with success and reluctant to call himself back down to earth. He waited until Kate had fastened her seat belt before he found the nerve to break the mood.

"You know what comes next, don't you?"

"What?"

"You're going to have to talk to Brandon. Until we know what happened at that party . . ."

She stared out the window. "I can't."

He started the car and sat for a minute, letting the engine warm up. "You have to. You're the only one who can. Enos won't question him and Brandon won't talk to me." He shifted into reverse and backed slowly onto the street. "You have to do everything you can to prove Joan was murdered, or her killer will go free. Don't you understand that?"

"I said I was *beginning* to wonder."

"For Pete's sake! You know as well as I do what happened, you just won't admit it."

She sat for a moment, not moving. "You don't understand the history we have, Brandon, Joan, and me."

"Tell me."

"No," she said sharply. "It's all too complicated and it has nothing to do with why Joan died. I'll help you a little while longer—just to see what comes up, but I won't talk with Brandon—now or ever."

twelve

Monday morning dawned gray and gloomy; a scant illumination of the clouds, nothing more. Almost before dawn Fred headed outside for his daily constitutional. He found himself back home in record time—before Kate even stirred.

He fixed breakfast and ate with relish—oyster stew from his secret supply in the garage. He liked it thick with crumbled crackers and black with pepper. He ate slowly, waiting for Kate to wake up. She didn't.

He cleared the dishes and left her a note telling her where to find everything he thought she'd need before he got back. He'd spent an entire weekend working on her, but she had no intention of giving an inch. Compromise obviously did not come easy to her. Forty-eight hours and they were right back where they started. She absolutely refused to speak with Brandon.

The last time he'd seen her, she'd been angry with him—again. She'd turned a deaf ear to all his arguments and had ignored his reasoning. Yet she'd stayed in Cutler all weekend. She remained infuriatingly mute, refusing to tell him what she thought or how she felt. But she stayed. Why? Four days ago, nothing had been more important than getting back to San Francisco.

Well, as he'd always said, if you want something done, you might as well buckle down and do it yourself because you can't count on anybody else to help you out. It didn't make sense to waste more time arguing with Kate. He'd just have to talk to Brandon himself.

Whistling a tune he remembered from boyhood, he headed toward the garage. The first few lazy flakes of snow fluttered past his eyes, soft and white. By nightfall ice would form black sheets across the roads, and blankets of snow would cover every surface.

He started the Buick and let it run for a minute to warm up before pulling out of the garage. Driving slowly through town, he checked the brakes three times before he reached Main Street. Those jokers at the garage told him they were in fine shape, but he couldn't hardly get stopped no matter how hard he pressed on the brakes. Fine shape! He made a mental note to drive the car down to Granby one of these next days and have the brakes checked by somebody who knew what they were doing.

He crept past Lacey's and looked for Margaret's Chevy. It stood in a spot near the front door. Right on schedule. He wanted to get to Cavanaugh's before she got up there to take care of Madison. After a week she was still taking care of the child. Doing too much, he thought. Hadn't even had time to make him his pot roast yesterday.

At Porter Lane he turned north and started up the mountain. Snow fell in light, dry, lacy flakes. Thick gray clouds hovered over the tops of the trees and dropped onto the highway occasionally giving the day an ominous feel. Fred turned on the headlights and hunched over the steering wheel, hoping any deer and elk out there would stay on one side of the road or the other until he passed.

Usually a fifteen-minute drive from town, the trip this morning took over half an hour because of the fog. In the gray morning light the Cavanaugh house looked uninviting. Though Brandon's BMW stood in the driveway next to Tony's sleek red car, no lights showed in the windows, no curl of smoke escaped the chimney.

The wind had picked up again, and the effect—the

deserted house, the heavy silence in the clouds, and the mournful cry of the wind through the trees—seemed unearthly.

Fred knocked on the door, so certain the house stood empty that when muffled footsteps sounded inside, they startled him. Brandon answered wearing a white bathrobe. His hair stuck out and creases lined his face as if he'd just been roused from sleep.

Fred tried to look pleasant, which wasn't easy considering Brandon's expression. Brandon looked over Fred's shoulder as if expecting to see someone else. Apparently he decided Fred had come alone. "What the hell do you want?"

"Can I have a word with you?"

"What about?"

Now, there was a stupid question. "Would you mind if I came in for a minute?"

Brandon's eyes narrowed suspiciously, but after a moment he shrugged. "I guess not." When he turned away, Fred pulled open the screen door and followed.

Brandon walked into the living room, crossed to the bar, and poured a shot of whiskey from the nearly empty decanter. Fred removed his coat and gloves and sat on the sofa. He waited, watching as Brandon tossed off the shot and poured himself another. The bitter aroma of liquor flooded the room.

"Where's Kate? Didn't she come with you?" Brandon asked thickly as his throat worked to get around the whiskey. His apparent interest in Kate made her refusal to see him even more peculiar.

"No." Fred waited until Brandon crossed the room and planted himself. His robe gaped open at his chest and fell away from one thigh. Brandon downed the second shot. The man had a problem, but it was one Fred understood. Whiskey hadn't been his medium, but he'd longed for something to cut the pain and shock of losing Phoebe. In the end, time had been the healer, but if he'd been a drinking man, alcohol might have dulled the pain for a while.

Brandon put his glass on an end table and ran his fingers through his hair as if realizing suddenly how unpresentable he looked. "Well, it's too bad. Tell Kate I'd love to see her again. How long is she staying?"

"I don't know," Fred answered truthfully.

"We've got a lot to talk about, Kate and me."

Something made Fred vaguely uneasy. Was it the tone of Brandon's voice? Or the look in his eye?

Brandon settled back in the chair. "So, what can I help you with?"

"I'd like to talk with you about the night Joan died."

Brandon's smile never reached his eyes. His mouth stopped its upward tilt, his body tensed. "What about it?"

"What happened?"

Brandon looked out the window in the direction of the lake. The clouds hung heavily, obscuring the view. "I wish I knew."

"I've heard, of course, that you think she committed suicide. Why do you believe that?"

With a huge sigh Brandon looked back at Fred. His eyes sagged downward at the corners. His entire face assumed a pathetic look. "Who knows? I never could figure out what upset her. Why do you care?"

"I knew her a little. It didn't seem like something she would do—as far as I knew."

"Believe me, she wasn't what she pretended to be."

"She just never seemed unstable to me. When Enos told me that she'd committed suicide, it came as a shock."

"So what's why you've been asking questions all around town?" Brandon's face softened, slowly, and took on a pleasant expression. Except his eyes, which remained guarded. "Her suicide wasn't surprising. She'd threatened it so often, I'd stopped paying attention."

"Why?"

"Joan had serious problems as long as I knew her. Her father . . ." Brandon lowered his head in a gesture of despair, but the emotion was not convincing. "Tell me, how well do you know Kate?"

"As well as I can in four days, I suppose."

"What do you think of her?"

The question caught Fred off guard. But before he could answer, Brandon went on.

"Their father destroyed them both. Classic case of emotional abuse. They each found their own way of dealing with life. Kate doesn't believe in love—not any kind. She'll do anything to avoid commitment. She can't give. That's how Russell screwed her up. Joan . . . well, Joanie was different. She wanted love. She *needed* to be loved, but nobody could ever love her enough. No matter what I did, it wasn't good enough. She wanted someone to coddle her and take care of her, but she didn't like the physical demands of marriage. While I—" He shrugged pitifully. "I found out too late that she didn't really want a husband—if you know what I mean."

Fred did. He didn't want to hear the details.

Brandon reached for his glass, remembered it was empty, and scowled into the bottom of it. "You must know how I feel. Didn't you lose your wife a few years ago?"

"Under different circumstances, yes."

Someone standing behind Fred cleared his throat. Brandon looked up, smiled weakly, and composed his face. "Tony. Fred's asking some questions about Joan."

Tony Striker came into the room, his face pleasant. "Really? What kind of questions?" He perched on one arm of the sofa.

"About the night Joan died," Fred said. "About what upset her and why you believe she committed suicide."

Tony smiled easily. "You know, when we first heard you were asking around about Joan, Brandon was pretty mad. But we never thought about Joan's friends. Like you. We never thought you'd be upset or that anybody else would even care. I had no idea you and Joan were so close."

"I haven't been able to sleep well since it happened. I couldn't imagine . . ." Fred let his voice trail away.

Tony smiled sadly. "It's a terrible tragedy for Brandon and for Madison. Did you know we found Kate's sleeping pills gone? She must have taken twenty or thirty of them. And I was the one who took her down to Granby to fill the prescription just a few days before she died."

But Fred hadn't asked how she committed suicide, he'd asked *why*, and nobody wanted to answer him. He rubbed one hand across his chin and tried to look thoughtful. "It's a terrible tragedy for everyone. But I still don't understand why she'd do it, and neither does Kate."

Brandon leaned forward, his eyes bright. "What do you mean?"

"Brandon, calm down," Tony warned.

"Calm down?" Brandon shot to his feet. "You want me to calm down when this old man is trying to make it sound like someone killed Joan? It's hard enough going through all this as it is." He pointed one finger unsteadily at Fred. "I don't need anything else from you."

Tony rose. "Calm down, Brandon. You're overreacting. Fred didn't say that, did you, Fred?"

Not yet. But he wanted to. He took a deep breath and let it out slowly. "All I asked was what happened here the night she died. I think it would help Kate if she knew."

Brandon's chest heaved for a moment as he struggled to compose himself, and the sound of labored breathing filled the room. "If Kate wants to know anything, let her come and ask me. I'm not talking to you about it. This is a family matter."

"Come on, Brandon. Talking with Fred won't hurt anything," Tony said reasonably.

Brandon glared at Tony for a moment. With visible effort he calmed himself and faced Fred again. "What happened here the night she died? She destroyed me. The biggest night of my life, my once-in-a-lifetime chance to make something of myself. *Me*, not Joan's husband. And what did she do? She refused to come down before dinner, barely spoke to any of our guests, and then disappeared right after dinner. Of course, I didn't know where she was or what she was doing, all I knew was that those people would never take me seriously again. She destroyed me, in more ways than one."

Tony sprang from the sofa and moved quickly to Brandon's side. He put an arm around Brandon's shoulders and forcefully ushered him toward the door. Looking back at Fred, he said, "If you'll wait a minute, I'll be right back. I think Brandon's had enough for now."

Fred inclined his head slightly, and the two men moved out of the room. Relieved to find himself alone, he pulled in a deep breath. His knees trembled. He pressed his hands against them and felt the trembling stop. By the time Tony returned, he felt better.

"Look, I'm sorry about that. But this whole thing has been rough on him. Not just Joan dying, but the last few months. She was like a different woman toward the end."

"Why?"

"I wish I knew. We all do. Something was obviously bothering her, though none of us knew how far it had gone. And of course Brandon feels guilty. He thinks he should have been able to recognize her problem and fix it somehow."

"Why did he say Joan destroyed him?"

"Their marriage had been on the rocks for several months, ever since Joan started suspecting him of cheating on her. She started taking sleeping pills to get through the night, and God only knows what else to get through the day. That's the truth, Fred, though whether you tell Kate or not is up to you. It might make it worse for her to know."

"Do you think Joan purposely ruined Brandon's dinner party?"

"No. She was genuinely upset that night, but I never knew why. They had some horrible arguments the last little while. I guess I just assumed they'd had another one."

"About what?"

"I don't know."

"Weren't you here?"

"Yeah. But I didn't hear them arguing—I just *assumed* they'd had an argument since lately that's what they seemed to do most."

"She had an argument with Logan Ramsey that night, too. Do you know what that was about?"

Tony's face froze, leaving his eyes the only part of his face that looked alive. "Logan Ramsey? Where did you hear that?"

"Around. I don't remember where."

"I don't think he was even here that night."

"I understand he left early. He said that Brandon and Joan *had* been arguing when he got here."

Tony's eyes narrowed. "What is this? *Are* you trying to make it look like somebody murdered Joan?"

Fred didn't respond.

Tony stood and moved about the room, agitated. "Do you know how ridiculous that sounds? Who on earth would want to murder her? What motive could there possibly be?"

"Money," Fred said simply.

Tony laughed shortly. "You think somebody killed Joan because of money? You didn't know her very well, did you? Nobody would have to kill her for money—she practically *gave* it away. If anybody wanted money from Joan, all they had to do was ask." He stopped pacing and rubbed his forehead. "You don't really believe somebody killed her, do you?"

"I don't know. Apparently she had arguments recently with a number of people."

"Ramsey? I didn't think he'd have the guts to kill somebody."

"If there's one thing I've realized the last couple of days, it's that I don't know people as well as I thought I did."

"Really? Lots of secrets lurking out there in our little village? Who else has surprised you?"

Fred waved his hand, pushing away the question. He had no intention of telling Tony Striker—or anybody else, for that matter—what he knew.

Tony opened his mouth to speak again, but stopped short at the sound of quick footsteps on the front deck outside. The front door burst open, and Margaret came in on a blast of cold air. She stomped her feet and looked up, her cheeks flushed pink from the cold.

"Dad? What are you doing here?"

Fred couldn't resist a smile. He'd never been able to keep from smiling when Margaret entered a room. She grew more beautiful every day. With her dark hair and eyes and her heart-shaped face, she looked like a young Olivia De Havilland, except Margaret's eyes were a little closer together and her mouth was a bit wider.

"Waiting to see you, sweetheart," he lied and immediately wished he hadn't.

Tony clapped him enthusiastically on the shoulder and mumbled something about errands he needed to run, leaving him alone in the foyer with Margaret. But Fred hadn't asked about everything he wanted to, and now he'd never get another chance.

thirteen

Fred tried to hide his disappointment. Besides coming up empty-handed in his search for new information about the night Joan died, he hadn't even had a chance to ask about the problem between Joan and Summer. Since Summer's version differed from Winona's, he'd hoped Brandon or Tony would shed a little light on the subject, but he'd lost his chance even to ask.

Margaret watched him, her eyes bright, her face expectant. Fred's anger dissipated. She had no idea what she'd done.

He fought to look stern. "So you're up here again today? Don't you think it's time some of the other ladies took their turn? You can't do it all."

As he'd known it would, Margaret's face fell. Her eyes clouded over and the smile slid from her lips. "Is that why you're up here?"

"Somebody's got to keep an eye on you," he teased. He wanted her to bristle at him the way Phoebe would have, but he should have known better.

Instead, she looked away. "Nobody has to keep an eye on me. I'm not doing anything wrong."

"Of course you're not." Never for one minute had he suspected her of doing anything wrong. "You're just doing too much. I wanted to make sure you're holding up."

He didn't say that he knew Webb would be too busy at the Copper Penny to look after her, because he knew how much it would hurt her.

But she knew what he meant. "Webb's angry enough at me, so don't you start."

Fred cursed inwardly at the thought of his son-in-law and wished for the millionth time that Margaret had never married him. "Why is *he* angry?"

Margaret shrugged out of her coat. "The usual. He says I'm not taking care of my own family. He wants me home." Her tone hinted at things she left unsaid.

"And?"

"And nothing."

If Webb had started acting up again, no wonder she spent every waking hour caring for these people. Fred pressed a kiss onto her cheek. "You're not angry with your poor old dad, are you?"

The worry eased from her eyes and she laughed, a wonderful laugh that ran up the scale of delight. Phoebe's laugh. It never failed to tug at Fred's heartstrings when he heard it, which was far too seldom these days.

"Were you really waiting for me or did I interrupt something else?"

"You didn't interrupt a thing."

"I don't believe you, but come into the kitchen and I'll make it up to you." She turned toward the back of the house. "Where's Kate? Didn't she come with you?"

"She wasn't up when I left."

"So you sneaked off without her? What are you up to?"

"Up to?" She looked too thin these days. Her jeans practically hung on her, and her sweatshirt looked two sizes too large.

Scowling over her shoulder, she scolded, "Don't act so innocent with me, Dad. I know you."

"I'm just trying to help Kate, that's all. She's a stranger in town, and she needs help figuring out what happened to her sister."

"There are plenty of other people who can help her. Enos, for example."

"She's staying with me. I feel responsible."

"Yes"—Margaret nodded at him and looked angry—"I heard all about how you managed that. Enos isn't pleased, to say the least."

"Can't help that."

"Why don't you just leave the whole thing alone? Enos is the sheriff. He's got everything under control."

"Under control? When he believes this cockamamy suicide story? If I leave it up to him, somebody's going to get away with murder."

"You're doing it again, aren't you? You've been up nights thinking about this and you're obsessed with it."

"I am not obsessed."

"Have you been sleeping? Don't lie to me. The last few weeks it's been the brakes on your car. Now it's going to be Joan's death. Just tell me one thing—how do you know she *didn't* commit suicide?"

Fred stared at her a moment and then looked away. He didn't know why he worked so hard to spare her feelings when she didn't give a thought for his. Behind him, he heard her sigh.

"Dad, you're not as young as you used to be. Your health isn't good. I worry about you."

"I'm not dead yet." He'd meant his words to sound light, but they came out harsh and bitter.

"Don't say that! I can't stand the thought of something happening to you."

He turned back to her, trying to ease the anger of his words with a smile. "I'm not going anywhere yet."

"How can you act so casual about it? Doc says you've got to take it easy. He says—"

"He says a lot of things, the old fool. Why do you believe him and not me? I know my own body. If there was anything wrong with me but this blasted arthritis, wouldn't I know it? If I hadn't known that joker all my life, I'd file a complaint against him for malpractice."

He lowered himself into a chair at the kitchen table near a large plate-glass window and stared at the granite face of the mountain a few yards behind him.

He heard Margaret moving around behind him, her actions slow. He knew how she felt about him, and he knew how losing her mother had hurt her. But he couldn't give up on life yet, not even for her.

Cupboards opened and closed, pans rattled, and silverware clinked as she worked. After a minute she spoke again. "So how are things going with Kate? Are you two getting along?"

Grateful for the note of normalcy in her voice, he turned to face her. "I get along with her as well as anybody could, I expect."

"What does that mean?"

"Kate's a hard one to figure out. She's unemotional. It's like she doesn't really care about Joan. But, then, I guess if she could go ten years without speaking to her sister . . ."

Margaret looked at him tenderly. "She's just a different kind of woman than you're used to. Women are different now. They have careers, they don't just stay at home all their lives washing dishes and cleaning up after men. You've just never seen anyone quite like her. You know, sometimes I wonder what I'd be like if I lived somewhere else or if I hadn't gotten married so young. Or even if I hadn't started having kids right off."

"You wouldn't like it."

"You never know." She sliced potatoes and looked at him thoughtfully. "I wonder what Sarah and Deborah will do with their lives."

"They're good girls," he reassured her. "You've got fine kids, all three of them."

She smiled at him, but she looked distracted. "Deborah's twelve this year. Sarah's off to college—at least, I hope she is—in another year. What am I going to do when they're gone?"

"What do you want to do? It's up to you."

"No, it isn't." She shook her head and looked away. When she spoke again, her voice sounded wistful. "You know, I envy Kate."

"Why? She's alone. No family, no children—"

"Nothing tying her down. Nothing keeping her—" She shook her head and smiled. "Never mind."

Nothing keeping her chained to a sour marriage. Fred didn't believe in divorce—under most circumstances. When his youngest son, Douglas, divorced his wife last year, Fred had been bitterly disappointed. He'd thought they should have stuck by each other and given themselves more time. But he didn't feel the same way when it came to Webster Templeton and Margaret. In fact, he often had to bite his tongue to keep himself from urging her to end the marriage.

He forced a smile onto his face and a bright tone into his voice. "How's Benjamin coming on cleaning out that shed for what's-her-name?"

"Summer? It's slow. Of course, everything Ben does goes slow. He spends more time daydreaming than actually working."

"Do you think it's a good idea to let him go over there?"

"Do you think I could stop him even if I didn't? It's okay, Dad. Summer's a little odd, but she's not dangerous."

With all his heart Fred hoped she was right.

Margaret scrambled eggs and lined a skillet with bacon. She diced an onion into the skillet with the potatoes, and soon the rich aroma of old-fashioned breakfast, the kind everyone ate before all the excitement about cholesterol and fiber, filled the air.

"Are you hungry?"

Though still pleasantly full from his contraband oyster stew, the meal smelled good enough to entice him. He nearly said yes when he saw her reaching for a box of the cardboard-tasting cereal she expected him to eat at home. In ten years some scientist would announce that fiber caused cancer and everyone would abandon their cereal boxes in panic.

"Why don't people just eat the way God intended them to in the first place?" he grumbled.

"God didn't intend for you to eat a gallon of ice cream a week."

He refused to grant that comment the dignity of a reply, but shook his head at the cereal she offered.

She replaced the box on a shelf. "Why don't you tell me what you're really doing up here?"

"I told you."

"No, you didn't. Not the truth anyway. You're still poking around trying to prove that Joan was murdered, aren't you?"

He thought about denying it, but decided against it. She'd never believe him anyway.

She wiped her hands on a towel. "Were you asking questions about it when I got here?"

He ignored her and looked around the room. She kept it neat as a pin, just like she did her own kitchen. Everything in its place.

"You were! I can't believe it! I can't believe they didn't kick you out of here! What were you thinking?"

Shadows from the half-light of morning haunted the room. She shouldn't be trying to cook in a dark room. He flipped the wall switch, but nothing happened.

"How long has that light been burned out?"

Margaret raised her eyes to the light fixture. "Since yesterday, but don't change the subject."

"The subject is closed. I'll put a new bulb in it for you."

"Forget the lightbulb, I'll do it later."

"You shouldn't be the one changing it." Fred looked at the vaulted ceiling with dismay. Just like with Webb, Margaret would end up practically breaking her neck trying to do everything while Brandon soaked up his booze. "Where does he keep his ladder?"

"You're not changing it for me."

From the back window he could see a corner of the garage. But before he got halfway to the door, Margaret guessed where he was headed.

"No! You stay here. Watch breakfast for me and I'll go get it."

He ignored her. But in that bullheaded way she'd developed over the years, she dashed past him and out the door. Now she'd strain her back trying to carry in a heavy ladder for him because she thought he was too old to do it himself. He crossed to the stove and gave everything a quick stir.

Potatoes and bacon sizzled happily, and the eggs began to gather substance. He stirred again and studied the view from the kitchen windows. It wouldn't kill him to carry the ladder, no matter what she said. And to leave him in here stirring breakfast while she did the heavy work—well, he just couldn't stand it.

He turned the heat down on everything and followed her. Rounding the corner of the garage, he ran headlong into her. Her eyes were wide, her face pale.

"Call Enos," she whispered.

"What happened?"

She didn't speak, but pointed behind her with trembling fingers.

Cautiously Fred entered the garage. She tugged him forward, urgently. In the corner a ladder leaned against the wall. Behind it Fred saw something dark.

He looked at Margaret, silently asking for an explanation, but she only pointed. "There. Behind the ladder."

By this time his eyes had adjusted to the darkness. With difficulty he squatted near the ladder. At first he saw only the blanket. It had once been folded neatly, but now its top layer had been pulled back to expose a broken table lamp.

The lamp looked new and expensive, but the blanket itself
held his attention. He looked up at Margaret, scarcely daring
to believe what he saw.

   Blood.

fourteen

"I'm going to call Enos," Margaret said, and this time her voice carried more conviction.

Fred shook his head. "Not from here."

"But he needs to see this."

"I don't think we ought to take a chance on calling from the house. What if Brandon hears us?"

"I can't remember the last time Brandon came into the kitchen. Or Tony either, for that matter. They're not very domestic."

But Fred would not be convinced. At last he had a clue, something concrete, and he wouldn't risk Brandon over-hearing him talking to Enos about it. Neither would he take a chance on Brandon moving the blanket before Enos could see it. "I'll go back into town and get Enos. You come with me."

"I can't."

"I can't leave you up here. Don't you realize what this means?"

"Dad, I can't leave. I'm here to take care of Madison, and if you're right, I can't leave her alone with them."

How could he drive away and leave her—or the child—here with Joan's murderer just a few feet away? Fred tried to think of an argument that would persuade her, but he knew that wouldn't be easy. She'd inherited her mother's stubborn streak.

She stared at him, her mouth stretched in a firm line, her eyes dark. She wore an expression he'd seen many times in forty-seven years of marriage. At this moment Margaret looked so much like her mother it hurt.

Calming slightly, he asked himself whether there would really be any danger to her if he left her here. Reluctantly he admitted there probably wouldn't be. Would it be safe to call Enos from inside the house? Probably. But Enos had been a little testy lately, and Fred would need to be awfully convincing to get him up here. Even with a find as big as this, he couldn't risk trying to talk to Enos over the phone. Fred knew he could be much more convincing in person. He had to go, and since Margaret wouldn't budge, he had no choice but to leave her behind.

When they reached his car, she kissed him gently. "I don't want you coming back up with Enos. Go home and rest, all right?"

He didn't answer. He could see no reason to make promises he wouldn't keep. Before she could push for a commitment, he shut the door and started the engine.

Before he'd gone a mile, Mother Nature unleashed the storm she'd been holding in check all morning. Within minutes snow covered the hood of his car and the roads iced over enough to make driving treacherous.

He touched the brakes once or twice, but the slight pressure he applied sent the car sliding toward the edge of the road. If he slid off the road now, he'd never make it to town, and no one would come along this road in a storm.

Downshifting into second gear, he felt the car jerk a little as it settled itself at a lower speed. The trees flanking the road served as a barrier to the wind, giving him a little visibility, but he could only see a few feet in front of him.

He crept down the mountain and chafed at the delay. After what seemed like forever, he reached Bergen's Meadow, a stretch of more than two miles through fields of grass. No trees lined the highway to deflect the wind. There was nothing to protect him from the elements.

Gripping the wheel hard enough to make his fingers ache

from the effort, Fred riveted his eyes on the swirling white fields ahead. Tall metal poles topped with red flags gave him only occasional reassurance that he hadn't left the road.

He pushed the windshield wipers onto high. They zinged back and forth with enthusiasm but without results. Wind buffeted the car, sliding it like a toy toward the edge of the road.

He tried to strike a bargain with God. If he made it down the mountain safely, he'd . . . he'd . . . He could think of no promise that he'd be able to keep. He begged God silently to help him. If he got into trouble here, he might not be found for a long time. He begged God to help Margaret, to keep her and the little girl safe until he could get help back up the mountain for them.

When the first dim streetlight glimmered promise of safety in the middle of the storm's frenzy, relief washed over him. Within minutes signs of habitation appeared regularly; a parked car, a front porch light burning feebly behind the snow, someone huddled into a coat moving toward home.

Enos's truck still stood in front of his office, its body outlined under the powder. The office windows glowed a warm welcome. Fred parked and hurried up the steps and into the door.

But Enos was not alone. Doc Huggins sat across the desk from him, deep in conversation. Both men looked up, impatient with Fred's interruption.

"Fred? What the hell are you doing out in this storm?" Enos's face puckered into a frown.

"I need you to come with me up to Cavanaugh's place."

Enos shoved himself out of his chair, his face red, his jaw clenched. "Cavanaugh's? Don't tell me you've been up there."

"Margaret's found something I think you need to see."

"Maggie? What—"

"You know she's been helping out with Madison for the

last few days? While I was up there with her this morning, she found a blanket in the garage—covered with blood."

Doc looked up, his eyes bright with curiosity. "Blood?"

"She's up there now. You've got to come with me."

Doc slumped back down in his chair.

Enos sat heavily. "Not in this storm."

"What? Maggie's up there alone with them. She may be in danger. You've got to come."

"Fred, whatever it is, it's not a clue to Joan Cavanaugh's death."

Anger at Enos raged through Fred. The man had lost his mind. He looked at Doc for support, for a rational reaction, but Doc looked away, studied his fingers, and dug dirt from under one fingernail.

Leaning back in his chair, Enos cleared his throat. "You want to tell him, Doc?" But without waiting for an answer, he went on. "We got the results of the autopsy back today. Even though I don't like to admit it, you were right. Joan was murdered."

Fred's heart began to pound. He sank gratefully into the chair next to Doc. "It's official?"

Doc nodded. "Just came in a few minutes ago." His brows knit and his expression grew grave. "Listen here, Fred, you've got to calm down a little. You're way too wound up." He reached beneath his seat, drew out his black bag, and proceeded to make a nuisance of himself taking Fred's blood pressure.

Fred tried to push him away. No time to worry about that now. Margaret's safety remained uppermost in his mind. He spoke her name aloud, pushing Doc away and struggling to his feet. He'd have to go back up the mountain himself if he couldn't get any help here. His knees buckled, protesting angrily from deep within his joints.

"Sit down, Fred," Enos commanded.

But Fred ignored him and pulled his gloves back on over stiff, resisting fingers.

Enos got to his feet and came around the desk quickly. Taking Fred by his shoulders roughly, he pushed him back into his seat. "Maggie's all right. I'll call her right now and set her mind at ease if it'll help you calm down." He looked at Doc. "What should I tell her?"

"Nothing more than you have to. We ought to break the news to Brandon first."

"I was planning to go as soon as the storm's over and the roads have been cleared," Enos agreed. When he moved toward the telephone, Doc took his place and kept the pressure on Fred's shoulders.

Enos had a lot of explaining to do. Fred had never known him to act so irresponsibly. The autopsy had come back and he knew Joan was murdered, so why didn't he show an interest in viewing a piece of the evidence? And why didn't he care about Margaret?

When Enos connected with Margaret, his voice carried across the room. "Maggie? Your dad's here. Look, he told us what you found, but don't worry. It's nothing to worry about. No . . ." Something she said drew a chuckle from him. "Believe it or not, he was right. No, it's not." Enos listened a moment and his face lit, as it always did when he talked to Margaret. "I'll make sure he does."

Enos broke the connection and Fred watched his face compose itself. But for the first time in years, Fred didn't care about Margaret and Enos. "How'd she die?"

Doc waited to speak until Enos had pushed the telephone back into a corner of his desk. "She was suffocated. The coroner's office fixed the time of death just about when I thought—somewhere between nine and eleven that night. Not a drop of water in her lungs, no sleeping pills in her system. Contusions on her skull. A small cut on one arm. Some skin under her fingernails. No significant blood loss."

Enos nodded, as if endorsing Doc's statement. "No significant blood loss, Fred. That means whatever you found up there isn't connected with her death."

Fred stared blankly until the import hit. The blood on the blanket wasn't Joan's. At least she didn't die from it. And Margaret really did not face any danger.

But where had the blood come from? And why had someone hidden the blanket behind the ladder in the garage?

Contusions on her skull, a small cut on one arm. Skin under her fingernails. Death hadn't come easily. She'd put up a struggle and her assailant probably had scratches to prove it.

All at once Fred felt sick to his stomach again. Pictures of Joan fighting for her life formed in his head. How long had she struggled? How long did it take to suffocate a person?

He shuddered and tried to rid himself of the image, but he couldn't. Her death must have been horrible. Had she seen her killer's face? Was it someone she knew? He couldn't even begin to imagine the terror she must have felt.

As the horror stabbed at him, he wanted to retch. He knew it was irrational, but he didn't want to be right any longer. He wanted more than anything for the autopsy to say that Joan had drowned, that she had committed suicide or had an accident on the steep lake shore that morning.

Enos rocked back on his chair, reached for a pencil, and held it between his fingers like a cigarette. Doc fell silent.

Fred breathed heavily, pulling deep draughts of air through his nose. "Who do you think did it?" he asked.

But Enos shook his head. "I don't have enough evidence yet to implicate anybody, but I'll get Ivan and Grady on it first thing tomorrow."

"He did it, you know," Fred mused.

Doc looked up, surprised. "Who?"

"Brandon. He did it."

Enos sighed. "I don't think so. He has an alibi, substantiated by a number of people for the time of death. Every one of his guests say that he didn't leave the party at any time."

"You've talked to them?"

"A day or two ago."

It was Fred's turn to be confused. "When did you say you got the autopsy report?"

"Just this morning. Lydel called me about a half an hour ago."

"But you've been questioning witnesses? Why? I thought you believed the suicide story."

Enos looked away for a second. When he met Fred's eyes, a sparkle lit his face. "I don't think I actually said I believed it, did I?"

"Well, of course you did—didn't he say so, Doc?"

Doc held up his hands to ward off the questions. "Don't get me in the middle of one of your arguments."

Enos scratched behind his ear with the pencil. "Even with a suicide, there's a certain amount of investigation that goes on. I talked with a few people. Everyone agrees that Joan was distracted and distant the night she died, but I also learned that Brandon never left his guests from the moment they arrived—when Joan was still very much alive—until they left, somewhere between one or two hours after she died."

"Why didn't you tell me? If I'd known . . ." If he'd known, then what? Would he have been content to do nothing until the autopsy report came back? Would it really have made a difference?

"What was I supposed to do, run around town accusing people of committing a murder that hadn't officially happened? You can't do things like that these days. Everybody's protected under the law. You step out of bounds once, accuse somebody, say the wrong thing at the wrong time, and the whole case gets thrown out because the law enforcement officer jumped the gun or got carried away. I did everything I *could* considering what I had to go on."

Fred leaned back farther in the chair, suddenly swamped by exhaustion. "You could have told me."

"I didn't have to tell you a blasted thing. You were

supposed to stay out of it, remember? As it was, I told you more than I should have."

Fred leaned against the back of the chair. He wanted to argue with Enos, but he knew he wouldn't get anywhere pushing this particular issue. He couldn't even be certain why it bothered him so much that Enos hadn't kept him informed about the investigation.

Gradually he relaxed and the sleep he'd been missing the last few nights tried to claim him. At least his part was over now, and life could get back to normal. No more questioning friends and neighbors. No more lying awake nights trying to figure out a way to convince Enos of the truth.

So why didn't he feel happy? Elated? At least he'd get a chance to read the whole newspaper in the mornings. He'd be home to see the John Wayne movie tomorrow afternoon, and he'd get to bed on time—no later than nine. Of course, he was tired. And he'd feel better once he got a little sleep.

But why did he feel let down? Left out? As if he wanted to keep going?

He might as well admit it—he wanted to keep going. He wanted to be involved. He liked having something to do in the mornings, something to occupy his mind, and he didn't want to read the newspaper all the way through—twice. He didn't even care whether he caught the John Wayne movie.

Against his will, fatigue overwhelmed him. He closed his eyes, promising himself it would be for just long enough to replenish his flagging energy. He drifted off listening to Enos and Doc.

Some time later Fred awoke, aware on some inner level that he'd been snoring. Doc had gone and Enos had his nose buried in *Vengeance Trail*, Deloy Barnes's latest western. Fred had noticed one or two copies left on the shelf at Lacey's the other day and meant to pick one up for himself.

Groaning, he pushed himself up in the chair with aching arms. The muscles in his neck burned, and his back had cramped while he slept. How long had he been sitting here? He glanced at his watch. Eleven o'clock? He'd been asleep the better part of an hour!

Enos looked up from the book, folded down the corner of the page, and placed it aside with a show of reluctance. "How do you feel?"

"I'm not sure," Fred admitted. "Stiff. Relieved." His disappointment at the recent turn of events would have to remain his secret or he'd never hear the end of it.

Enos smiled. "Well, you were right." Getting up from the desk, he strolled to his window and stood there a moment, looking out. "It's too bad this storm's come up. It's going to make going back over the crime scene almost impossible."

"Yep," Fred agreed.

"As soon as it lets up, we'll have to get back out there. That's the worst thing about this job, you know? Nothing at all to do for weeks on end and then, all of a sudden, wham!"

"Well, if you're short-handed—"

"No."

"I've been all over the scene of the crime and then some. Remember how I told you that I'd been all along the west shore?"

"No, Fred. There's an official investigation now, and you absolutely can't interfere with it. If you do, I'll lock you up just to keep you out of my way."

Fred straightened his coat and readjusted the collar. "It was just a thought. I wasn't the one who said you had too much to do. By the way, have you told Kate yet?"

"No. I suppose there's no reason I can't tell her before I tell Brandon. I'll come along with you and do it now."

Struggling to his feet, Fred tentatively moved his knees, unsure how they'd react when he got them moving again. "Want a ride?"

Enos grabbed his coat off the back of his chair. "I'll give you one in the truck. No sense trying to drive your car home in this storm if I have to go out anyway." He turned on the answering machine and locked his desk drawer.

Fred pulled open the door and recoiled when the wind whipped inside. Cold burned through his clothing and settled into his bones. Enos grabbed his old, black cowboy hat and settled it on his head. He drew on his gloves and clapped one hand on Fred's shoulder. "Ready?"

Fred nodded and lowered his head. With Enos at his side, he moved into the storm.

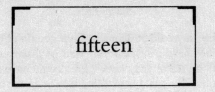

fifteen

Fred pushed the Mute button on his remote control. In forty-eight hours the strange sense of lethargy he'd felt in Enos's office hadn't lessened, and he despaired of its ever going away. He changed the television channel, but an old episode of "Perry Mason" lit the screen, and he pressed the Off button. He didn't want to watch Perry solve a murder this morning.

As he had a dozen times before, he thought about walking over to the sheriff's office—just to see what was going on. But Enos would be angry if he did, and as always, he changed his mind.

Enos had warned him away, and now he had no reason to stay involved. When he'd been trying to prove that Joan was murdered, he had an excuse. Now he had none. Kate had her answers. Enos had found the right track. And Fred had never felt so miserable.

Thinking of Kate, he frowned. Her things still occupied space in Margaret's old room, but he hadn't seen much of her since Enos told her about the autopsy. She'd left the house early yesterday morning and had come back late. And she'd done the same thing this morning. She hadn't eaten a meal with him since Sunday night.

He dug through a stack of magazines, looking for something interesting to read. He'd read them all.

Maybe he should walk to Lacey's and pick up that Deloy Barnes western. If Janice happened to say anything about the investigation—and if anyone in town knew how things were going, it would be Janice—Enos couldn't blame Fred.

Did Enos have a suspect yet? Had he discovered all the information Fred already knew? Fred could have saved him a lot of time. He could have filled him in on the breakup of the Cavanaughs' marriage, about the relationship between all of Russell Talbot's daughters. He could have told Enos about the so-called artwork of Summer's that was stolen, the threatened lawsuit, and Ramsey's involvement in Shadow Mountain.

But Enos didn't care what Fred knew.

Frustrated, Fred walked aimlessly around the house for a few minutes. There must be a hundred things he needed to do. He might as well get started on some of them today.

His slippers scuffed on the floor as he located paper and pencil to make a list. He settled into his rocking chair and chewed the eraser, thinking. After a few minutes he pushed the list aside with a sigh.

He couldn't pretend life was back to normal. No matter what he did, he couldn't get his mind off the murder. And he couldn't think of any way to get himself involved again.

The creaking of his chair broke the silence. Across the room his clock ticked off the seconds hollowly.

On the street he heard someone shouting. Even at this distance the voice sounded anxious. Suddenly he sat up straight.

"Grandpa . . . Hey, Grandpa!" Rapid footsteps thundered onto the front porch. Fred pushed himself out of his chair just as Benjamin threw the front door open with a crash. "Grandpa!"

"I'm right here. What on earth—?"

"Grandpa, look!" Panting heavily, Benjamin thrust out his hand. In it he held a small, dark object. Fred moved a little closer, narrowed his eyes, and adjusted his glasses.

A heel broken from a woman's shoe lay in Benjamin's hand.

Fred's heart hammered. It had to be Joan's. "Where did you find that?"

"Miss Dey's old workshed down by the lake." Benjamin's narrow chest rose and fell rapidly as he worked to catch his breath.

"We'd better call Enos. No, let's take it to him. Hold on just a minute. Sit down while I get dressed and I'll go with you."

Benjamin nodded and plopped into Fred's rocking chair, his face alight with pride. Benjamin shouldn't have moved the evidence, the only piece of physical evidence Fred had seen so far, but he didn't have the heart to tell the boy he'd made a mistake.

He dressed quickly, suddenly energetic. Within minutes he rejoined Benjamin and they set off on foot for Main Street.

Bright winter sunlight reflected off the new snow, giving the world the look of an overexposed snapshot. Fred shielded his eyes; Benjamin's squinted into the glare.

Placing a hand on the boy's shoulder, Fred said, "All right, boy, tell me what happened. How did you find it?"

Benjamin shrugged, trying to look nonchalant, but the gleam in his eyes betrayed his excitement. "I was looking for her snow shovels, you know? She said they were probably in the workshed? So I went out there and I looked around for a while. You know, dug into piles of stuff and looked behind things? I didn't really know where to look, but there's this sort of empty spot toward the back? You can't really see it from the front. So I went back there and started looking around. I didn't really expect to find 'em, but I thought I ought to look. Well, anyway, I saw this thing lying there on the floor off to the side—kind of shiny?" He held up the black patent-leather heel. "I picked it up, you know? To see what it was? And then I remembered Mom talking about the sheriff finding Mrs. Cavanaugh's shoes over by the lake? But she said one of them didn't have a heel and I thought—I don't know." He paused, then cocked one eye at Fred. "Do you think it's hers?"

Fred nodded and tried not to smile. He knew this was serious business, but he couldn't help being a little grateful for the chance to get involved again—even remotely.

Benjamin shuddered and stuffed the heel back into his pocket.

Fred patted the boy's shoulder. Murder might be a frightening business in reality, but it had to seem exciting in the abstract. "We'll get it to the sheriff and he'll know what to do with it. Did you move anything else in the shed?"

"Lots of stuff. I was digging around, like I said, looking for those stupid snow shovels."

When they reached the sheriff's office, the door was locked. Dismayed, Fred led Benjamin into town. They looked at the bank and at Lacey's. Fred used the pay phone at the back of the store to call Enos's house, but he got no answer. They peered up and down every street from Lake Front to Estes and finally ducked into the Bluebird to warm up.

At a booth in the corner under the movie poster from *Kissin' Cousins* of Elvis in a blond wig, they found Enos. Across from him, speaking rapidly and gesturing wildly, Kate had claimed a spot.

Fred took Benjamin's elbow and propelled him across the room. As they approached, Kate faltered, then stopped speaking.

Without the slightest hesitation at interrupting their conversation, Fred said, "Benjamin needs to talk with you, Enos."

Enos jerked his head toward the other side of the room. "Go sit at one of those tables, and I'll be right with you."

"This is important," Fred warned.

Enos sighed heavily and looked at Fred with barely concealed impatience, but Fred refused to back down.

Kate straightened her spine and put on her haughty face. "So is this."

Fred ignored her. "Benjamin's found some evidence I think you'll be interested in."

That caught Enos's attention—finally. "What you got, Ben?"

Benjamin started to reach into his pocket, but Fred stopped him with a shake of his head. "Scoot over and let us sit down. I don't want the boy bringing it out right here where everybody can see it."

Enos scooted toward the window, and Kate, reluctantly, did the same. Fred slid in beside her and nodded at Benjamin to take the seat beside Enos.

Almost reverently the boy withdrew the broken heel from his pocket. Kate's quick intake of breath did Fred's poor old heart good.

Stumbling a little over his words in his excitement, Benjamin told them his story. Enos met Fred's eyes, mirroring the concern Fred felt. Benjamin had inadvertently stumbled upon the place where Joan had been killed. Lab tests would prove it conclusively, but in his soul, Fred knew it. And he could tell that Enos did, too.

Liz wandered over with a coffeepot and a steaming mug of cocoa for Benjamin. She filled Fred's cup, ruffled Benjamin's hair, and left without a word.

Enos turned the heel over and over in his hand, looking at it from every angle, as if it held the answers to all the questions. "Will you show me right where you found this?"

Benjamin nodded. His eyes had lost their sparkle and his skin looked pale. When he raised his mug to his lips, his hands shook. Reality had hit him.

"Do you want to finish your cocoa?" Enos asked.

Benjamin shook his head uncertainly.

"Let's get going, then. Don't worry," Enos added to Fred, "I'll take him home. It looks like you're out of a job, Ben.

No more cleaning things up at Summer's—for a few days anyway."

Benjamin stood up shakily and looked to Fred for reassurance. Fred nodded at him and winked, but the boy still looked uncertain. Enos slid out from behind the table and placed his big arm around the boy's shoulder, guiding him gently toward the door.

Fred watched them go, but even when the door closed behind them, he didn't move to the opposite side of the booth right away. He didn't want Kate to leave just because Enos had gone.

When they'd left Summer Dey's house, he'd almost believed they could team up. But the minute she learned about the autopsy results, she'd frozen up again.

Kate shifted toward the edge of the booth but stopped when she saw he had no intention of moving.

He sat back and tried to look casual. "What were you two talking about when we came in?" He expected resistance, surliness, even antagonism. And he readied himself for battle. He was quickly losing patience with her attitude.

But she turned to him almost eagerly and a little of her animation reappeared. "I spent all day yesterday at the county recorder's office. You remember the file we found at the bank—the Shadow Mountain one with Joan's name on it? Well, I wanted to find out more about what she was doing with her money, what she had invested in, that sort of thing. Joan did own Shadow Mountain and she bought another piece of land next to it within the last couple of months."

"Are you sure?"

"Positive."

Impossible. He would have heard about it. Cutler was no place for secrets.

"Not only that," Kate went on, "but somebody else recently bought several other large tracts surrounding Shadow Mountain—another Cutler resident. Any guesses?"

"Brandon?"

Kate shook her head eagerly. "Logan Ramsey!"

Ramsey? It couldn't be. He'd seriously overextended himself a few years ago, made some bad investments, suffered a few losses, and he'd been struggling ever since to maintain his standard of living on a shoestring.

"Not Ramsey. It must have been the bank."

Kate rolled her eyes at him. "Within the last three months he's invested close to a million dollars in property around Shadow Mountain. Cash. No lienholder listed and it's all in his name."

Fred whistled. "A million? He doesn't have that kind of money."

"Well, he got it somewhere. Private loan maybe. All I know is that after I bribed the clerk with lunch and pretended to be on the lookout for an investment in property that would almost guarantee a big return, she told me all about it. She gave me the names of the people I ought to contact. It seems that plans are in the works to develop Shadow Mountain as a ski resort. They want to make it another Aspen—maybe bigger."

"What?"

"Thousands of condominium units, ski runs, an airport, restaurants. They even want to recreate old Silver City's Main Street."

"That would ruin the entire area!"

"It would change it, that's for sure."

"You know what's happened in Aspen, don't you? They've increased property values so much the families who've lived there forever can't afford to stay. Everything that made the area interesting is being destroyed. That's exactly what would happen here!"

"If a big development comes in here, Fred, you'd make a lot of money off that lakefront property of yours."

"My property wouldn't be for sale."

She shrugged indifferently.

"You don't understand, do you? You think everything is about money. Doesn't tradition mean anything to you? Or security?"

She looked blank.

"You don't understand about people like me whose roots have grown so deep we never want to leave."

"Why don't you face reality? The world isn't like that anymore. People are mobile. Society is based on change. If I had to live in a place like this, I'd lose my mind!"

Fred stood and looked down at her. "Let's not ever test it." He turned on his heel and walked toward the front door. Behind him, he heard her scramble out of the booth and run after him. Ignoring her, he stepped outside.

She caught up easily and fell in step with him. "Look, I know you don't like me, but I'm going to ask you for a favor anyway."

"What?"

"I've gone as far as I can go with this thing alone. I tried to talk to a couple of people earlier today, but they won't tell me anything. But people like you. They'll talk to you. When I try to ask questions, everybody suddenly develops amnesia. I need your help."

Not for the world did he want her to know how attractive that sounded to him. He frowned at her and made his voice gruff. "To do what?"

"Find out about Shadow Mountain."

"Why?"

"Maybe I want to invest in it, get in on the ground floor."

"Forget it."

"What? You're kidding?"

Fred stopped and looked at her. People never ceased to amaze him, even after all these years. Without saying a word he moved on.

"Why won't you help?"

"Because I'm not going to do anything to help somebody destroy this land for a profit."

"Okay. What if the real reason I need your help is because I think there's something fishy going on with the development and I want to find out what?"

"Why should I believe that?"

"Because it's the truth."

"Why do you think there's something suspicious going on?"

"Because you obviously think at least one of the people involved in this thing shouldn't be. And somehow Joan was involved in it. And because the developers are trying to destroy all this beauty for a profit."

He'd almost believed her until then. He kept walking.

She stopped. "All right, you want the truth?"

He hesitated, then turned to face her. "The truth."

"Because I have to *do* something. I can't sit here in this podunk town and rot on your front porch while I wait for your sheriff to make an arrest. Because I want to know why Joan was involved with this project. Because nobody involved in the actual development is talking, at least not to me, and that makes me suspicious. And because I don't trust the developer."

"Who is the developer, did they say?"

Kate's lips curved upward slowly. "They said." The smile reached her eyes. "A company called Basin Development. Its general partners are listed as Brandon Cavanaugh and Tony Striker."

sixteen

Fred believed in putting first things first, and he didn't propose to tackle this any differently. Kate had asked for his help solving the Shadow Mountain puzzle, but he knew—they both knew—that they really wanted to figure out who murdered Joan. And they believed the murder was somehow connected to Shadow Mountain. Find the answers to one and he'd find the answer to the other.

He sat across from Kate at the kitchen table with a sheet of paper between them. They needed to make a list of the suspects. Then they could identify possible motives and alibis.

He pushed a pen toward her, but she pushed it back. "This isn't what I had in mind."

Would it kill her to agree with him sometime?

She glared at him. "Can we just put the paper away? What good is it going to do us to sit here and make a list? There are probably half a dozen people we need to talk to, so let's go!"

Didn't she wear herself out, always being in such a hurry? She didn't even take the time to think. Her legs started getting nervous if she sat still for more than thirty seconds. If she kept going at this rate, she'd be old before her fortieth birthday.

He pushed a piece of paper at her. "Slow down. There's no need to go rushing off half-cocked. First we'll work through it on paper, then we'll go."

Kate expelled her breath and rolled her eyes. "By the time

you get around to doing anything, the development will be finished and a hundred families will have moved in."

He looked up and smiled. "I don't think so. Life moves at a different pace up here. We've got plenty of time."

"I've got less than a week, or have you forgotten? I've got to be back in San Francisco next Tuesday night."

"I haven't forgotten. That's why I think a little preparation will save us time when we're actually out there talking to people."

She threw up her hands. "Okay. You want to make a list of suspects, we'll make a list of the suspects. One. Brandon."

Fred reached for the paper. "Brandon Cavanaugh," he said slowly as he wrote the name. "Motive?"

"Maybe he really was having an affair with Winona Fox. Can you believe that woman? How could she have done it to Joan after Joan took her in, set her up in business—"

"We'll get to her in a minute. Stick with Brandon for now. The affair. What else?"

"Money."

"Why?"

"Why what?"

"Why would he kill her because she found out about his affair? Why would he kill her over money? Come on, now, Kate—work on it a little."

She jumped up and began to pace as she thought. After a moment she stopped in front of him. "They could have been having an affair and Joan found out about it, but that still wouldn't be enough of a motive—unless it affected Brandon in some way."

"It would have if Joan threatened to divorce him. He'd lose her money."

"He's lived the good life for a long time, and he'd do anything to keep things the way they are. But I don't believe Joan would have divorced him."

"Even if he was sleeping with her sister?"

Kate's eyes narrowed and darkened before she turned away. "I doubt it."

"Well, I don't. I can't imagine many women finding something like that out and being happy about it." He wrote rapidly. "And if she did file for divorce and wanted to take the Shadow Mountain property— Just imagine this, Kate, what if you're wrong? What if she did? What would that have done to Brandon?"

"Basin Development still wouldn't have been affected unless they'd already sunk money into the property. They probably never signed a contract or made the agreement binding since Joan and Brandon were married. And if Brandon already plowed money into Shadow Mountain, he might take a hit financially."

"Wait a minute." He held up one hand and wrote furiously. "You're going too fast." He finished making his notes and then looked at her curiously. "If she did divorce Brandon, wouldn't he still be a wealthy man?"

Kate shook her head. "They signed a prenuptial agreement. You can bet he didn't want to, but at least she listened to my father's attorneys about that. Joan's money was well protected against a possible divorce settlement."

But not against death. They stared at each other in silence as if each had reached the same conclusion.

Fred looked away first. "Who's our next suspect?"

"Winona."

"I didn't think she was involved in the deal."

"If she's sleeping with Brandon and he was involved, she had a stake in it somehow. Women like her always do."

You'd never believe Kate and Winona were sisters to hear either one of them talk. Fred shook his head. "Winona had to have a stronger motive than that. After all, Joan did sign the store over to her. Sounds like they were fairly close."

"Close?"

"Well, why else would she give the store to Winona?"

"Guilt maybe. Maybe she felt sorry for Winona because

of the way Father treated her in his will. Joan had a bleeding heart when it came to stuff like that."

"Okay, so why would Winona want her dead?"

"I said Joan had a bleeding heart, not Winona. Maybe she didn't think Joan gave her enough. Maybe she wanted Joan out of the way so Brandon could inherit all her money. Then he'd be free and she could move in and become the next Mrs. Cavanaugh."

"Or," Fred said slowly, "what if Winona was actually the one stealing the art from Summer and Joan found out? But that still doesn't explain why she'd give the store away."

Kate's voice came softly, her eyes dark with hatred. "If she did it, I'll kill her."

Fred looked up. Though her eyes had darkened and her voice held a note of steel, he didn't believe she actually meant it. "That's a good idea," he said. "That'd solve everything."

"Be quiet."

"Then talk sense. I'm not going to help you if you're going to talk like that."

She curled her lip and turned away. "Fine."

"Who's next?"

"What about Summer Dey?"

"Motive?"

"Her stolen art."

Fred made a face. "It's hard to believe she'd kill Joan because of those horrendous paintings of hers, isn't it?"

"The quality of her work is beside the point. The art theft upset her enough to make a lot of noise about Joan. Enough noise that Joan threatened her with a lawsuit just days before she died."

"Anybody who'd paint those awful things is probably capable of anything." Fred added her to the list. "Who's next?"

"Logan Ramsey. He's been buying up property around

Shadow Mountain, and you say he's heavily overextended. He's got a lot riding on that development."

"Then why kill her? It sounds to me like she was the only one who could make it happen. Without Joan, the whole thing would fall apart."

Kate stopped pacing and stared at him. "What did you say?"

"Without Joan—" He met Kate's eager glance and felt his pulse quicken.

Kate finished the thought for him: "—the whole deal would fall apart. What if Joan pulled out?"

"Would she?"

"I don't know, but what if she did? Who's going to lose if she did? Brandon. Ramsey."

"Tony Striker," Fred reminded her.

"All right. Brandon's partner in Basin Development. Same as above. Come on, Fred, just make the little ditto marks and let's get on with it."

Fred wrote it all out, thought a minute, and added a few more lines. When he'd finished, he had a list of suspects and possible motives and a list of questions he wanted answered. Had anybody in town heard either of the Cavanaughs talk about divorce? Why did Logan Ramsey visit Joan the night she died? How much money were Summer's paintings worth? And had Joan actually filed suit against her? Was it possible that Brandon had disappeared for a few minutes during the party that night?

Fred wanted to know why Logan Ramsey argued with Joan and what he wanted to stop her from doing. And why Summer thought Joan would steal her paintings and whether anyone else believed her accusations.

He wanted to find Joan's truck and have Enos check it for fingerprints so they could find out who drove it to Summer's house at one-thirty in the morning—*after* Joan died.

Kate sat across from him. She looked at him strangely, her eyes deep and swimming with an odd expression. "Are you sure you want to do this? You know the sheriff isn't going to like it."

Of course he wanted to. He wanted this more than anything he could think of at the moment. Investigating this murder, dealing with Kate, arguing with Enos, eavesdropping on conversations, all of it had brought him more fully to life again than he'd been in years.

A few days ago he'd thought it was over and life had slipped back into its routine. Now, with Kate dragging him back into the investigation, he realized that for more years than he cared to count, he'd been painfully bored.

He smiled, feeling almost tender toward her. "I want to do this."

She returned his smile. "Then do you mind if I ask you one thing?"

"Sure."

"Can we *please* do something now and quit making these lists?"

Fred pushed himself to his feet and reached for his jacket. "A few days ago when I wanted you to go to one or two places with me to ask a few questions, did you want to go? No. But now—now that it's all your idea, you expect me to run out the door at the drop of a hat."

"You've made your point. *Now* can we go?"

Fred pushed past her and out the back door. He heard her coming after him, but he didn't wait. "One more thing," he called over his shoulder. "I'm doing the talking."

The door banged closed hard enough to rattle its window. "Oh, no, you're not."

But this time he didn't intend to let her get the best of him. "You asked me to help you because nobody in town wants to talk to you. If you start asking questions, you'll ruin everything. You don't have what it takes to get along up here. You don't have the slightest idea how to treat people."

"I get along very well with people. I don't need lessons on social graces from you."

Fred crammed his cap on his head. At least he asked how people were before he started pumping them for information. Most of the time. "Your problem is that you don't respect these people. I haven't figured out yet whether that's the way you are with everybody or whether you just think folks who live here aren't as smart as the ones in San Francisco. Maybe you are more pleasant with folks there."

"I don't think I've acted any differently toward you and your friends than I do toward anyone else."

"Then you do have a problem," Fred said and set off toward town.

They quarreled all the way to Main Street, loud enough to bring Loralee Kirkham to her front door as they passed. Like children, they argued almost for the sport of it. Fred baited Kate and took great delight in watching her attempts at controlling her anger. And he enjoyed every minute of it.

They'd walked almost to the east end of town without resolving the question of which suspect to talk to first. Ahead of them, between the slush-covered pickup trucks parked in front of the Frame-Up, Brandon's silver BMW stood out like a sore thumb.

Couldn't the man show a little restraint? Maybe play the part of the grieving widower for a few weeks before he paraded his infidelities before the entire town? Reluctantly Fred met Kate's eyes. She must have read his suspicions in his expression, because her eyes widened. She looked at the car for only a second or two before she sprinted toward the store.

Trailing her, he hoped she really hadn't meant it when she said she'd kill Winona. She certainly looked capable of it at the moment.

The showroom stood empty. Even the merry tinkling of the bell over the door didn't bring a response. If he'd been alone, Fred would have waited until someone appeared, but Kate didn't share his reservations. Crossing the room, she darted behind the curtain.

Fred followed, clinging to the hope that he'd be able to stop her if she did anything foolish. At the back of the storeroom a stairway rose to the second floor. Showing no signs of hesitation, Kate took the stairs two at a time.

Fred's alarm grew. He took the stairs more slowly, reaching the top just as Kate disappeared through a door that led to the room over the first floor showroom. Before he could reach the door, shouts erupted. Shrill voices grated the air. A man's voice punctuated the cacophony with obscenities.

Fred stepped through the door into pandemonium. Kate stood just inside, her arms folded tightly across her chest, a gleam of triumph and some other emotion, something unsettling in her eyes. Brandon scrambled with his underwear while Winona lay on a sofa, a blanket draped casually over her.

"You'll never change, will you?" Kate said bitterly. Without mercy she watched Brandon's frantic attempts to dress.

Fred wanted to turn away out of decency, to give the man a chance to cover himself, but he wanted to keep an eye on Kate more. He had no idea what she might do.

She stepped toward Brandon. "You couldn't even wait for Joan's memory to fade before you went panting after somebody else, could you? You can't even *pretend* to be sorry she's dead."

Struggling, Brandon managed to get into his briefs and came out from behind the sofa at last. He moved toward Kate, his hands out, imploring. "You don't understand . . ."

Fred reached out to restrain her—too late. She slapped Brandon full across the face. "Don't tell me I don't understand! I understand everything. I always have. I know exactly what you are, and I'm only sorry Joan didn't find it out before it was too late."

She turned to Winona, who hadn't moved from her

provocative pose on the sofa. "I just had to see for myself what kind of woman you are."

Winona smiled wickedly. "Well, now you know. One who doesn't spend her nights alone."

Or her mornings, from the look of things. Fred looked away, uncomfortable with her state of undress beneath the skimpy cover, hoping she wouldn't move and dislodge the blanket.

"What did you promise him to get him in bed with you?" Kate demanded.

Winona brushed back her hair in a lazy movement. "*I* didn't have to promise him anything. I'm not in the habit of buying my men." She moved as if to sit up, let the blanket edge lower, and caught it in the nick of time. At Fred's flush she laughed throatily. "Isn't he sweet? You ought to take up with this one, Kate, he's such an innocent old thing."

Fred's face burned with embarrassment. He felt Kate look at him before she shifted her gaze to Brandon again.

"It's not what you think—" Brandon began.

Kate swore. "Save it. I've heard it all from you before." Without another word she left the room.

Relieved to have the scene over with relatively little damage, Fred nodded clumsily at Brandon and went after Kate. He had more questions for Brandon, but they'd have to keep. This didn't seem like a good time.

When he reached the top of the stairs, he saw Kate near the bottom. She leaned back against one wall, hugging her knees to her chest. She watched him walk down to meet her and for a moment he wondered if she were on the verge of tears.

"Well," he said with a little laugh, "that was a shock."

"I knew what I'd find the minute I saw his car outside."

"Then why did you barge in there like that?"

Kate shrugged. "Maybe I had to see it for myself."

Knowing would have been enough for Fred. Seeing went

a bit too far. She rocked herself gently and stared at her knees. He'd never seen her so quiet before.

"How long are you going to sit here?"

"I'm ready," she said, but her voice sounded flat.

"What's wrong?"

"Besides the obvious? It brings back too many memories. I'll be all right in a minute."

"Listen, let's get one more thing straight before we go any further. I'm willing to help you, I told you that, but I'm not going to do it unless you tell me everything. Like what happened between the three of you. And I don't want to hear that it was a long time ago or that it doesn't matter."

He honestly thought she'd refuse. He expected her to rise to the bait and stand up fighting, or tell him to forget it.

But she only shrugged. "I might as well tell you, I guess. It can't hurt anymore. I was married once—briefly. It didn't work out and we split up after only three years, but I still loved him even though I knew the marriage would never work. He married me for my money. He admitted it. The day the divorce was final I came home to find him with Joan. Oh, she never slept with him while we were married— I'll give her that much credit, but he didn't even let our marriage die before he went after her."

She tilted her head and looked up at Fred with a distorted smile. "Brandon married Joan less than a month after he divorced me."

seventeen

"I never had any idea how she felt," Kate said to Fred later. "We both met him one summer at Bar Harbor, and I fell head over heels in love. He wanted me because I was the oldest, and of course, he thought I would get the money." She shrugged almost sheepishly and kicked at a chunk of ice on the trail.

After the scene with Brandon and Winona, Kate had needed to pull herself together, and in desperation Fred had led her to the lake. They walked the north path, away from Fred's place, away from the spot where he'd found Joan's body.

He waited for her to continue, but she remained silent. "So you both fell in love with him."

Kate nodded, but kept her eyes on the path. "He was handsome and exciting. He said all the right things, did all the right things. Much later, of course, I recognized what I should have noticed from the beginning, but at first, all I saw was his charm. I felt so lucky to have him."

"What about Joan?"

"I didn't care. No, that's not right. I would have cared if I'd realized. But I only saw that he loved me and I loved him. I would have done anything for him."

"Didn't your parents see through him?"

Kate laughed scornfully. "If my father thought about me at all, he would have been glad to have me off his hands. My mother was dead. Joan was all I had until Brandon came along."

He touched the back of her elbow, wishing he had the courage to offer her comfort. "Maybe you were wrong about your father. We don't always know what another person feels. . . ."

"I know what *he* felt."

"That's probably what my kids think." He smiled, trying to lighten the moment.

She didn't smile back. "You're lucky, Fred. I've watched you with Maggie, and I've seen how much you love her and how much she loves you. I wish I knew how that felt. I don't feel anything but disgust when I think of my father."

"Why?"

She shook her head, but didn't answer. Shoving her hands into her pockets, she stepped ahead of him on the path.

Fred increased his own pace to catch her. "I've never understood how you and Joan could go ten years without seeing each other. Even thinking about my kids doing something like that tears me apart."

"Your kids won't."

"Didn't you miss her?"

"No. Not at first, anyway. I was too angry. Later I wondered if I'd been wrong, but I couldn't have done anything to prevent what happened and couldn't let myself feel bad about it forever. I've learned not to worry about things I can't change."

"But you could have changed that."

"Not while she was with Brandon. He didn't want Joan to have anything to do with me, and she seemed happy enough to go along with him. He convinced her I was jealous and that I'd try to ruin their marriage, but he just didn't want me to tell her the truth about him. He didn't need me to do that, though, did he?" She swung away from him and took a few steps off the path into a grove of aspens.

Fred watched her in silence as she walked through a pile of leaves and snow. Even wearing his boots, his toes felt like ice. He needed to get her indoors soon or she would freeze.

She looked forlorn standing in the middle of the snow, her arms at her side, her head drooping. He wished he could think of something to say that would help her.

It couldn't be good for her to be so self-contained, to lock everything up so tightly inside herself. By some odd circumstance he'd been thrown in the middle of this crisis in her life, and probably because he was responsible for urging her to stay, he felt responsible for helping her overcome it.

"I should be angry with him, shouldn't I?" she said over her shoulder a few minutes later. "I can't feel anything for Joan but pity. And Brandon disgusts me. No matter how hard I try, I can't make myself feel truly sorry that he hurt her."

Fred went to her. "Well, she hurt you. It's hard to feel sympathy for somebody who's offended you."

"Harder for some than for others, I suppose."

"Probably. So I guess that explains why you never came to see her—why you never called her in ten years—because she married Brandon?"

"Partly." She twitched her lips in a hint of a smile. "Mostly, I guess. I tried to tell her what he wanted from her, but she wouldn't believe me. She kept saying that I was jealous because she had him and I didn't. I don't know, maybe I was at first. But I knew what he wanted and I hated him for using her to get it." She knocked the snow from a low-hanging branch with one vicious movement. "I wish I'd never inherited that filthy money."

That surprised him. He always assumed she cared a great deal about her wealth.

"It's all we ever got of my father. Oh, I took it. He owed it to me. In fact, he owed me more than that, but the money was what I got, and I don't intend to share it with anyone—especially Winona Fox." She took a deep breath and looked away. "I didn't find out about her until I was seven. She must have been eleven or twelve, I don't know which."

Her expression changed and pain skipped across her face. Tears gathered in her eyes and spilled onto her cheeks. For the first time since he'd known her, she lost control and Fred suspected she'd needed this for a long time.

"Nobody ever bothered to tell me about his other family— about my *sister*. You know how I found out? Somebody brought a pony to the house one day. I thought it was for me. I can't tell you how excited I was. And happy. He'd never done anything like that for me before. He actually came home that night—which was pretty rare in itself. I ran to him and threw my arms around him and thanked him. I kissed his cheek over and over. He pushed me away and yelled at my mother for letting me mess up his suit and then he left. Afterward, my mother told me the pony was for Winona. That's how I found out."

Her shoulders slumped, but Fred didn't go to her. He held back, telling himself that she needed to let everything out. If he put his arm around her and offered her comfort, she would pull away and lock everything inside again. Later, when she'd let it all go, he could comfort her.

"My mother *knew*. She knew about Dierdre and Winona. And she stayed married to him. She said she stayed because she *loved* him. Can you believe that?"

When she met Fred's eyes, the tears had disappeared, and in their place, hatred glittered. "All I wanted after that was to look down on his face when he died—to see him in his casket and know he was gone."

Fred couldn't move, but he struggled with her hatred and tried to understand how a child could feel such anger toward a parent.

Kate's lips curved upward, but no warmth shone from her eyes. "From the time I was old enough to understand, I hated seeing what he did to my mother. She married him believing he loved her, but he'd been sleeping with Dierdre for years before he married my mother. Winona was born before he married my mother, but Dierdre didn't come from the right type of people, so he had to marry my mother—for appearances. My mother didn't know at first, of course, and after a while I think she stopped caring. When she explained it all to me, she said that Dierdre and Russell were the same type and they'd probably never get over each other. So she took the money and the big house and let him leave us to go to them. She learned to love the jewelry and clothes he gave her in exchange for holidays with them. I can count on one hand the number of Christmases we had together. I *hate* the money, but I'll be damned if I'll let her have any of it!

"When my father died, he left everything to us—Joan and me. We were his legitimate daughters, so we got it all. Winona couldn't stand it. She's tried everything to get a share of the money. She believes one third of it should be hers."

Which gave her a convincing motive for wanting Joan out of the way. But could she have overpowered Joan and carried her lifeless body to the lake? Or did she have an accomplice? Maybe she and Brandon were in this together.

Kate smiled up at him; the moment for comfort had passed. "You're thinking Winona killed Joan for the money, aren't you? But unless Joan left the money to Winona in a will, which she didn't, Winona had no motive."

"Actually, I'm trying to imagine Brandon and Winona working together. Between the two of them—"

"I don't know. Maybe." She shook her head, unconvinced. "I talked with my attorneys yesterday about Joan's will. I wanted to know how much Brandon gets—whether it would be worth it to him to kill her. They told me that everything from my father's trust goes to Madison."

"Not to Brandon?"

"Not a cent. The only thing he gets is the property they owned together, and there's not a lot of that. Not enough to kill for."

"Who can say what's enough to kill for? I read in the paper once about a lady who killed a friend over a game of

Scrabble. But maybe you're right. Maybe it wasn't the money."

"Summer?"

Fred shrugged. "If she believed Joan was destroying her, she might have done it. Besides, she doesn't have an alibi for the time of the murder, only her story about hearing noises outside of her house that night."

"I don't know," she shook her head, "there's no proof Joan actually stole any of Summer's art."

"Joan? I don't believe it. Winona? Maybe. She could have been skimming money off the top from the sales she made. She's the one with the contacts around the country. So she's the one most likely to be involved in this business."

Kate's eyes blazed. "Either way, she was using Joan's reputation and the store to take money that didn't belong to her and setting Joan up for the fall. But that only works if Joan still had an interest in the Frame-Up."

"We only have Winona's word for it that she didn't. She never let you look at the documents."

"If she's lying about that, Madison should inherit Joan's share from the store, too."

"Right people, wrong reason?"

"Something like that."

He cast a sideways glance at her and took a deep breath. "What will you do now? About Madison, I mean?"

"What is there to do?"

"You can't just leave her up there with Brandon and never see her."

She turned to face him. "What do you want me to do? Knock on Brandon's door and tell him I came to see her? Or maybe I should come to visit her twice a year. I know—I could stay with Brandon for the holidays!"

"I expect you to do whatever you can to see that she has a better life than you had."

"She'll have a wonderful life. She'll have all Joan's money eventually. What more does she need?"

He gripped her arm and brought his face close to hers. "She deserves more than a bank full of money. She deserves to be loved."

Her eyes glittered as she pulled her arm from his grasp. "Well, I'm not the person to give it to her. I don't know the first thing about children except that they're demanding and selfish. They want everything they see and they're never satisfied."

Fred bit back the words that rose to his lips, aware that they were born of anger and were probably better left unsaid. Selfish and demanding? Unlike some adults he could name, he supposed. He fought to calm himself, aware that she was watching him, and finally turned away, unable to look at her without voicing his opinion.

He didn't hear her come up behind him, and when she touched his arm, it startled him.

"You're angry with me," she said simply, as if she were surprised by his reaction.

"Yes."

"Why? Why do you care how I feel about Madison?"

What could he say? That he cared because he didn't like to see Kate so cold and unfeeling and because he thought Madison could bring her out of it? Or that she had only to look at her own painful childhood to find the answers? Better to say nothing at all.

"You think I ought to go see her?"

"Yes."

"And you believe that when I see her, I'll be swept off my feet and experience a surge of maternal instinct?"

"No."

"Then why do you keep bringing it up?"

"I just think it would be the best thing for both of you."

"Why?"

He'd tried to keep his mouth shut, honestly he had. He'd tried to keep his nose out of Kate's business, to let her handle her family the way she saw fit, but with Madison involved, he really had no choice. "Because you're going to do to her exactly what your father did to you. Because she's going to grow up empty and alone—just like you."

"You think I'm empty?"

"Yes."

"And what would make me 'full'? A husband and a dog and two-point-three kids in a little white house with a picket fence?"

"No." There was no point in even trying to talk to her. She'd closed her mind long ago to what he had to say. He walked away.

"I wouldn't even know how to love her, dammit!"

"You could try," he called back over his shoulder. He should have known better than to say anything.

Behind him, he heard the sound of her hurried footsteps. She fell into step beside him. "If the only thing of Joan's that Brandon inherits is the property he and Joan owned to-gether, that means the house, the money—all of it—goes to Madison. Do you know what that means?"

"It means Madison is a wealthy young woman."

"Yes. And it means that whoever controls Madison controls Joan's fortune."

"Did Brandon know about the will before Joan died?"

Kate shrugged. "I don't know for sure, but I imagine he must have. And if he did, Winona did."

"But Winona would never get her hands on it."

"Not directly. But if they got Joan out of the way, taking care of Madison's money would be easy."

That logic made Brandon's motive weaker, but still strong enough to be believed. The problem was, too many people were involved and too many people had motives for killing Joan. And the more Fred dug, the less he knew.

Maybe they should go back and talk to the others again. Logan Ramsey, for instance. Maybe they should find out just what connection Logan Ramsey had with Shadow Mountain and Joan. Maybe they should find out where he got a million dollars to invest and how desperate he was for the Shadow Mountain project to go through?

He matched his stride to Kate's and shoved his hands into his pockets. He probably ought to go home and warm up, get his hands and feet warm, but he couldn't. Not yet.

"Are you ready to hit it again?" he asked.

Kate turned to him and smiled. "I thought you'd never ask."

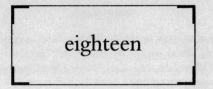

eighteen

Logan Ramsey did not look pleased to see Fred and Kate a second time. Scowling, he led them into his office and dropped into his seat. His starched white shirt stretched across his abundant middle. "What can I do for you this time?"

Fred settled into a chair and met Ramsey's wide, too-innocent gaze. "We need to ask you one or two more questions."

Ramsey worked his big face into an expression of confusion. "I can't imagine why you'd need to talk with me, but I suppose I have a minute or two." He made a show of clearing the center of his desk, arranged his hands carefully on the blotter, and turned a bland face in their direction.

"We want to know about Shadow Mountain," Kate said.

Ramsey's eyes narrowed. He looked from Kate to Fred,. trying unconvincingly to look perplexed. He shook his head vaguely. "Shadow Mountain? The old abandoned mine? What about it?"

He was good, and if Fred hadn't known the truth, he might have been fooled. "We want to know about the project Basin Development is working on."

"A development? I—"

"And about your plans for the property you've purchased on either side of it," Kate added.

Ramsey's face twitched. He twisted in his seat and rubbed the back of his neck with his big, open palm. "You must be mistaken. I don't know what you're talking about."

"We know you've been buying land around Shadow Mountain," Fred said. "We know the Cavanaughs owned Shadow Mountain and that Basin Development plans to build a resort community over the old mine."

Kate interrupted. "We know that Brandon Cavanaugh and Tony Striker *own* Basin Development. We know you're all involved with Shadow Mountain and that you, and a few others, argued with Joan the night she was murdered. What we want is for you to tell us what we don't know. For instance, what did you argue with Joan about?"

Ramsey pulled a handkerchief from his pocket and mopped his forehead. "I didn't argue with Joan. And I don't know why you're asking me about Shadow Mountain."

"But you did argue with her and we have witnesses who'll testify to that. And we're asking you because you're in a position to know," Kate insisted. "You're involved."

Shifting uneasily in his chair, Ramsey shook his head. Spots of color crept into his cheeks. Fred raised a hand to stop the exchange. He'd warned Kate to let him do the talking, but as usual, she hadn't listened. "There are just a few things—" he began, but again Kate cut him off.

"You've heard about the autopsy, I suppose. No secrets in this town, are there? You were one of the last people to see Joan alive. Don't deny it again—we've talked with witnesses who say you threatened her just a few hours before she was killed."

"I never threatened her!"

"There are witnesses who heard you—"

Fred dropped his hand on Kate's arm firmly. When she would have spoken again, he applied pressure and shook his head. She had to back down a little, or they'd never get the answers they needed.

Ramsey's eyes followed the exchange and flickered toward Fred. He swiped at his forehead with his handkerchief and made an attempt to pull himself together, but he seemed to have disintegrated under Kate's assault. He reached up with one trembling hand and rubbed his temple. Beneath his thick fingers, a vein throbbed and his skin had taken on a mottled look.

Kate had pushed him too far. She still thought she could play with city tactics in a place like Cutler. If she didn't back down a little, the situation could easily blow up in their faces.

"Just tell us what you know about Shadow Mountain," Fred urged.

"I don't know much. I'll admit I heard rumors that there might be something happening up there, so I used a little extra money to pick up some property. I thought it sounded like a good deal."

Kate raised her eyebrows. "A million dollars is a little extra money?"

Ramsey's face closed down. His eyes blanked and his jaw set firmly. Now she'd pushed too far.

Fred jabbed her with his elbow and wished vainly for something to stuff in her mouth. "Where did you get that kind of money?"

Ramsey stood and shoved his handkerchief into his pocket. "I think this conversation has gone far enough. I have no intention of answering any more of your questions. I want you to leave my office."

Fred shook his head at Kate. He might not be ready to toss accusations around, but he had no intention of backing down completely. "Everybody knows you and your family had financial trouble earlier this year, but suddenly you've got a million dollars to invest. There's only one place I can think of you could put your hands on that kind of money."

"Where I got my money is none of your business."

"Maybe not, but I think I'd be wanting to clear up any misunderstandings about it if I were you. Just in case anybody had the wrong idea."

Ramsey's lips thinned and tiny lines formed around his mouth, but his eyes widened, whether in anger or fear Fred couldn't be certain. "I arranged a number of short-term loans."

"Through Silver City Bank?"

"No. Through a bank in Denver I sometimes use."

Just when he had everything going so well, Kate couldn't resist adding her two cents' worth. "You'll want that information available for the sheriff. I'm sure he'll want to check out your story. Now, what did you and Joan argue about the night she died?"

Flushing darkly, Ramsey pulled open a desk drawer and rummaged through it. "I don't have to talk to you."

Kate's eyes narrowed. "No, you don't, but you should. I have to warn you, I'm not a nice woman when I'm crossed. Someone in this town murdered my sister and I won't rest until I know who did it." She sat back in her chair and crossed her legs. "I'm not Fred, Mr. Ramsey. I don't live here and I don't like you people. I don't know your wives and children. I don't have anything to lose by hounding you until I get the truth. Now, let's try it again. Why did you threaten Joan the night she died?"

Ramsey hesitated, but the hard glitter in Kate's eyes apparently convinced him to cooperate. "I didn't mean I'd *kill* her!" He looked from Kate to Fred frantically. "She called me that night and told me she'd decided to back out of the deal. I went up there early, before the other guests arrived, to talk some sense into her. She'd found out about Brandon and Winona, and she'd told him she was going to divorce him. He'd begged her to stay with him one more night—so that he could get financing for Shadow Mountain from some of the guests they'd invited to dinner. She told me she'd agreed because he promised he wouldn't put up a fight over custody. Anyway, by the time I got there, she was running around like a crazy woman. I think Brandon must have hit her because she had a split lip and it looked like she'd had a bloody nose. They must have had a real bad fight—there was blood and glass everywhere."

His eyes darted between the two of them almost pathetically. "I didn't care if she divorced Brandon, but they weren't the only ones involved in the project. She didn't have to pull out and leave everybody else hanging. Without her the whole thing crumbled and the property I bought became virtually worthless."

Kate looked disbelieving. "Aren't you exaggerating a little? Property in this area would never be worthless."

"It might as well be. Eventually it'll be worth a lot, but I need a quick turnaround. I figure I've got six months, maximum. I can't wait years for someone else to come along with enough money to develop the land. But Joan didn't care about anything but destroying Brandon. She knew if she pulled her money out, she'd ruin him. He'd already borrowed heavily and used the money to begin reclamation at the mine, but he needed more. Lots more. I begged her to reconsider, but she refused. She wouldn't even listen. I thought she might hurt herself—really. That's why I wasn't surprised when they said she'd committed suicide. Anyway, after I'd tried to talk with her a while, I gave up and went downstairs. I'll admit I was angry, really angry, but I didn't mean that I'd try to stop her *that* way."

"Is Basin Development going ahead with the project now?" Fred asked.

Trembling, Ramsey turned to him. "They have to. If they get back on track, I can sell my property at a decent profit within a few months and I can pay back . . . my loans."

Fred turned away. If his suspicions were correct, Ramsey had a lot of suffering ahead and a long way to go before things looked up for him again.

Kate looked disgusted, but it didn't stop her from launching another volley of questions. "How did Joan find out about Brandon and Winona? Who told her?"

"Everybody knew. She *must* have known before that night, but maybe she couldn't admit it. You know, ignore it and it will go away? I remember thinking maybe she'd caught them together, you know, and she couldn't deny it any longer and that's what upset her so much. I don't know. Like I said, we didn't exactly have a coherent conversation. I couldn't have cared less about her and Brandon, I just wanted to save Shadow Mountain. But she didn't care about anyone but herself. When she wouldn't listen to me, I got mad and left."

Kate looked as if she might be sick. She turned away from Ramsey, as if she couldn't stand to look at him any longer.

"Brandon should have done something," Ramsey whined. "He's the one at fault. If he hadn't screwed around on her, none of this would have happened. I just wanted him to talk some sense into her, keep her from pulling out, that's all. You've got to believe me—I didn't kill her."

"The trouble is we only have your word that you left Cavanaugh's then," Fred said. "Did anybody see you leave?"

"I left before dinner. I was so angry I decided to drive for a while. I ended up in Denver—I told you that already."

"No witnesses?" Kate asked.

Ramsey shook his head. Suddenly his eyes widened. "Wait a minute! That artist—what's her name? Summer Dey! She was coming in just as I came out. We nearly ran into each other on the deck. She saw me!"

Summer Dey had gone to Cavanaugh's? "I didn't realize she was a friend of theirs."

"I don't think she was. I don't think they invited her to dinner, anyway. She looked pretty rough—like she'd been crying. And she was angry, I can tell you that much. She was swearing up a storm and nearly ran right into me. I had to jump out of the way or she would have knocked me flat. She can tell you when I left."

"We'll check with her," Fred promised.

But Ramsey wasn't finished. "You want to know who killed Joan. Talk to Brandon. She was ready to cut him off without a dime. Do you know what that would do to a man like him?"

"Are you saying Brandon killed her?"

"I'm saying that if you're smart, you'll talk to him and quit harassing innocent people, that's all."

"Do you believe him?" Kate asked when they had escaped the stuffy atmosphere of Ramsey's cramped office.

Fred thought of Ramsey's face, twisted with pain, white with fear. "About which part? About the loans? No. I think he's been playing with money that doesn't belong to him and got caught with his fingers in the cash drawer. Now his back is up against the wall, and he can't do a thing to fix it. His wife will never stay with him through this. He'll lose his kids, his home. He'll definitely lose his career."

How far would a man go to escape a prison sentence? More particularly, how far would Logan Ramsey go?

Fred took Kate's arm and led her away from the bank. "That man's a wreck. He's ruined his life and he knows it. I believe he'd do almost anything to change things. Whether that includes murder—I don't know."

"People do strange things over money. He certainly had motive enough—and opportunity."

"But why would he take the money? How could he let himself get so deeply involved in something like that?"

Kate pursed her lips. "I know it's hard for you to believe, but some people find this kind of life a little stifling. I think Ramsey's one of them. I think he wanted a better life—all right, a different life. He knew he'd never get it here, not in this town. When he heard about Shadow Mountain, he saw it as his chance. There are a lot of people who can't resist money and power. He probably thought he could get in on the ground floor and when it became bigger than Aspen, all his troubles would be over."

"And instead, he created more problems for himself. He juggled the books at the bank, took money that didn't belong to him, and believed he'd never get caught. I don't know how he thought he'd get away with it."

Kate smiled wryly. "People do that kind of thing all the time, Fred. Somehow, in our own minds, we're invincible. We don't believe the bad stuff will happen to us. Most of us tear through life without ever stopping to really think about consequences. Otherwise, we'd probably never do anything at all. Life would scare us too much. You do it with your heart condition. You can't face it and continue to function, so you deny it and you keep on living the only way you know how."

"Foolish, foolish people," he said softly, not entirely certain whether he included himself.

Kate stopped walking. "So now what?"

"You're not going to like it."

"Brandon?"

Fred nodded.

"Why not Summer again? She's got a few secrets. She neglected to mention she'd been at Cavanaugh's the night Joan died. Why did she go there? Did it have something to do with her paintings? Did she confront Joan again and kill her this time? Or did Joan threaten her again and frighten her? You aren't forgetting about the heel Ben found in her shed, are you? Don't you think we ought to check into that? We probably ought to follow through with Enos and see what he found."

"We will. But I think it's time Brandon and Tony answered a few questions."

Kate fell silent. Fred didn't press her, but walked at her side listening to the syncopated rhythm of their feet on the boardwalk. Out of the corner of his eye, he watched the emotions cross her face, watched her make up her mind.

She smiled bitterly. "I hate him, you know."

"I know."

"I don't want to see him."

"You've already seen him."

To Fred's surprise, Kate laughed. "Quite a lot of him, huh?" She sobered and glanced at him. "I told you up front I never wanted to talk to him."

"You're the one who broke that rule. I didn't drag you into the Frame-Up this morning. Look, I know it will be difficult, but I think we'll get more out of him if you come along. Besides, he won't refuse to speak with me if you're there."

"I don't like it."

"I never asked you to like it." He stopped and took her by the shoulders. "Listen, Kate, we're going around town asking questions because we say we want to know who killed Joan—or that we want to understand about Shadow Mountain. Well, there's just no way to do that if we keep tiptoeing around Brandon. So do you want to find out who killed Joan, or do you want to keep fiddling around?"

She glared at him. "You're pushy, you know that?"

"It's one of my better qualities."

She laughed without humor. "And if I refuse?"

"I'll keep pushing you. You know as well as I do that you have to do it some time."

She walked away from him, but her step held little conviction. He followed at a discreet distance, knowing what her answer would be but content to wait until she knew herself.

After several minutes she stopped and faced him. "All right. But I have a terrible feeling I'm going to be sorry."

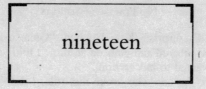

nineteen

Behind them Enos climbed out of his truck and strolled toward the Buick, his face sullen. He tapped on the window and motioned for Fred to roll it down. Fred lowered the automatic window, and Enos leaned his elbows on the car door, nodding a brittle greeting to Kate.

He made a slow survey of the car's interior before finally meeting Fred's eyes. "What brings you two up here?"

Kate's face composed itself in stony lines and she managed, somehow, to look offended. "I want to speak with my brother-in-law, Sheriff. I asked Fred to come with me. Is there some problem?"

Enos pushed back his old black hat and looked surprised. "Well, now, that's a change of tune for you, isn't it? Why do you suddenly want to talk to him?"

She sent him a scathing look that he pretended not to see. "My sister was murdered in this town and my only living relative happens to be Brandon's daughter. I imagine you can figure it out if you try hard enough."

Fred smiled sheepishly at Enos. "Don't let her bother you, son. She's just upset. This has all been pretty hard on her. She wants to make sure Madison is taken care of before she leaves town. We've heard one or two things that kind of worry her about the child."

Enos looked skeptical. "I wish I could believe that was all you had in mind."

Somehow Kate managed to look down her nose at Enos

even though he towered over her. "Have I ever given you reason to doubt my word?"

Enos tipped the brim of his hat. "No, ma'am. But Fred—well, he's a horse of a different color, so to speak."

Fred opened the car door and pushed it against Enos's legs. "I've never lied to you and you know it."

Enos stepped out of the way with a nod. "No, that's true. You just forget to tell me things. And you forget the things *I* tell *you*. I'll bet you already forgot that I told you to keep your nose out of this investigation."

Fred took a deep breath of clear mountain air, too thin and cold to give him a good lungful. "Speaking of the investigation, what did you find when Benjamin took you over to Summer's? Anything interesting?"

Enos patted his jacket, searched his pockets, and came up with a piece of Doublemint. "Plenty," he said, "but nothing I'm going to tell you about."

Behind them Kate climbed out of the car and slammed the car door. "Are you ready?"

Fred waved a hand at her. "Just a minute." Excitement pumping through him with every heartbeat, he turned back toward Enos. "That's where it happened, isn't it? That's where Joan was killed."

Enos shoved his hands into his pockets and walked toward the edge of the parking area. He stood quite still for a moment, looking over the treetops toward town. Fred followed more slowly. He wanted desperately to know what Enos had learned, but he also knew Enos wouldn't confide in him if he felt pressured.

Craning his neck, Fred looked over the scene that stretched far below. In the distance the lake glittered like a jewel in the winter sunlight. Heavy, dark pines capped in white stood guard on its shores. An occasional wisp of smoke marked the location of a house, but the forest still grew thick enough to cover most of the evidence of civilization.

What would happen to this place if Shadow Mountain became a reality? Fred visualized other once-remote mountain areas that now teamed with life. Six- and eight-lane freeways sliced through the mountains, condominiums scrabbled over the hillsides. People—everywhere the people wanting, hungry with greed—buying up every parcel of land until the locals, whose families had lived in one spot for a hundred years, could no longer afford the taxes or the cost of living in their own homes.

How long would it be before they devoured this forest? He sighed. Enos looked over at him, and the sadness in the younger man's eyes convinced Fred that he'd been having similar thoughts.

"It's going, Fred," Enos said. "Some day this will all be gone, and I don't think there's a blasted thing you or I can do to stop it."

Fred squinted into the sunlight, lifted his face toward it, and reveled in its fragile warmth. He could hear Kate moving around behind them, could feel her anxiety growing. This was one of the things she couldn't understand; the luxury of standing still in the sun for a minute. He didn't think she felt any joy in nature or in the act of living itself. She felt only the pressure of the moment and the need to accomplish—to excel. From achievement she derived her pleasure. But once her ability to achieve diminished, so would her happiness.

"Are you coming, Fred?" she called. He recognized the tension in her voice and responded. Patting Enos lightly on the shoulder, Fred turned back toward the house.

Kate waited for him near the porch as patiently as she knew how. Deep furrows creased her forehead, a frown puckered her mouth. Fred didn't look back at Enos; he would follow in a minute.

They climbed onto the deck. Tension flowed from Kate, making every movement precise. Fred knocked and almost immediately the door flew open. He had expected Brandon, maybe Tony, but Madison caught him off guard. She held the doorknob in both hands and stared at them with doe eyes, big and dark and wounded. Her tiny face puckered in a frown.

Kate gasped audibly and Fred put an arm to steady her.

They stared at each other, the child and the woman, taking each other's measure. Fred watched Madison, but remained acutely aware of Kate standing at his side.

When it became apparent that Kate would not speak, he broke the silence. "Hello, sweetheart. Is your daddy here?"

Madison's dark eyes turned to him. She nodded solemnly.

"Can we come in and talk to him?"

She shrugged and turned to Kate. "You look like my mommy," she said softly, and her little voice wavered slightly. She didn't wait for a response, but turned and ran down the hall. In the distance Fred could hear her child's voice calling for Brandon.

Kate stared after the child, her breath shallow, her eyes wide. He'd known how she would react once she saw the child. Madison's wide brown eyes and long blond hair created a startling effect. But more important, she looked almost exactly like Joan. He'd believed that if he saw it, Kate would, too. She had. It had shaken her.

He listened to the interior of the house, silent now. Even the sound of Madison's voice had faded. Enos climbed the steps and joined them, but Kate barely seemed to notice. She still looked stunned when heavy, adult footsteps approached the door and Brandon greeted them.

He gave no hint of embarrassment at their last meeting. Leading them into the living room, he grinned easily. "What's this, Enos? I didn't know you'd joined their little group. Is it the Three Musketeers now?" He chuckled at his own joke and then looked around the room. Piles of papers littered the coffee table. Someone had unpacked several large crates in the middle of the floor and exposed the backs of two large framed paintings. Packing material littered the floor; other artwork of various sizes leaned against chairs and the sofa.

Fred hadn't seen such a mess since they'd visited Summer Dey's art studio. In fact, the longer he stared at the mess, the more familiar it looked. "Aren't some of these Summer's work?"

Brandon smiled. "Ah, I see you're a man of many talents. You're an art expert on top of everything else."

Enos held his hat in both hands and looked at one of Summer's drab splatter paintings. "Why do you have these up here?"

"I wasn't aware there was any law against purchasing art." Brandon smiled broadly, but something dark hid behind his eyes. "These are just a few paintings Winona suggested I look at to begin my collection."

Enos looked up sharply. "Those?"

"They don't look like much, do they? But I'm told they fetch quite a price in Boston." Brandon chuckled. He seemed to be greatly amused.

"You're kidding?"

"Not your style? Not really mine, either, but I'm looking for an investment, and Winona says people are willing to pay through the nose for these things if they're marketed right."

Though he couldn't imagine anyone wanting to spend more than a few dollars, if that, Fred asked, "How much would these go for?"

Brandon scowled at him. "Why? Do you want to buy one?"

Before Fred could answer, Enos stepped forward, coming effectively between them. "Are you buying them from Winona?"

"Well, of course. That way everybody's happy."

Kate raised her eyes to Brandon's. "Why did Summer accuse Joan of stealing some of her paintings?"

A secretive smile tugged at the corners of Brandon's

mouth. He looked at her with hungry eyes. "Because, darling Kate, she's crazy as a loon, that's why. Joan never stole her paintings. Why should she? It's not like she needed the money or anything. But that crazy woman wouldn't believe it, and she damn near destroyed my dinner party when she came up here that night. It was all we could do to get rid of her."

Brandon watched Kate greedily, and a shiver of apprehension stole up Fred's spine. If Brandon's interest disturbed her, she gave no sign.

Enos scratched his head, bemused. "But you're going to buy her paintings. Why?"

"Because Winona says they're valuable, and when it comes to art, I trust her judgment."

Winona. Everything kept pointing back to Winona and to Summer. Either Summer killed Joan because she believed Joan had stolen the paintings, or Winona killed her because Joan discovered what Winona was doing. "When did you get these?"

Brandon's eyes narrowed almost imperceptibly. He didn't like that question, but why not?

Before Brandon could answer, Enos motioned to Fred to be quiet, and Fred bit back his next question angrily.

Kate moved toward a stack of paintings against the window, and Brandon's eyes followed her every move. Did he still feel an attraction for her or did some other emotion cloud his features? Fred couldn't be sure, but the dark look on Brandon's face bothered him. Worst of all, Enos didn't act like he noticed anything.

Kate looked thoughtful, then turned toward Fred. "Do you think these are the ones Summer accused Joan of stealing?"

"Could be."

"How much does Winona claim these would bring you if she sold them?"

Brandon named a figure, an outrageous figure. Fred

whistled. He'd never imagined this stuff was worth that much money. One or two sales could have made Summer very comfortable for a long time.

"I knew she had something to do with Joan's death!" Kate whirled back to face Brandon, her face dark. "What happened? Did Joan find out and Winona had to kill her to keep her from talking?"

"Ever the dramatic, aren't you, Kate? Joan found out what?"

"That Winona was selling these paintings and pocketing the money."

"Joan knew that, yes. There's nothing illegal about collecting a commission when you act as an agent."

"But she stole these, didn't she? And she made it look like Joan was responsible," Fred interrupted. "And when Summer found out about it, she thought it was Joan."

Enos folded his arms over his chest. "I think you'd better fill me in on the whole thing, Brandon."

Brandon looked away from Kate with some effort. "Joan figured it out herself when Summer came to her that first day. She came home upset and angry with Winona and threatened to force her out of town. Winona promised to make everything up to Summer, and Joan calmed down about it, but she never felt the same about things after that. Joan blamed herself. She felt responsible for Winona, like she owed her something—not money exactly, but something. She knew it was the money that drove Winona to steal the paintings. Joan believed that if she could give Winona something, set her up with her own business, she'd either stop or she'd run herself into the ground. That's when she signed the store over to Winona. She said she didn't want anything to do with it any longer. I thought Winona had taken care of everything, but when Summer showed up here at dinner the night Joan died, I realized she still didn't know the truth. After Summer finally left, Joan and Winona had another one of their arguments. Joan took off and that was the last I saw of her."

"And in spite of that," Fred said, "you still tried to claim that she committed suicide? Why?"

"I thought she had! There were the pills and—"

"—and your affair with Winona?"

Brandon looked away. "Winona told her about it. I don't think Joan believed it at first, but later . . ." He strode toward the fireplace and leaned his arm on the mantel, the picture of dejection.

Enos stepped forward and Fred bit back his next question. He hoped Enos knew enough to ask the right ones himself. He wished Enos knew as much about all this as he did.

Enos moved to a position behind Brandon and when he spoke, his voice carried a hard edge. "When did Winona tell Joan about your affair?"

Brandon shrugged and turned a tired-looking face toward Enos. "I don't know. A few weeks ago, maybe."

"Not the night she died?"

"No, it was before that."

"You're sure?" Enos looked thoughtful. "I don't think that's exactly right. Think about it again, will you? I don't think Winona ever told Joan about your affair. I think Joan found out for herself when she went to the Frame-Up and found the two of you together. She was shocked and angry, wasn't she? She came home and you followed her. When you got here, she told you she wanted a divorce."

Brandon shook his head, but Enos pressed on. "You argued with her and then you struck her, didn't you? And later, somehow, when your guests were all being entertained, you slipped out and killed her."

Brandon's eyes had widened with fear. "No. No, it wasn't like that at all."

"I've got a witness who will testify that you and Joan had a violent argument here on the night she died," Enos said.

A hushed stillness settled over the room as Enos's words

died away. From behind them all, a voice broke the silence. "I had to tell them the truth, Brandon. But I *never* wanted to believe it."

Fred turned in what seemed like slow motion and saw Tony standing in the doorway, his face twisted with emotion. He looked at Brandon, his eyes deep and sad. "Joan was terrified that night. Everyone in the house could hear you two. I stayed with Madison—you know how she hated it when you argued. Afterward, when you came downstairs, so upset about Joan and what would happen to Shadow Mountain, I got worried. I talked to Joan that night after dinner. I'd never seen her so upset. That's why *I* believed she'd killed herself. Especially when I found the bottle of sleeping pills . . ." His voice broke over a choked sob.

Fred didn't dare speak. He'd been right all along. About everything. The realization made him light-headed. He looked back at Brandon, whose eyes had grown even wider.

Without warning, Tony sprang from his position in the doorway and rushed across the room at Brandon. "You son of a bitch! You killed her, didn't you?"

Enos reacted quickly, but not quickly enough to prevent Tony from landing a blow to Brandon's abdomen.

Fred and Kate responded at the same moment. Fred grabbed Tony's arms and pinned them behind his back. The younger man twisted and fought, but Fred gritted his teeth and held on, hoping his strength would last.

At first he thought Kate was helping him, but after a few seconds, Fred realized she had rushed past him. While Enos grappled with Brandon, he tried to fend off Kate's blows, which, though aimed at Brandon, fell with disturbing regularity on Enos's head and shoulders.

It wasn't until he saw that Enos had Brandon in custody that Tony stopped struggling and, gratefully, Fred released him.

Enos produced a set of handcuffs and locked them on Brandon's wrists. "I'm taking you in, Brandon, on suspicion of murder. We've located the spot where Joan died, and we've found tire prints outside that match those on your car. We have witnesses who heard you arguing and who will testify that you struck your wife the night she died. We know about your involvement in Shadow Mountain and about Joan's threat to pull her money out of the deal. We know about your affair with her sister. The only thing I don't know yet is how you managed to kill her in the middle of the party, but the evidence says you did just that."

Brandon raised his head and the look in his eyes caught Fred off guard. "I didn't kill her," he whispered. "I never left the party until long after she died. You have to believe me! I didn't kill her."

Enos produced a small slip of paper from his shirt pocket and read Brandon his rights. The right to remain silent. The right to have an attorney present. Just like on television.

At the end Enos gave a sharp tug on Brandon's arm. Brandon stumbled slightly as Enos led him away. Fred became aware of the hushed breathing of the other two occupants of the room and then something else, the soft sound of muffled crying.

He found Madison huddled behind a chair in the hallway. When she saw Fred, she turned to flee, but he scooped her into his arms and held her against his chest. Whispering soothing, grandfatherly words, he calmed her slightly and brushed her hair back from her eyes.

Turning back to Kate, he met her frightened gaze. "She's got to stay with you now. You're all the family she's got."

Tony struggled to compose himself and held out his arms for Madison. "Don't you think she ought to stay here? This is her home."

"She needs to get away from here, Tony. I know you're her uncle of sorts, but Kate is her aunt and right now I think Madison needs the nurturing of a mother figure more than anything else."

Tony backed away and nodded. "You're right, I guess. I just hate to see her go through any more."

"We'll fix up a bed at my place for her. Kate, I think you ought to go find her some clothes and a few toys."

Kate shook her head and took a step backward. "I don't know anything about caring for children. I can't do it. What about Maggie?"

The strain of the last couple of weeks proved to be too much. Losing control, Fred shouted, "Dammit, Kate! Stop thinking of yourself and spare a thought for this poor child!" Madison flinched in his arms. He softened his voice, but spoke no less firmly. "Go upstairs and find some of her things."

Kate sent him a biting look, but climbed the stairs anyway, and Tony followed, quietly offering to help.

Suddenly the atmosphere in the house felt uncomfortable, overheated, and stuffy. Fred longed to get back outside into the fresh air. He patted Madison on the shoulder and held her against his chest, trying to calm her. Her lip trembled as she fought tears. "Did they scare you?"

She nodded and snuggled closer. He hated to see her so frightened. Children shouldn't have to see things like she'd seen the last few days. Poor little kid. He hugged her closer to him and wished he could make everything all right.

He could do one thing, though. He could get her out of this house with all its glass and expensive furniture and take her someplace warm and comfortable. A place where things had been made for kids to touch, where the floors were scratched and the carpets worn from years of knees scooting across them. A place where the closets still held blocks and trucks and ragged dolls with faded smiles—the kind of place where every kid deserves to spend time—to grow up.

He could take her home.

twenty

Doc closed his medical bag and turned around. "He's doing fine, Margaret. Nothing to worry about. Maybe a little more excitement than I'd normally prescribe, but he's all right. No need to change anything he's doing as long as he feels good."

Fred buttoned his shirt, aware that Doc's assurances carried little weight with Margaret. She'd believe what she wanted to.

"I don't care. I still think you need to cut back, Dad." She sent a pointed look in Doc's direction. "Do you know how close you came to . . . to . . . I can't believe you let yourself get in the middle of a fight! Thank heavens Enos called me when he did."

And Enos would hear a thing or two about calling her, too. "For Pete's sake, Margaret, I'm all right."

"If you were all right, Doc wouldn't need to be here, would he?"

"Doc doesn't need to be here. He's only here because you flew off the handle and called him."

Doc smiled as he shrugged into his coat. "Your dad isn't that bad off, Maggie. He still needs to watch what he does, and eat a little healthier than he likes to, but he isn't at death's door."

Margaret ignored him and turned on Fred angrily. "I'm going to talk with Enos about this. I don't know what he's thinking of—letting you get involved in all this murder business. And then to let you start fighting . . ." She crossed to the window and lowered the blinds.

Fred pushed himself off the bed and tucked his shirttail into his pants. "Leave the blinds open."

"You need to get some rest."

"I'm not going to rest and I want the blinds open."

"Dad—"

Fred's patience finally cracked. He'd had it with people treating him like an invalid and was even more fed up with Margaret treating him like a child. "Doc, would you please tell my daughter *again* that I'm not ready to die? I've got too much to do to spend the rest of the day lying in bed."

"He's no worse than he was last week, Maggie," Doc said as he grabbed up his bag and headed for the door. "He's getting moderate exercise every day and that works in his favor. The only thing you need to watch with him is his caffeine intake. Try not to let him have too much. . . ."

They walked into the hallway, and a moment later, Fred heard the front door close behind them. Margaret probably decided to walk Doc to his car so she could convince him to order Fred to bed.

Fred slipped into the living room. Kate sat cross-legged on the sofa studying the Yellow Pages and didn't look up at Fred's approach.

Fred came up behind her and looked over her shoulder. "What are you doing?"

Her head came up with a jerk and with one hand she smoothed the hair out of her eyes. "I'm making reservations for my return flight. Now that Brandon's been arrested, there's nothing else I need to stay for."

"You're leaving?"

"I have to be back to work in two days. I've put this off as long as I can, and now that it's over I need to go home."

"What about Shadow Mountain? What about Madison?"

Kate looked perplexed. "Shadow Mountain? What has that got to do with me?"

"What about Joan's interest in it? Aren't there loose ends you need to tie up or something?"

"The whole thing is Brandon's worry now. He can do whatever he wants with it. I'm not involved."

"Then what about Madison?"

Kate looked back at the book and turned a page. "I don't know what's going to happen with her yet."

"What do you mean? You're taking her with you, aren't you? She can't stay here."

Kate's eyes met his and hers flashed, dark and angry. "Why not? Tony says—and I agree—that it would be too difficult on her to move her away from her home at a time like this. He's perfectly willing to see that she's taken care of—at least until after Brandon's trial."

Fred snorted. "Tony? You'd leave that little girl up there with him? He doesn't know the first thing about taking care of a child."

"Neither do I, or had you forgotten? I think she'd be better off staying here. This is her home."

"She wants to stay with you."

"She's a child, Fred. She doesn't know what she wants. She'll be better off at home than in a strange place with a bunch of people she doesn't know."

"I don't think you should leave yet. At least stay until everything's settled."

"I don't have an option!" Kate cried. "I have to be back at work. I can't just stay here indefinitely. I have deadlines, commitments. People are waiting for me to get back to the city."

"When are you coming back?"

Kate laughed in derision. "Here? I am not coming back to . . . this place. Once I leave here, that's it."

"But—" Fred protested.

"I'm granting Tony a power of attorney so he can deal with anything that might come up."

"You're doing what?" Fred shouted. At the sound of

footsteps approaching through the kitchen, he reined in his temper and repeated, more softly, "You're doing what?"

"It's no big deal, Fred. It's just good business sense. He's already involved in the development. He knows what needs to be done. Who else would I have do it?"

"You shouldn't sign away your rights like that. That's ridiculous."

Margaret stepped into the room, her face a mirror of concern. "Dad? What are you doing?"

"Nothing—"

"He's trying to talk me into staying a while longer," Kate interrupted. "He's also giving me business advice. He doesn't think I can make intelligent decisions."

"I'd say that's pretty obvious, judging from the ones you're making right now," Fred snapped.

"I think you ought to let Kate make her own decisions, Dad. She's not a child."

"Excellent advice, Margaret. You ought to listen to it yourself sometime," Fred grumped.

Kate flopped back onto the sofa and leaned her head back. "Who do you want me to leave the power of attorney with? You? Mr. Progress? I'm sure you'd look out for my best interests."

"I don't want your power of attorney. I don't want Tony to have it. I wouldn't want you to give it to Enos. I want you to keep it and handle things that come up as you need to."

"Dad—" Margaret warned as the sound of little footsteps reached them. Madison, fresh from a nap, scuttled into the room and raced toward Kate, hugging her legs with two chubby arms. Kate clicked her tongue in annoyance and looked back at the Yellow Pages.

Fred called Madison to him, but she shook her head, unwilling to leave Kate's side. "Can't you pick her up for a minute?"

Kate ignored him and concentrated on her reading. Margaret disappeared into the kitchen again at the sound of the back doorbell, and a moment later, Fred followed, at his wit's end.

In the kitchen he found Margaret and Enos huddled together over the table, their heads together, their voices low whispers. Margaret looked up and stopped in the middle of a sentence.

Enos flushed, embarrassed to have been caught in the conspiracy with Margaret. "Is Kate still here?"

"In the living room."

Enos moved past Fred and Margaret turned toward the sink, pretending a sudden interest in Fred's few unwashed dishes.

"Leave them," Fred ordered.

"It's all right, Dad. I'll do them quickly before I leave."

Tired and emotionally exhausted, he couldn't take much more of her well-meaning concern. "Go home, Margaret. I'll do my own dishes."

"I don't mind."

"Margaret, go home. I *want* to do my own dishes." He turned away quickly, afraid to see the hurt fill her eyes, and followed Enos into the living room. From the kitchen came the sound of the back door opening and closing quietly.

Enos's glance flickered toward Fred as he entered the room, but returned immediately to Kate. "I've had to release Brandon from custody."

Kate bolted to her feet. "What?"

"I had no choice. The lab results came back. The tissue we found under Joan's fingernails doesn't match his. At best, the evidence against him is inconclusive. Until something else comes up, I can't hold him."

How could this happen? Fred had been sure they'd arrested the right man. The evidence seemed to point right to Brandon. "You mean Joan had someone *else's* skin under her fingernails? Is that what you're saying?"

Madison looked up at the sound of her mother's name.

"Mommy?" she asked, moving away from Kate voluntarily for the first time.

Fred had forgotten her for a moment. They couldn't talk about this now. Not in front of her.

Enos apparently reached the same conclusion. He patted Fred's shoulder and nodded toward the kitchen. "Fred, would you mind . . . ?"

"Yes, I'd mind."

But Enos waited, not speaking, expecting Fred to comply. In the end Fred scooped Madison up into his arms and retreated into the kitchen.

He poured a glass of milk, dug one of Margaret's homemade chocolate-chip cookies out of the jar, and placed them both in front of her at the table. Then he crossed the room and put his ear to the door.

Enos's voice came through only slightly muffled. Fred could hear well enough to catch most of the conversation. Would he always be reduced to eavesdropping on important conversations—even in his own home?

". . . checking into his allegations that Ramsey embezzled funds from the bank," Enos's voice rumbled. "He claims to have proof. He says that Joan knew about it—that she's the one who told him. If it's true—"

"I think it is," Kate interrupted. "Fred and I have both wondered how he got all that money. I'll bet a bank examiner would find Ramsey's books very interesting."

Silence for a moment, then Enos's voice came again. He did not sound happy. "Maybe you ought to tell me what else the two of you learned while you were *not* investigating Joan's death."

And to Fred's chagrin, Kate didn't hesitate. She told him everything they'd learned, everything they'd seen. She talked about their latest visit to the art gallery, their conversations with Ramsey, and their visit to Summer's house. She even explained Winona's various connections.

"We actually sat down and made a list," she said at last.

"Suspects, motives, that sort of thing. I'll get Fred to get you a copy of it."

"You've been busy," Enos grumbled.

"I had to do something, especially after I found out about the will. Brandon controls everything, of course, but if anything happens to him before Madison is twenty-five, Joan named me as his successor. . . ." Her voice dropped and Fred couldn't hear what she said next.

He looked over at Madison, where she smacked her lips over the cookie. She gave him a chocolate grin and lifted the glass of milk.

Kate's voice rose again, loud enough for Fred to hear her last few words. ". . . pretty sharp for an old man."

That was the last straw. The whole younger generation seemed to think mental agility disappeared when skin began to wrinkle. And they acted so amazed if a senior citizen showed any signs of intelligence. Even Kate sounded surprised that he was still alert at seventy-two.

But who had been right about the murder in the first place? And who'd been responsible for finding out all that information she'd just rattled off to Enos? An old man, that's who! He snorted in derision and turned back toward Madison.

The full humiliation of his situation hit him. Banished to the kitchen with a child—and in his own home! Who did they think they were—and why did he let them get away with it? Maybe it was time for this old man to straighten a few things out.

He wiped away the cookie crumbs and put his hand on Madison's shoulder. "Want to go for a walk with me?"

She nodded happily. "Can Kate come?"

"Not this time, but we'll be back in a minute. We'll be back before she even misses us."

He retrieved their coats from the back porch and zipped Madison tightly into hers. He stuffed mittens on her tiny hands and tied her hood until it puckered around her little face. With utter trust, the kind that frightened him for his own grandchildren, she reached up and took his hand.

He led her down the driveway and wondered how long it would take Kate and Enos to discover they were gone. When they came to look for him, he wouldn't be sitting there waiting.

He'd suffered enough indignity allowing Margaret to treat him like a child. He wasn't going to let Enos and Kate join in. It was time to do something about it.

And in the meantime he intended to have a banana split with hot fudge and half a pot of coffee at the Bluebird. And he defied any of those kids to find him and tell him he couldn't.

twenty-one

In the big corner booth beneath the *Blue Hawaii* poster at the Bluebird, Fred started to feel a little better. In the background Elvis sang "Let Me Help" while Lizzie brought two glasses of water and a straw for Madison. Fred ordered coffee, but Lizzie shook her head.

"Can't," she said.

Fred sighed. "Don't you start—"

Lizzie dropped into a chair beside him and covered his hand with hers. "I can't do it, Fred. Doc told me about you getting in that fight up at Cavanaugh's, and he said he'd close me down if I served you coffee any time in the next two weeks."

"He can't close you down, for heaven's sake."

"I know that," she said and looked offended that he would even suggest such a thing. "But he's worried about you. We all are. And I'm not giving you a drop of coffee for two weeks—until the seventh of November. I've marked it on my calendar." She patted his hand roughly. "Now, don't you get mad at *me*. If I didn't care . . ."

She left him to draw his own conclusions. Pushing herself to her feet, she nodded toward Madison. "That Joan's little girl?"

"That's right."

"Looks just like her mother, don't she?"

Fred sipped his water and made a face. Maybe it was time to leave Cutler and move someplace larger, someplace where the people wouldn't care whether he had a cup of coffee or not. Someplace where nobody would feel the compulsion to baby-sit him or where they wouldn't worry about answering to Margaret if they accidentally treated him like an adult.

Lizzie reached a hand toward Madison and stroked her cheek. "Cute little thing, isn't she?"

Madison accepted Lizzie's attention solemnly. She held her water glass in two hands and tried to lift her mouth high enough over the rim to take a drink. Water dribbled down her chin.

Lizzie chuckled. "Let me know when you're ready to order."

"I'd be ready now if you'd give a man what he wants."

"Sorry. Some other time." She walked away, not even looking back.

If there had been any other place to go in town, he'd have taken his business there.

Madison turned her big brown eyes in his direction. "Where's Kate?"

"Back at my house. We'll go back in a minute."

The child nodded. "Are you mad at her?"

Fred smiled. "No. I just wanted to take a walk." And to get away from his own house.

Madison kicked her short legs and pondered his answer. The straw in her water glass distracted her. She dribbled water across the table, before she spoke again. "I don't like people to be mad."

"Neither do I," he said absently. Sometimes a man just couldn't help but be mad. Sometimes a situation called for anger.

"Everybody was mad at Mommy."

Fred wiped the water on the table with his napkin. He didn't want to be angry with Margaret or Enos, but he had to do something.

Madison pulled her straw out of her water again. "Mommy didn't like people to be mad, either. It made her cry. I want her to come back, and I want everybody not to be mad at her anymore."

Fred took the straw away. What could he say to Margaret that would make her understand? He stopped and looked at Madison, realizing for the first time what she'd said.

"How did you know everybody was mad at your mommy?"

"'Cause I heard 'em. I don't like people who get mad, and I don't like people who make Mommy cry." She picked up her spoon and walked it across the table. "Do I have to go back to my house?"

"Don't you want to?"

"No." She picked up her fork and made it dance with the spoon.

Fred took the fork away and left the spoon dancing by itself. "Why not?"

"I just don't." The spoon stopped dancing. "He maked my mommy cry, and then he taked her away, and I don't like him anymore."

Fred's pulse stuttered and began beating a rapid tattoo. How much did she know about what happened to her mother? What was she—four? five?—old enough to be aware of what was going on in her home. But did she understand that someone had killed her mommy?

"Who took your mommy away?"

"A very bad person."

"Do you know who?"

After a moment's hesitation she shook her head.

"Did somebody tell you not to tell?"

She nodded.

What idiot would tell a small child something like that? And what effect would it have on her? Would she carry scars forever? Would she have trouble adjusting? Be a rotten teenager?

In his day people always said kids were resilient, that they could bounce back from anything. But these days they thought kids couldn't handle a blasted thing. Every time he turned on the television or the radio, somebody had something to say about it. About how every little thing you did around a kid affected their life somehow.

Madison reached for her fork. "Can we eat now?"

Chalk one up for the old-timers. She seemed normal enough, as long as people stopped filling her head with horror stories.

He turned in his seat, intending to signal Lizzie that he was ready to order. The window behind Madison looked out over the street. Through it, he saw someone moving around. He focused slowly.

Brandon had parked his BMW in front of the Frame-Up again—as bold as brass. While Fred watched, he disappeared into the store. Doing what? Another clandestine meeting in full view of the entire town?

Just as well Kate hadn't come with them. She'd have bolted out of her seat if she'd seen this. Fred's eyes rose to the second-story window. He couldn't see anything from here, but he wondered whether they'd gone up there again.

A minute later the front door of the store opened, and Brandon emerged carrying a box. At least this time they must have stayed on the main floor.

Brandon's weight shifted as he carried the box. He paused once or twice on the way to his car to catch his breath. Whatever the box held must be fairly heavy.

Brandon lifted his head and looked up and down the street furtively, then balanced the box against the car while he opened the trunk and put it inside.

He hurried back into the store, and a minute or two later he reappeared carrying another box. What on earth were they doing over there? Clearing out?

With Brandon out of jail, it meant he'd come after Madison next. But Fred couldn't return Madison to Brandon's custody—not now.

Determined to put off the inevitable, Fred reached behind Madison and pulled down the blind, both to shield her from

Brandon's view and to prevent her from seeing her father on the street. Until he knew what Brandon's intentions were, Fred wouldn't make any decisions about Madison. Until he had to, he wouldn't do anything about giving her back.

For the first time that day he wished Kate was with him, but as quickly as the thought came, he buried it. For what he had in mind, she would have been in the way.

He wanted to know what Brandon and Winona were doing, but he couldn't do anything about it as long as he had Madison with him. He cast about for other possibilities.

Margaret. But Winona and Brandon might leave any minute; he didn't have time to call her.

George Newman sat at the counter, hunched over a plate. Fred knew George and trusted him, but he wasn't going to thrust an already frightened four-year-old at him. It wouldn't be good for either of them.

The song on the jukebox changed and the opening stanzas of "Suspicious Minds" blared from the speakers. The frantic music only increased Fred's sense of urgency. What should he do? Brandon and Winona were obviously removing something from the Frame-Up and he couldn't let them load up and drive away without even trying to find out what they were up to.

Lizzie.

Where had she gone? The kitchen. Cautioning Madison to stay at the table, he hurried toward the kitchen. Behind a swinging door, he found Lizzie before a sink filled with soapy water, thick rubber gloves on her hands.

"I need a favor."

She waved a gloved hand in his direction. "Get out of the kitchen."

"I need to check on something, but I can't do it if the girl is with me."

"I'll keep my eye on her."

"I won't be long."

"Go on."

"You're sure it's okay?" Lizzie nodded and he started out the door. "I promised her some ice cream," he called back to her. "Will you give her some?"

"Get out of my kitchen before I change my mind," she grumbled, but one hand had already reached for the freezer.

"Don't let her go with *anybody*."

"Don't worry, she'll be all right."

"I mean anybody—okay?"

"I got it."

"Thanks, Lizzie."

She sent him away with a scowl.

He quickly returned to the table where Madison waited for him, her eyes wide and trusting.

"Lizzie is going to bring your ice cream," he told her. "I've got to run outside for just a few minutes. If I'm not back by the time you've finished yours, tell Lizzie to bring some for me and you can eat it, too. Okay?"

Madison nodded, but her eyes reflected uncertainty.

He bent over her and hugged her quickly. Her little lip quivered. He hugged her again and only when Lizzie started toward the table with a dish of strawberry ice cream did he let himself leave the restaurant. Behind him, the music faded away as he crossed the street.

He should probably call the house and see if Enos had left yet. But why? What would he say? That Brandon had gone to Winona after Enos released him? What if he had? That Brandon had loaded two big boxes into the trunk of his car? That didn't mean anything. That he had a bad feeling? That wouldn't get him anywhere.

Besides, he didn't want to call Enos. He ducked into the shadowy doorway of the shoe repair shop just as the door to the Frame-Up opened again. He hoped Brandon hadn't seen him from the window. This time Winona followed Brandon into the street.

Brandon carried another heavy box to the car and spent a minute or two arranging the trunk while Winona watched, hands on hips. Twice she lifted her gaze and studied the street. Twice Fred pulled back into the shadows, hoping she wouldn't see him hiding there.

When Brandon had arranged the boxes to his satisfaction, he closed the trunk. Winona went to him, and he took her into his arms tenderly.

Brandon kissed her forehead and pressed her from him. "Do you need to do anything else?"

"Not a thing." Winona twined her fingers through his hair. "I can't believe this is finally happening."

After kissing her again, Brandon released her, but he looked worried. "Darling," he hesitated and reached one hand out to trace her lips with his finger. "I've decided to leave Cutler right away."

"Six more months, sweetheart, and then we can leave. By then everything will be done on the mountain and they'll be ready to start construction. They won't need us here for the first few months."

"No." He turned away from her. "I mean that I want to leave—now. I'm not going to finish Shadow Mountain."

Winona looked as if he'd hit her in the face. She recovered after a moment, smiled, and wrapped her arms around him. "You scared me. Don't do that—I thought you were serious."

Brandon didn't return her smile. He held her hands and pushed her away from him again. "I am serious. This project just isn't worth the trouble it's causing. I've decided to cut my losses and pull out." His hands slid up Winona's arms in a caressing motion.

Winona didn't move for a long time. The words must have registered as slowly as the smile slid from her lips. Her brows knit in confusion, as if she still battled to convince herself Brandon had told her a hideous joke. At last anger replaced confusion.

"You bastard!"

Brandon tried to gather her into his arms again, but she

pushed him away roughly. "After all we've been through? After everything we've done?"

"Trust me," he said. "I know what's best for us. I've found another property in Phoenix. It's wonderful—a dream come true. Wait till you see it."

"*This* is my dream come true. This is what I've worked toward for the last two years." She took a few steps away from him. Brandon reached for her, angry with her now, but she twisted away from him. "You can't throw it all away."

Brandon looked over his shoulder, as if checking to make sure they hadn't been overheard. He smiled, but the anger that boiled below the surface was barely concealed. "I can do anything I want. I've put up with a woman telling me what to do for the last fifteen years of my life, and I'm not going to take it from you now."

"You're pathetic." Winona turned away and walked quickly back toward the Frame-Up.

Brandon ran after her, grabbed her by the shoulders, and turned her toward him. "Don't play games with me. You're in this as far as I am. You'd better be grateful I'm getting rid of the books before someone tries to prove what happened to those paintings."

She struck him viciously across the face. "*I* didn't do a thing—yet."

Winona ran back inside and slammed the door behind her. Brandon stood in front of his car, red-faced. He clenched and unclenched his fists repeatedly as if struggling against some violent urge.

Fred longed to escape the cramped doorway before Brandon discovered him there. His back and knees ached, and he needed to take the load off his feet. He wanted to go home and get warm. He wanted to forget about Enos and Kate and Margaret and murders and suspects and illicit love affairs and Shadow Mountain and art theft, but he couldn't. He'd think about it all night. He wouldn't sleep. By morning, he'd be a wreck.

He waited for Brandon to get into his car, impatient now to get out of his hiding place. But when Brandon turned, a shout from behind stopped him. Letting go of the car door, Brandon stepped away and out of Fred's sight.

Leaning forward, Fred strained to see Brandon's companion. A pair of thick legs, shiny black leather shoes, gray trousers with a crease . . . Logan Ramsey. Now, this was an interesting turn of events.

Fred strained to hear their conversation, but they stood too far away. He could hear only a word or two, but enough to know they weren't having a friendly conversation.

Brandon moved backward and Ramsey followed, stepping fully into Fred's view for the first time. His arms gestured wildly near Brandon's face. His mouth moved rapidly, angrily, stretching wide as the words tumbled out.

Brandon pushed Ramsey in the chest with both his hands and turned away from him. A mistake.

Ramsey exploded. His face twisted in fury and he rushed at Brandon, hitting him just as Brandon reached the BMW. The two men fell heavily against the car, and Ramsey used his bulk to hold Brandon against the car.

Brandon struggled, but Ramsey held him there. "You're not going to get away with this, Cavanaugh!"

Fighting to push away his attacker, Brandon might have won if Ramsey hadn't been the bigger man. He held fast.

From where he stood, Fred could only see the back of Brandon's head. He couldn't tell whether Brandon spoke or not, but after several long seconds, Ramsey released Brandon and pulled himself up unsteadily.

"Tonight then!" Ramsey shouted. "And you'd better be there." As suddenly as he appeared, Ramsey turned away, leaving Brandon alone.

At last Brandon ran his fingers through his hair, slid behind the wheel of his car, and drove away.

Relieved to be alone, Fred gave Brandon a few minutes to get out of sight before emerging from the doorway. His knees were cramped and stiff and his neck hurt. Unfortunately, he had no better idea what had happened to Joan than before. Everything he heard, everything he saw, turned him in a different direction. He suspected first one neighbor, then another.

He walked slowly back to the Bluebird, pondering, questioning, trying to piece together the puzzle. He had all the pieces, but he didn't know how they fit.

Tempers still ran high and he suspected it wasn't over yet. He felt uneasy, apprehensive. Like watching stormclouds roll across the mountains and watching the sky darken and not being able to do anything to stop it from coming.

twenty-two

From somewhere in the night a rhythmic pounding roused Fred from a sound sleep. He wondered if he'd imagined it and looked at the illuminated face on his alarm clock beside his bed. Two-fifteen. He'd never get back to sleep now.

The pounding came again, and he stumbled from his bed and down the hall, barely awake enough to identify the direction from which it sounded. He hurried to the front door and switched on the outside light. Under its harsh white glare Enos waited impatiently, his breath visible in the icy night air.

Opening the door, Fred drew his robe tightly across his chest. "What on earth . . . ?"

Enos barged through the door, the scent of the night on his clothes. "Where's Kate?"

"It's two o'clock in the morning. Where do you think she is?"

"Go wake her."

Another time Fred might have protested, but Enos's manner seemed too urgent. He turned to go, but Kate entered the room, disheveled from sleep.

Enos scarcely greeted her, he just motioned her toward the sofa. She sat and waited groggily for him to speak.

Worry lines etched a pattern across Enos's forehead and around his eyes. A cold finger of apprehension ran up Fred's spine.

Enos pushed his fingers through his thin hair and looked

at Kate apologetically. "I've got some bad news. Brandon's body has been found at the bottom of that sinkhole at the abandoned mine."

Kate shot up from the sofa, her eyes wide. "What?"

"Brandon's been murdered."

Wide awake now, Fred crossed to the sofa and pressed Kate back into her seat. "How did it happen?"

"Winona called in earlier. She was worried about him. She said he'd gone out after dinner to meet someone at the mine site. When he didn't come back, she got worried and called me. Grady and I went looking for him and we found him—dead."

Kate's hand shook and her lip quivered slightly when she spoke. "How could you let this happen?"

Enos removed his hat and turned it in his hands in a way Fred had seen him do many times—a signal that he was struggling to control himself. "There was no way I could have known this would happen."

"Any clues?" Fred left Kate's side and lowered himself into his rocking chair.

"Not many. Signs of a scuffle near the edge, enough to make us believe Brandon didn't go over on his own. Nothing else to speak of. Winona couldn't tell us anything."

Fred thought of Ramsey's parting words to Brandon earlier that afternoon. He'd have to tell Enos about his latest escapade, he supposed.

Kate propped her elbows on her knees and buried her face in her hands, more upset than Fred expected her to be.

"Winona didn't know who he was meeting?"

Kate looked up. "Does she have an alibi, or do you think maybe she pushed him over and then came back home to play the part of the grieving lover?"

"I don't think she's guilty." Enos looked worn out.

But Kate didn't seem to care. "Why not? Who would be more likely to kill him? Where was she when he was killed? How did she know where to find him?"

"I've told you what I know."

She shot to her feet again. "What are you doing *here*? How do you know she's not skipping town right now?"

Enos answered with infinite patience. "I've got one of the boys keeping an eye on her. She's not going anywhere. I have someone on Ramsey's house and Summer's cabin, too."

Kate glared at him. "Well, go arrest her. What are you waiting for? Do you want her to kill again?"

Fred set the rocking chair in motion. "I have to agree with Enos. She might have killed Joan, but I don't think she killed Brandon."

Kate made a noise of disgust and turned away. "I don't believe you two. The woman is a parasite. All she's after is the money. Joan's money—*my* money."

"She's your sister, isn't she?" Enos's brows knit in confusion.

"*Half* sister. For all that meant to her. She never cared about anything or anybody except herself in her entire life."

With a shake of his head Enos replaced his hat and started for the door. "I've got lots to do still and it's getting late. I thought you ought to know. You've still got Madison here with you, don't you?"

Fred nodded absently, but Kate said, "For the time being. Tony doesn't think we should move her out of her home on top of everything else. I've been wondering if he isn't right. . . ."

"But you are her closest living relative, isn't that right?"

"Other than Tony, yes."

"And Winona."

"You wouldn't give Madison to *her*?" Kate's eyes widened. If Fred hadn't known her better, he might have suspected some genuine concern for the girl.

"For now I think it's best to leave Madison right where she is. We won't do anything about moving her until we have to. It's all right if she stays here a while longer, isn't it, Fred?"

"Of course. She's happy here." He refrained from adding that she ought to stay with Kate, whether Kate wanted the responsibility or not. Instead, he brought the conversation back to Brandon's murder. "Do you have any idea who might have done this?"

"A few," Enos admitted.

Fred struggled to make sense of it. The last time he'd seen Brandon alive, he'd driven away in a BMW loaded with books and records from the Frame-Up he and Winona wanted to hide. He'd just been in a terrible argument with Winona, and Ramsey had fought with him in the middle of Main Street. Now he was dead. The connection ought to be obvious. Instead, it left him as baffled as ever.

Enos reached the door and turned back to face Kate. "Just one more thing. Were you here all evening?"

"Of course I was. Why are you asking that?"

"And Fred was here with you? He can vouch for your whereabouts?"

Fred's head snapped up. "She was here with us all evening."

"You think *I* killed Brandon?" Kate's voice grew shrill.

"Routine questions, Kate. Everyone who was involved with Brandon and Joan in any way is going to have to answer the same questions."

"I'm one of your suspects?"

"It's common knowledge how much you hated Brandon. You've made no secret of that."

Maybe Kate didn't realize how angry she would make Enos by challenging him, but when she dashed across the room and positioned herself in front of the door, Fred groaned inwardly. She stuck her chin up and fixed Enos with one of her stubborn, challenging looks. Enos didn't move. Between the two of them, this could prove to be a long night.

Enos studied her for a minute with the muscles in his jaw clenched.

Kate didn't flinch. "*Winona* did it."

"How would killing Brandon now put Winona any closer to your money?"

"I don't know, but she did it."

Fred cleared his throat. Maybe the time had come to tell Enos what he knew. "I heard a couple of things earlier today you might be interested in."

At first he thought Enos hadn't heard him. In fact, he had second thoughts about saying anything when Enos finally dragged his gaze away from Kate.

"I happened to be coming out of the shoe repair shop just as Winona and Brandon were loading some boxes into the trunk of his car."

Enos didn't look as impressed with the news as Fred had expected him to. "The shoe repair shop? The one that's been closed for the last two weeks?"

"I forgot Spence was on vacation. I tried to take a pair of boots in and I happened to get caught in the doorway while Brandon and Winona argued. Naturally, I didn't want to just barge out and interrupt them."

"Naturally. But why didn't you tell me about this before now?"

"I didn't think you'd be interested. After all, you'd cleared Brandon of Joan's murder and you told me to stay out of your investigation. I didn't figure you'd want to hear a bunch of gossip."

Even with the sugar coating, Enos didn't like Fred's answer much. His face grew craggy, deep lines crisscrossed above his eyes, across the bridge of his nose, and formed twin crevices on either side of his mouth. "I think you'd better tell me what you overheard."

Fred told him, briefly. When he got to Ramsey's parting words, Enos's scowl deepened. It was a damning piece of evidence.

"Ramsey's a desperate man. As long as Brandon went ahead with Shadow Mountain, Ramsey stood a chance of repaying the money he embezzled from the bank. But when Brandon pulled out—just like Joan did—he got desperate," Fred finished.

Enos toyed with his hat brim, a sure sign of agitation. "I wish you had come to me sooner. We might have been able to save the man's life."

"I honestly didn't expect this to happen."

"From now on, if you know something material to my investigations, I expect you to come to me. Otherwise, stay out of it. No more overhearing conversations—nothing." He jammed his hat onto his head. "I've got to go. I just came to let Kate know about Brandon."

Fred pushed himself out of his chair. "Well, you've done that," he muttered.

"You say you found him at the bottom of a sinkhole?" Kate demanded.

Though it had been years since he'd last been there, Fred tried to picture the layout of the surface mine at Shadow Mountain. "I thought they'd filled that in."

"They've started reclamation, but they haven't done anything with that part of it yet. You're talking about a sixty- to seventy-foot drop in most places and no easy way to make the land stable."

"How did you find him down there?" Kate asked.

"After Winona called, we went up to the mine. We couldn't see anybody at first, but Grady and I found signs of a struggle near the edge, and we found Brandon's body below."

"So what next?" Fred asked.

"Nothing, as far as you're concerned."

"I guess this eliminates Brandon as a suspect in Joan's murder."

With a heavy sigh Enos turned an impatient face in his direction. "Don't start."

"I'm just trying to help."

"Help? All you've done the past week is make more problems for me." Enos zipped up his coat. "Don't help. Don't do anything. Just stay out of my way—please." And with that he left, slamming the door behind him.

Fred stared after it, afraid to turn around and let Kate see the pain he knew must show on his face. In all the years he'd known Enos, he'd never known him to lose his temper at him. Not really.

Granted, he'd been upset by two murders in two weeks. And he was still a touch ornery from not smoking, but everything Fred had done, he'd done with the best of intentions. He'd only tried to help. Never once had he thought that ignoring Enos's advice might make Enos's job harder.

Kate moved somewhere in the room behind him. "Well," she said bitterly, "let's hope he can do better with this murder than he did with Joan's. It's not like he has even a thousand suspects. He's got what—four? five?—and he's no further along than this after all this time—"

Wearily Fred turned to face her. "Enos Asay is the best sheriff you'll find anywhere in this country."

Kate made a contemptuous sound and turned away.

Fred turned back to the door and turned the lock. When he was certain Kate had left the room, he leaned his forehead against the cool glass and struggled with the most difficult decision he'd had to make in a long time.

At last he drew a long, shuddering breath and made a vow. No matter what happened from here on out, he would not let himself get involved in the murders again.

twenty-three

Fred turned his face toward the bright winter sunlight and felt it on his skin. He breathed deeply. The clear mountain air carried frost in it this morning; the temperature probably wouldn't get above freezing all day. Old snow squeaked under his boots as he walked the path. It had lost its moisture in the dry, icy weather and sounded more like rubber than snow.

He followed his usual path and rounded the curve near the lake where he'd found Joan's body just two short weeks ago. Hard to believe so much had happened in that time. Hard to believe the murderer had struck again, but two unrelated murders at the same time in a town the size of Cutler would be too much of a coincidence.

He didn't feel the same about Cutler or about Spirit Lake as he had two weeks ago. He'd changed. Cutler had changed. He looked at things differently now and knew he'd never be the same again.

He wanted more than anything to solve the murders. He'd put them so high on his list of priorities that he could hardly think of anything else. Someone he knew had committed murder. Twice. The thought obsessed him, to use Margaret's word for it. And he knew the murderer had to be one of four people: Logan Ramsey, Winona Fox, Summer Dey, or Tony Striker.

After Kate left tomorrow, things would get back to normal. Maybe he'd learn to be content sitting in his rocking chair every day. Maybe he'd find fulfillment looking out over the world on Lake Front Drive. And maybe he wouldn't.

He walked on. Past Summer Dey's cabin, where the smoke from her morning fire curled lazily into the cloudless sky. Past the path that led from the lake to her house. Almost past the work shed.

He stopped and looked at it. In that ordinary-looking building someone had suffocated Joan in the middle of the night. Its doors hung open on lazy hinges, exposing its interior. Fred looked around to make sure nobody saw him before he left the path.

Someone had removed the crime tape. There didn't seem to be any reason for him to stay out. Besides, he just wanted to see what it looked like.

Inside, the shed smelled slightly musty, of old wood and rusted metal tools and infrequent airings-out. Benjamin had gotten a good start on cleaning it. He'd piled boxes neatly against the sides and gathered garden tools together. But against the back wall piles of rubbish and old junk covered with cobwebs looked as if they hadn't been touched in years.

Had Joan come here with someone she trusted or had she been brought here against her will? Why had the killer chosen this spot when there were other places, perhaps more convenient, even more comfortable places along the lake? Fred would probably never know.

Someone had stacked a pile of old lumber against one wall. From one of the pieces near the top, someone had recently cut away a piece of wood. The gaping wound in the lumber looked fresh and raw. It had probably had some clue to the murder on it—skin tissue, blood, or hair—and Enos or one of the lab boys had taken it away to run tests on it.

So much junk crowded the tiny shed, the only space left where Joan and her attacker could have moved around that night was right where Fred stood. Had it happened here?

Did his foot rest on the spot where Joan's life had been brutally stolen from her?

Uncomfortable with the thought, he stepped backward just as the sound of footsteps reached his ears. Hurrying toward the doors, he reached the front of the shed just as Summer came around the corner.

She cried out when she saw him, obviously startled. "What are you doing here?"

Fred glanced over his shoulder into the shed. "Just wanted to look at the place, I guess."

Squinting through the open doors, she grimaced in obvious distaste. "Why do you want to see in there?"

"Curiosity, I guess."

"*She* hasn't been here yet. Why hasn't she come to see the spot where Joan died? She should come."

"Who? Kate?"

"The angry one."

"Kate."

"She shouldn't let her sister's life slip away without communing with the vibrations. They could tell her so much."

Fred felt sorry he'd stopped to look at the shed. Maybe if he just walked away . . .

He tried it, but Summer stepped in front of him, blocking his exit. "How do you feel about this place? What does it do to you to think that someone was murdered in there?"

"It doesn't do anything to me."

"Really? How odd. It spooks me. I haven't slept well since it happened, imagining someone attacking her, suffocating her with a garbage bag right here."

Fred's pulse quickened. A garbage bag? How did Summer know that?

"She must have been working off some powerful karma, that's all I can say."

"Karma?"

Summer stepped aside to let Fred leave the shed. She

pushed the doors closed, fastening the clasp and the padlock into place. "You know, from a previous life. Like if she was a man in a previous life and she—I don't know—maybe she killed her wife or beat her or something and now in this life, she had to pay that debt before she could progress. Only she wasn't paying the debt, so she had to be killed."

Fred tried not to let the horror that grew inside him show on his face. "This life?" He shouldn't have asked. He could have kicked himself.

"Our spirits are as old as time. Don't you feel it? I can put you in touch with your higher state of consciousness and all will be explained to you."

"I'm not interested." He already had an explanation and it had suited him just fine for seventy-two years. He shouldn't even be listening to this folderol.

"But you miss so much when you go through life only experiencing the obvious, the things your lower state of consciousness can understand. If you knew about the lives you'd lived before this one, you'd be free."

"Are you talking about reincarnation?" Every time she opened her mouth, she said something crazy.

"Don't you ever think about it? Don't you ever wonder why your life is the way it is here? Why your wife had to die and leave you alone? Or why your daughter had to marry a man she doesn't love? Karmic debt. If we don't pay the debt in this life, we'll come back again and again until we do." Her eyes burned with some kind of fanatic enthusiasm.

Fred turned away. She made him very uncomfortable. He wanted to leave.

"Haven't you ever wondered what debt you're working off right now? What you were in a previous life that brought you here?"

"No, never."

"Joan had a serious debt to work off, but she wasn't interested in making amends. She only wanted to follow her own interests. I tried to reach her, but she turned away from me. She wouldn't listen. I could see it. I could see what she needed to do, but she thought I was crazy."

He had to get away from her.

"I like to think that those of us who know each other in this life probably knew each other before and we're here to help each other. What should we do when we see someone following the wrong path? Should we allow her to keep going? Or should we take it into our own hands to help her to work off her debts?"

Fred decided not to acknowledge her; it seemed a safer course of action than actually carrying on a conversation with her. She was crazy! He took a step or two away, and when she didn't follow, he worked to increase the distance between them.

She called after him. "Don't let yourself get too upset about Joan. In the end she'll be grateful this happened."

Fred stumbled over a hidden root on the path and inadvertently looked back at her over his shoulder. Summer watched him, her eyes dreamy and glazed over.

Fear suddenly pounded in his throat. It wasn't Ramsey who killed Joan—it was Summer! She'd killed Joan, believing that she had to help her work off some ancient debt and he'd underestimated her all this time. Everyone had.

"I've got to get back," he stammered. "I still have guests."

Summer smiled. "Kate. She has much to work through herself. She's carrying a heavy burden. It's almost overpowering. She owes a lot to people. Can't you feel it when you look at her? Can't you feel the tragedy surrounding her?"

She paused and raised her arms above her head, lifting her face to the sun. "I see you every morning when you walk along the path you know. I've always wanted to come out here and talk with you." She lowered her arms and stared intently at him. "We have a lot to talk about."

Starting tomorrow he'd find a new path. Absolutely. Now

he had to get out of here as quickly as he could. He half-jogged back the direction he'd come, hoping she didn't believe he'd ever done anything that needed paying back.

He reached the house in record time, out of breath but relieved to still be in one piece. He'd expected Kate and Madison to be eating breakfast, but the house stood empty.

He checked his watch. Only eight-thirty; too early to do much of anything in town. In fact, the only place open at this time of day was the Bluebird.

As soon as he thought of it, he knew that's where Kate and Madison were. He hadn't made coffee before he went out, and Madison probably woke up ready to eat. Kate's skills in the kitchen had turned out to be practically nonexistent. Even pouring cold cereal and milk in a bowl seemed more than she could handle.

Enos would be there, too. Fred had no time to lose. He hurried toward the garage and fired up the Buick, backing it carefully onto the street. He didn't have time to waste walking when Summer might be getting ready to even the psychic scores again any minute.

Every car in town must have been in the Bluebird's parking lot when he got there. Breakfast was Lizzie's best meal of the day. He finally had to settle for parking across the street on Estes and hoping nobody would slide into the car if they took the corner too fast on these icy streets.

Most of the tables had already been claimed, but a small booth by the window and a couple of tables at the back by the rest rooms stood empty. Near the window Kate and Madison sat with Tony Striker. The child shrieked with delight when she saw Fred. Enos occupied a table with Ivan and Grady. Logan Ramsey ate his lone breakfast stuffed into a booth two sizes too small for his ample frame. And to Fred's surprise, Winona sat alone beneath the *Blue Hawaii* poster, her untouched breakfast cooling on the table while she dabbed repeatedly at her eyes with a handkerchief.

Fred dragged a chair over to Enos's table and nodded to

Ivan and Grady. "I have to talk to you," he whispered urgently to Enos.

"After breakfast. The boys and I were up most of the night and I don't mind telling you, we're tired and hungry."

"This is important."

Grady snorted and slid down on his backbone, sharing an amused glance with Ivan who raised his coffee cup to hide his smile. Couple of young bucks!

"Why don't you go get some breakfast?" Enos said. "I'll talk with you in a bit. You haven't eaten yet, have you?"

"No, but listen—"

Enos looked up from his plate, and the look on his face gave no hint of encouragement. For one split second Fred thought he saw a look in Enos's eyes, something almost secretive, a glance in the boys' direction, a nearly imperceptible shake of his head. Banking that Enos had sent him a message, Fred relented and went back to the empty booth.

He ordered white toast and an egg. Lizzie brought him wheat toast and cereal and sat it before him with a meaningful look. He barked an order for coffee at her as she walked away. She didn't look back, and he knew she wouldn't bring it.

Angry and frustrated, he tugged on his coat. It had twisted under him as he slid into the booth and pulled uncomfortably at his arms. Something hard pressed into his hip. Feeling more than a little put out by Enos's attitude, he reached into his pocket for the offending object and pulled out the pen he'd picked up several days ago by the lake. In all the excitement of the last few days, he'd forgotten he put it there.

He held it toward the light for a good look. He hadn't taken the time before to look at it well. It bore no initials or other identifying marks, but even in the cold fluorescent lighting, it looked new.

He placed it in front of him on the table where he could

study it while he ate. He slathered his bread with butter and used every drop of strawberry jam he could scrape from the little packets that came on his plate.

He timed his breakfast, watching Ivan and Grady, eating steadily but not too quickly, so as to be finished when they were. Just as he polished off the last bite of toast and Ivan pushed back his chair and Grady mopped his mouth with his napkin, George Newman pushed himself away from the counter and came to Fred's booth.

He slid in behind the table and leaned his elbows onto it. "Say, Fred, I've been meaning to ask you about that hunting rifle of yours. Didn't you say you wanted to sell it last year? Did you get any takers?"

"No, but—"

"My son-in-law's interested in buyin' hisself a rifle. I told him he could do a sight worse than to buy yours. At least he'd know it had been took care of, if you know what I mean."

Fred watched Enos wipe his mouth and hands on his napkin, settle his hat on his head, and toss a couple of bills on the table before he walked out into the cold.

George rattled on, warming to his subject. "Isn't this the one you got that buck with? What was it, an eight point?"

"Four."

"Only four? I thought it was bigger'n that. You sure it was only four? Didn't you get a bigger one the last time you went out?"

"No, George. Four's my biggest. The rifle's a good one and he's welcome to buy it, but I really—"

"Well, now, I don't know if he'd be willing to pay so much for it seeing as how you only got a four point with it when I told him it was an eight."

Through the window Fred watched Enos climb into the cab of his truck. Across the street Ivan and Grady raced away in Grady's car. Just inside the window Winona folded her napkin and stood. As she passed his booth, she nodded coldly.

"Maybe if you'd drop the price a little," George pressed.

"Look, George—" Fred tried to rise.

George raised a hand in surrender. "All right, if you're going to be that way, I'll just have to tell him you won't negotiate. But listen, I wondered whether you could show him a thing or two on it so that if he decides he wants it . . ."

Kate zipped Madison into her coat. Madison waved shyly and Fred blew her a kiss.

". . . you going to sell the scope with it? It won't be much good without the scope, will it? I'd think for that price . . ."

Tony peeled a couple of bills off the roll in his pocket and tucked them under the rim of his plate. Placing his hand almost intimately on the small of Kate's back, he guided her past Fred's booth. Madison stopped to give Fred a hug and then ran after the adults. Tony reached a hand toward Madison, but she ran to Kate's side and tugged at her coat. Kate grudgingly put out her hand, and Madison took it contentedly.

". . . course the case automatically goes with it, doesn't it? I mean, you wouldn't have a need for the case without the rifle and the scope. . . ."

Logan Ramsey sucked in his stomach and hoisted himself from the booth. He caught Fred's eye and looked away hastily.

". . . at least one box of shells, or he won't be able to try it out. You wouldn't want them in your garage once the rifle's gone, and they're probably so old, they're not worth much anyway. . . ."

Ramsey settled his tab with Lizzie and looked back at Fred once more before walking out the door.

". . . so what do you think?" George finished and leaned back on his chair.

Fred dragged his attention back to George with some difficulty. "What?"

"What do you think? About the rifle?"

"I don't know." Fred reached into his pocket for his change, left enough to cover his bill, and walked toward the door.

George scrambled to keep up with him. "He's going to want to know soon."

Fred pushed open the door and stepped out into the cold with George only a step behind.

"If he doesn't buy your rifle, he's got his eye on one in Granby. Frankly, I think yours is better—"

Behind them, Lizzie pushed open the door and called Fred's name. He turned. She took a step forward, holding the pen out toward him. He reached for it just as she let go, and it fell to the ground with a clatter. He leaned over just as something buzzed past his ear, a high-pitched humming sound and a split second later, a popping noise.

George made a funny sound, a deep, groaning noise. Fred straightened, pen in hand. Lizzie pushed past him and rushed toward George, catching him as he fell. A dark red stain spread across his shoulder and onto his chest. After that everything happened in slow motion. Fred stared at George, unable for a moment to comprehend what had happened.

Lizzie fell to the boardwalk and cradled George's head in her lap. She looked up at Fred and spoke, her mouth stretched wide as it formed the words he couldn't hear over the buzzing in his ears.

She looked down at George and then back up again. This time when she spoke, Fred understood. "He's been shot. Find Enos. Dammit, Fred, go find Enos!"

twenty-four

Margaret did not look happy. Enos had called her the minute he'd shut George into Ivan's car and sent him on his way, shoulder bandaged, to the hospital. Margaret had rushed to Fred's side, and the way she kept fawning over him, you'd have thought he'd been shot, not George.

Margaret sat with Enos on the sofa, scheming against Fred, their heads close together. Her eyes strayed occasionally to Fred's face as if reassuring herself he was still alive.

To tell the truth, Fred knew the bullet had been meant for him. George just happened to be in the wrong place at the wrong time. If Lizzie hadn't dropped the pen, if Fred hadn't bent over to pick it up just when he had, he would be on his way to the hospital. And he'd probably have worse than a shoulder wound.

But he didn't know why. What made this morning different than any other? The obvious answer—the only answer—had to be that he knew something now he didn't know before. But whatever it was, he didn't *know* that he knew it. He'd struggled with the question all day.

He rocked unhappily in his chair where Margaret had moved it, well away from the front window. She shook her head at something Enos said and rubbed her forehead with her fingertips. She looked tired.

She looked up again, met Fred's eyes, and choked back a sob, as if she pictured him lying dead on the ground. He'd never meant to put her through this. He'd never intended for somebody to want him out of the way.

Enos put an arm across her shoulder; an offer of support and comfort. But Margaret pushed his arm away and strode angrily across the room, her eyes flashing, her face accusing.

"What on earth have you been doing? Why couldn't you listen to Enos and just stay out of this mess? Now look what's happened! George has been shot, and thank God he's all right. But, Dad, it could have been you!"

What was he supposed to say? That he hadn't meant for things to get out of control? That he couldn't have stopped himself any sooner? Neither answer would make her feel better. One thing he sure couldn't tell her, after this, was that he wasn't about to back down.

He'd been drawn back into the investigation, through no fault of his own. His life had been threatened. Poor, innocent, boring George had been shot. And nothing Margaret said, nothing Enos said, would make him turn tail and run.

But they would try. He had only to look at their faces to know what they had up their sleeves. She didn't intend to let him out of her sight again. She'd inherited that nasty stubborn streak from her mother.

Enos's radio, hanging from a belt loop, squawked and crackled. He hunched over, speaking softly. No doubt coordinating the search for George's assailant. Had they asked the suspects about their alibis? Had they checked and double-checked their stories? So much to be done, and Enos expected Fred to sit here and watch it all.

Well, it wouldn't work. Fred had been shot at, and he knew the prime suspects. He could help.

He pushed himself to his feet. Immediately Margaret moved to his side and took his arm. "Are you all right, Dad?"

"Of course I'm all right," he snarled at her.

He reached for his jacket where it had landed on the sofa

earlier. Margaret snatched it away from him, her face grim. "What do you think you're doing?"

"I'm going out. I've got to talk to some people, ask around . . ."

Enos reached them in two strides, his face looking unpleasant again. "You're not going anywhere. Someone took a shot at you. Someone tried to kill you, and if you think I'm going to let you go out after that—"

"Where were they all when George was shot? Have you found that out yet? What about Ramsey? Or Tony? Have you checked the angle from the art gallery? Could it have come from there? Does Winona own a gun?"

Margaret's face crumpled. "Enos, do something with him, please. What's gotten into him lately?"

When had the roles reversed in their lives? When had Margaret decided to be *his* parent? When had it become acceptable for her to speak of him as if he were a bad-tempered teenager in need of discipline?

Enos put an arm across his shoulder. "Fred, you've got to stay here. I can't protect you if I don't know where you are at all times. You've got to stay inside."

"Who said I need you to protect me?"

Enos's face had an argument with itself, struggled to look patient, and almost succeeded. He cast an imploring glance at Margaret.

Displaying an ample amount of virtuous patience, Fred waited for Margaret and Enos to come to their senses. "Where's Kate," he asked, "and Madison? Why aren't you out looking for them? Are you sure they're all right?"

"Ivan picked them up just outside of town. He's bringing them back here right now."

"Dad," Margaret pleaded, "please be reasonable. I worry about you. You could get yourself hurt—or killed."

"What's reasonable about asking me to stay locked up here where I'm nothing more than a sitting duck? I should be doing something." He pointed a finger in Enos's face.

"And don't you go telling me I've been in your way. You and I both know that's not true. I'll admit, though, it almost worked. You almost convinced me I'd been more hindrance than help."

"Good billy hell, Fred," Enos began, "you know how much I think of you, and how much I respect you. But in this one thing—this *one* time, I'm not going to let you get your own way. There's too much at stake."

Margaret nodded vigorously.

Fred stared at her for one long minute. "I'm still your father, young lady. Don't you forget that. I'm not senile and I'm not on my deathbed and I'm tired of you acting as if I'm too old and feeble to do more than sit in this damn chair and rock."

"If you won't take care of yourself, then I'm going to have to. Running around town playing detective at your age is not rational behavior. Whatever else you may think, I love you. I'm concerned about you. Dad . . . you're all I've got left! I couldn't stand it if anything happened to you."

"Nothing's going to happen to me unless I die of boredom."

She turned away from him.

"I've tried hard not to ever dictate to you, Margaret. I made it a point to treat you like an adult from the minute you reached the age. I let you make your own decisions once you became an adult, even though you made some downright foolish ones. You've done some things I don't agree with, but never once have I demanded that you do things my way."

"This isn't the same thing at all. I never wanted to do anything that could have cost me my life. If I had—and if you hadn't stopped me—*that* would have been wrong."

Fred looked to Enos for support, to provide the voice of reason, but Enos looked away, and in that moment Fred knew he'd lost.

In all her life Fred had never felt so angry with Margaret.

Not the time she took the car before she got her driver's license and ended up broadsiding Earl Ramsey's new Cadillac. Not the time she borrowed five hundred dollars from Enos because she didn't want to admit to Fred she needed it. And not the time she turned Enos down and decided to marry Webster Templeton.

He stormed down the hall and closed the door to his bedroom with a little extra emphasis. Several minutes passed before he could make himself cross to the window and lower himself into Phoebe's old chair. What would she think of the way Margaret was treating him?

He watched the sky darken with heavy, lead-colored clouds. The trees began to sway gently as the wind rose, and he felt, through the window, the temperature drop as another storm moved toward Cutler.

Long before twilight the sky had darkened ominously, yet when Margaret knocked furtively on his door, he ignored her. He paid no attention to her imploring whispers to come into the kitchen and eat.

As the storm increased, he found himself thinking of the murders again. And the onset of this new storm mirrored his inner turbulence.

He heard Kate and Madison return, exclaiming in high-pitched voices about the shooting in town and the weather. He heard Madison, stocking-footed, run up and down the hall repeatedly and the murmur of voices in conversation.

He knew when Enos left and when Webb called demanding that Margaret return home. For the first time ever Fred agreed with him, but Margaret stayed long after the call, and Fred knew she'd have trouble later.

He heard the telephone ring and heard Margaret call Kate to take it. He heard Kate agree to meet someone—to meet Tony—so they could finish tying up the loose ends. Her schedule called for her to leave town in the morning.

Not until he heard Madison crying for Kate after she left did he emerge from his self-imposed isolation.

In the living room Margaret struggled with Madison, whose tears and frantic thrashing against Margaret's hold on her seemed out of proportion to Kate's leaving. Margaret looked up, saw Fred coming, and smiled broadly. She looked relieved until he tightened the scowl on his face, lest she think he'd forgiven her.

Surprisingly, Madison came to him willingly when he reached out his arms and burrowed her tiny head under his chin. Her body shook until her tears subsided, and even then it shuddered with an occasional leftover spasm.

Rocking her gently, he quieted her fears, intensely aware of his own uneasiness. Surely the storm had brought it on, this sense of impending disaster. The storm and the tempest earlier on the streets of this innocent, quiet town where nothing ever happened.

Margaret retreated to the sofa, her eyes wide and childlike as she watched him. His big old grandfather clock ticked in the silence, measuring time against the wind that buffeted the house. The window rattled and he jumped, unaware until that moment how jangled his nerves were. Turning a sheepish eye toward Margaret, he saw her clutching her hand to her breast.

Madison stirred on his lap and yawned, and something inside him gave way to her utter trust. Tightening his arms around her, he kissed the top of her head.

Margaret shifted position, and the scratching of her denim jeans against the crushed velvet sofa sounded loud in the ominous quiet. Their eyes met, neither one able to look away, yet neither willing to be the first to smile and forgive.

Madison reached a chubby fist to her face and rubbed her eyes tiredly. "Is Kate coming back?"

"Of course she is," Fred assured her. "She won't be gone very long."

Her wide brown eyes opened, and she looked at him earnestly, as if pleading for reassurance. "Mommy didn't."

"This is different, sweetheart," Fred said soothingly.

"Mommy didn't come back and I don't want Kate to go away, too. I want Kate to come back," she wailed.

Fred brushed her hair from her forehead. "It's all right," he said softly.

"I didn't like Mommy to go."

"Of course you didn't."

"And I don't want Kate to get hurt. Will Kate get hurt?"

"Of course not."

She settled back against him, nearly satisfied. "I don't like him very much. I didn't want Mommy to go with him. His eyes looked funny and he scared me."

"That's all over now, sweetheart." He kissed the top of her head again.

She jerked up again and looked at Margaret. "Did his eyes look funny again tonight?"

"It wasn't—" Margaret began.

"But Mommy didn't go with—" Fred said.

He stopped, vaguely aware that Margaret had stopped at the same time. His eyes explored Madison's concerned face, searching for something—anything—to tell him he was wrong.

He lifted his eyes to Margaret. Fear radiated from her face. He wanted to believe that he'd misunderstood the terrified child, but he knew. In that moment, he knew.

He tried to still his racing pulse, tried to catch his breath, but couldn't. The feeling of disaster he'd been courting all evening had mushroomed, enveloping his senses.

"Sweetheart," he said softly as he turned Madison to face him, "when Mommy went away, did you see her leave with somebody?"

Madison nodded.

"Who did she go with, honey? Can you tell me?"

Madison shook her head.

"You can't tell me?"

Another shake of the head, more vehement this time. Margaret stood and slowly crossed the room. As she approached, Fred saw his own terror mirrored in her eyes. He shook his head, wanting to stop her from coming closer, not wanting to upset the child any more than necessary.

"If I guess it, will you tell me if I'm right?" Fred pleaded.

Madison tipped her head to one side and looked at him. He tried to smile, but his lips felt stiff and unwieldy. He tried to relax his hold on her arms, aware that his fingers gripped her too tightly.

Madison nodded slowly.

"Did Mommy go away with Uncle Tony?" he asked quietly, hardly daring to voice the words.

Madison frowned into his face. "I promised I wouldn't tell anybody."

He could hear Margaret breathing raggedly above them. He struggled to stay outwardly calm, knowing he shouldn't pressure or upset Madison, and fearing the danger Kate faced if he had guessed right.

"You're not telling, sweetheart. We're playing a game. All you have to do is say yes or no—okay?"

Madison studied his face unblinking. He smiled encouragement. *Come on,* he urged silently, *come on.*

She closed her eyes. "Yes," she said softly.

Fred's heart froze.

"Kate!" Margaret breathed.

With infinite care he lifted Madison from his lap and handed her into Margaret's trembling arms. He removed the pen from his pocket and showed it to Madison. "Have you ever seen this?"

She nodded solemnly. "Tony's."

He must have seen the pen on the table at the Bluebird. He thought Fred knew it was his, or suspected it wouldn't take him long to figure it out, so he'd shot at him.

"Where did they go?" he asked Margaret.

She shook her head. "I don't know. They were going to finish signing the power of attorney Tony had drawn up for her. I assumed they'd be going up to Cavanaugh's. . . . You're not going?"

"Of course not. I'm going to call Enos and pray he can get there on time."

He punched the numbers with fingers that suddenly seemed too large for the buttons; the clumsy fingers of an old man.

No answer.

He tried again, more slowly this time, in case he'd misdialed. Nothing. He tried Enos's home number. He had to shout to make Jessica hear him over her television. She shouted back that she hadn't seen Enos all day and slammed down the receiver.

Margaret looked troubled, as if she already knew in her heart what Fred began to suspect.

He dialed the Bluebird. Lizzie hadn't seen Enos, hadn't heard from Grady all night, didn't know where they were.

Margaret clutched Madison to her and watched Fred with pain-filled eyes, as if willing him not to go. And for her, despite their earlier disagreements over this very subject, he would have stayed. But now he had no choice.

He reached for his jacket, and Margaret let out a sob of protest. "Dad, please don't."

"Kate's in danger. I have to go."

"But—" she began, then looked away.

"You're aren't going to try to stop me?" Fred asked, shrugging into his jacket.

"Could I if I wanted to?"

"No."

Gripping her shoulders tightly, he kissed her cheek and her forehead. "Keep trying to reach Enos."

She nodded. Tears slipped from her eyes onto her cheeks, leaving silvery tracks as they traveled toward her chin.

As he opened the door, she called after him. "Dad? Be careful?"

"You bet." He stepped out into the storm and closed the

door. The wind whipped furiously, tearing at his jacket, pulling his cap off his head and forcing him to concentrate on walking just to get to the car.

He stopped by the garage to get his hunting rifle and scope and the box of shells George wanted so badly. He carried them in the front seat with him and propped the unloaded rifle against the passenger door, praying he wouldn't have to shoot anything.

Sheets of ice covered the roads, and he drove more rapidly than felt comfortable. He scanned the streets for Enos's truck, for a sign of Grady or Ivan. But by the time he made the left turn and headed up the mountain, he knew he was on his own.

twenty-five

The wind howled around him angrily, pushed at his car as if it were nothing more than a toy. He gripped the wheel, fighting against the wind and the black ice on the highway. Thank goodness it hadn't started to snow yet.

Seven-thirty. He'd been on the road over half an hour already, and only now did he see the turnoff to Cavanaugh's place.

Had Margaret reached Enos yet? He hoped so. With luck Enos might get here not far behind him. With luck.

As a precaution, he shut off the car lights and continued up the drive in the dark. He had difficulty making out the edges of the forest and had to force himself to drive slowly, hoping the sound of the car approaching wouldn't carry into the house.

It loomed before him, ablaze with light. The glow radiated from every window, warm and inviting and golden. Fred's spirits soared. He'd made it in time. The place looked ordinary and inviting.

He relaxed a little, feeling the tension leave his back and neck before he noticed the back door swinging open in the wind. A chill crept down his spine.

Soundlessly he pushed open the car door, holding his hand over the dome light. He eased the door closed until he heard a faint click and walked as quickly as he could across the frozen mud to the open door. He left the rifle in the car, not wanting to start trouble by appearing at the door with a gun. But he would have felt safer with it.

Steadying himself, he looked into the kitchen. Disarray greeted him. Two chairs lay on their sides, overturned in a mess of flour, sugar, and rice that must have come from the now-empty canisters on the floor. The breakfast counter had the appearance of having been swept clean, but everything lay scattered on the floor.

He was too late. He couldn't pretend any longer that Kate wasn't in danger. Whatever happened here, it hadn't been an accident. These were the signs of a struggle. Could she have been through this and still be all right? Or had she been injured?

He tiptoed into the house, his heart racing high in his throat, his mouth dry. Silence stretched before him, deep silence. And the absence of sound, so absolute and unnatural, heightened his awareness of the danger.

Where were they? Surely he would have heard them by now if they'd been in the house. Unless the house was too large for that. Or unless they'd heard him arrive.

He stepped cautiously, careful not to slip on the mess. He needed to find them—quickly.

He stole into the hallway and peered into the living room. The earlier disarray had disappeared; the paintings, the crates and packing material. It looked as pristine as it had the day Enos came to break the news of Joan's death.

At the back of the house he found the office, and he found signs of the struggle here, too. Files had been emptied onto the floor. Desk accessories—stapler, scissors, pencils, and pens—lay scattered across the floor.

His own breathing sounded so loud he could hardly draw a breath, fearing that it would give him away and endanger Kate. He pictured her, terrified and hurt, and remembered Joan's death.

Turning away from the desk, he saw a small, dark spot on the carpet. Apprehension nearly choked him, but he crouched beside it and touched it. His worst fears were confirmed. Blood.

Another spot appeared near one of the chairs by the desk, and another. For the first time he noticed a small trail of blood leading toward the door. Then it stopped.

Kate's blood? He fought back the fear and forced himself to move on. Frantic now, he searched the two upper floors of the house. Though every light had been left on, he found no sign of either Kate or Tony.

In a way he felt curiously relieved. As long as he didn't come upon Kate's body, he might still be in time to help her.

Hurrying back down the stairs, he cursed at his old knees and legs and how slowly they made him walk. If only he could run, but even his best efforts yielded little in the way of results.

He went out the front door and hurried back into the night. For the first time he realized that all three of the Cavanaugh vehicles stood in a row in the parking area.

His lungs burned as he gasped for breath. He'd pushed himself harder physically, trying to hurry, than he had in a long time. He listened, hoping for a sound that would tell him where to look next, but the wind moaned too loudly for any other sound to carry. Even if Kate could cry for help, he'd never hear her.

If the cars were here, Tony and Kate had to be close. Suddenly, in the distance through a break in the trees, he made out a faint light moving jerkily as a flashlight would in the hands of someone walking a rough mountain path.

Wrenching open the car door, he took his flashlight out of his glove compartment. Perching on the edge of the seat, he opened the box of shells and loaded his rifle with trembling fingers. He'd done it a hundred times before, but not since the war had he contemplated shooting another human being. Even now, he wondered what he would do when he finally found Tony.

As quickly as he could, he followed the path, unsure at first where it led. Not more than fifty feet from the house he found footprints, and he closed his eyes, thankful that there were two clear sets. One, bold and strong, a man's prints, had sufficient space between each footfall to convince Fred he moved with speed. The other set stumbled erratically.

Why didn't Kate fight him? Why didn't she break away and run? It made no sense to Fred, who knew Kate only as the feisty, stubborn, strong-willed woman who would never do anything subservient. Yet it didn't look as if she'd struggled since they got outside, and he couldn't be certain whether she'd fought him in the house or whether Tony had done all that damage by himself.

But the only way Kate would do *anything* without a fight was if she'd been forced. Because Tony had already shot at Fred, he couldn't rule out the possibility that Tony was using that gun on Kate to get what he wanted.

Behind the Cavanaugh property the path rose and fell, wound in and out of the trees, and headed north. Fred's boots clung to the ice and snow as well as anything he owned, but not well enough to give him any real traction. Still, it might be enough. In Kate's fair-weather clothes, she wouldn't be able to walk fast.

The cold seeped through his gloves and bit at his ears beneath his hat. His toes numbed in the ice. Kate must be frozen. Even if Tony didn't kill her, she'd soon die of exposure in this weather.

Fred rounded a bend in the path and hit a patch of ice. His legs flew out from under him, and he slid several feet down the mountainside, stopping only when his foot hit a tree and broke his fall. For countless agonizing minutes he struggled to drag himself back up the hill to the path, but the icy surface nearly defeated him. Several times he fell back several feet and had to begin the task again. Digging his feet into the frozen ground, he hoped for enough traction to climb out. Pulling on rocks and trees with his hands, he scratched his way to the top, inch by painful inch.

On the crest of the hill he stopped to catch his breath, but he'd already lost so much time. . . . He'd never catch up with them at this rate. He'd never find them.

Pulling the frosty air into his lungs, he tried desperately to control his breathing so he could move on. Already, his arms and legs ached with the unusual strains he'd placed on them. His muscles burned. If he survived this escapade, he'd be stiff for days.

Margaret's face flashed into his mind, the way she'd looked when he left the house. Terrified. She'd probably lost control of herself by now, worrying about him. She didn't expect him to come back. She didn't expect him to survive, but he would. He had to. She still needed him. All his kids needed him. The boys—Joseph, Jeffrey, and Douglas—still needed him around.

At last his breath came easier, and he started out again. Where did this path lead? What lay north of the Cavanaugh property? No other houses lay beyond theirs, because their property adjoined the Shadow Mountain property. Nobody wanted to live near that old mine, except the Cavanaughs.

He fought the wind and ice up and down the trail until he doubted he could make it any further. His fingers burned from the cold, his lungs ached from the effort of breathing the icy air.

After what seemed an eternity, he rounded a bend in the path, and the abandoned mine yawned below him. Even in the moonlight he could see the gaping wound in the side of this once beautiful mountain.

He struggled to get his bearings. Far below on the valley floor, the two-lane highway cut through the rock. Here, it ran parallel to a shallow fork of the Arkansas River. He crept closer to the edge of the mine face and looked over. Even with part of the reclamation completed, the mountain had lost its natural protection against erosion. The entire mountainside crumbled in the face of nature's assaults.

The old mine consisted of two sections. Fred stood at the highest point overlooking the upper quarry. A hundred feet below, the lower quarry stretched toward the riverbed. Between the upper quarry and the lower, the sinkhole into which Brandon Cavanaugh had been pushed to his death gaped, a large, dark hole maybe sixty feet in diameter.

Fred crouched on the unstable edge of the mountain. The wind tore at him, coming at him from all sides. The moon disappeared behind a cloud, leaving him in total darkness except the pinpoint beam his flashlight provided.

Had he been wrong? Had Tony taken Kate someplace else? For one long, dreadful moment he thought he'd lost them. He leaned back on his heels, cursing himself. He'd been so sure. When had he lost their trail?

He swore aloud, striking his leg with his fist in frustration. At that moment the light from the other flashlight appeared far below and moved out of the trees toward the edge of the sinkhole.

How did they get to the bottom? The path he'd been on had ended here at the quarry ledge. He ran back a few feet, but he could see nothing but trees—far too many of them.

Returning to the ledge, he looked over again, holding his breath until he caught a glimpse of the light. He might still be in time, but he had to find a way to the bottom.

He ran toward the southern ledge again, and this time he found the trailhead to the lower quarry. Quickly he started down the mountain, trying not to give himself away by making too much noise, but aware that he had, at the most, a few minutes before Kate met her death.

His foot slipped on an icy patch of ground, and because he was moving too quickly, he couldn't catch himself. His knee stretched, twisted away from his body at an impossible angle, and he fell to his other knee in pain. The rifle slipped from his hands and slid on the ice down the side of the mountain. He lunged for it, but pain in his leg forced him to his back.

He lay there for several seconds blinking back tears, knowing that each moment wasted on self-indulgence could endanger Kate's life, but unable to move. He gritted his teeth and forced himself to test his knee. The slightest movement brought a groan to his lips, and he wondered whether he would be able to get to his feet again.

Using the trunk of a small aspen tree for leverage, he tried to pull himself up. Pain tore at his knee and clutched at his abdomen, making him retch. He stopped halfway up and gave in to the nausea, but refused even then to slide back to the ground.

When the feeling passed, he forced himself to stand. Still holding the tree trunk, he tried to step, but his knee buckled beneath him and nearly sent him forward into the snow. Now what? He was hurt, useless, and unable to help Kate.

But he had to. He couldn't count that Margaret had been able to reach Enos. If he didn't reach Kate, she would die.

He managed to break a fairly sturdy limb from a nearby dead tree. Using it to steady himself, he made his way down the path. Every step caused his knee to throb and burn. Every jarring movement sent waves of agony up and down his leg.

At last he reached the end of the path and saw Tony and Kate silhouetted just a few feet in front of him at the quarry's edge. Sending a prayer of thanks upward, Fred moved slightly off the path, nearly biting through his lip as every movement on the uneven ground jarred his knee.

Though he managed to get close enough to see them clearly, the wind carried away their voices. Tony leaned close to Kate, his manner threatening. He pushed her toward the ledge, and for one sickening moment, Fred thought he would push her over, but he pulled her back and tipped his head back, laughing. He slapped her roughly and laughed again.

Look at him. He enjoyed hitting her and making her afraid. The sight of him sickened Fred. Tony had lived for years off Joan's bounty, a parasite. But he'd killed her when he saw his meal ticket disappearing into the mist with Joan's threats of divorcing Brandon.

Fred watched Tony as his face twisted with rage. What did he want from Kate? He'd lured her up here to get her power of attorney for Shadow Mountain—something she'd been only too willing to give him a few hours ago. What had changed?

He must have wanted something more from her, something she refused him. But other than the power of attorney—to deal with some minute portion of Shadow Mountain—what did Kate have that he wanted?

Madison.

With Kate out of the way Tony would be her only surviving relative, and he would have it all. He would own Shadow Mountain and control Madison's trust until she reached twenty-five, and by that time there would be nothing left.

Whatever he did, Fred had to save them both. But having him on their side didn't seem like much. Even if his knee had been in working order, he didn't see what he could do. If he tried to reach Kate, Tony would send her over the edge to her death. Or shoot her. Or shoot him.

Cursing the loss of his rifle, Fred realized he had no weapon except his tree branch while Tony had a lot going for him. He had youth and strength. And he had Kate as a prisoner. Other than the element of surprise, Fred didn't have one thing in his favor.

Tony pulled Kate to her feet and held her by her thin blouse, her face close to his. His mouth twisted with words Fred couldn't hear. He pushed her away roughly, and she fell to her knees.

Tony moved slightly, turning away from Kate until moonlight glinted off the metal in his hands. Fred had been right—he still had the pistol.

Where in the hell could Enos be? Hadn't Margaret found him yet? He was probably with the boys, safe and warm in the Bluebird having a piece of Lizzie's carrot cake and a cup or two of coffee when they should be out here doing their jobs.

He couldn't wait much longer. He'd have to do something soon or Kate would die. And then, without warning, Fred's time ran out. While he watched in horror, Tony raised the pistol and pointed it at Kate's head.

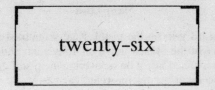

twenty-six

Fred heaved himself up, using the branch for leverage. He'd never make it in time to stop Tony from shooting Kate, but if he could distract him, it might buy a little time.

Fred limped toward them, each step agony, each step incredibly slow. Miraculously, Tony didn't hear him coming. As if he watched himself in slow motion, Fred plodded on.

For some reason Tony hadn't pulled the trigger. If Fred could reach them before Tony saw him, he might still be able to do something to save her. Knowing he'd have to hit Tony hard enough to knock him out, Fred raised the branch and swung it backward over his shoulder.

Closer. He needed to get closer before he struck. If he struck too soon, he wouldn't hurt Tony enough.

Kate hadn't seen him yet, either. Shadows from the trees hid him for a few feet, but once he left their protection, Tony would see him immediately.

He lunged, the branch poised to strike, when Tony turned. Aware of Fred for the first time, the younger man ducked and leaped to one side enough to deflect Fred's blow. It landed on Tony's arm with a sickening crack.

Fred knew he'd hurt him, but not enough to stop him. Tony turned, ignoring Kate now, the pistol aimed at Fred's chest. Fred stopped.

Kate scrambled up and threw herself at Tony's legs, knocking him slightly off balance. Surprised by her attack,

Tony lost his grip on the pistol. Kate scrambled after it as Fred brought the branch down on Tony's left shoulder.

Tony remained intent on recovering the pistol. Struggling with Kate for it, he overpowered her easily. He wrenched the gun from her grasp and shoved her toward the edge of the sinkhole.

She scrambled to maintain her foothold, her arms swinging wide, her feet seeking purchase on the loose dirt. Fred lunged toward her, grabbing for any hold that would keep her from falling over just as Tony's fist crashed into his face.

His vision blurred. Kate's scream tore through the air. Before Fred could clear his sight, Tony's fist hit him again, this time in the stomach. His breath left him. He gasped, desperate for air, but his stomach clenched and refused to allow his lungs to drag in any oxygen. He fell to the ground, doubled over with the pain in his stomach, his knee. His face throbbed where Tony's first blow had landed.

He hadn't saved her. He hadn't been strong enough to save her. He'd been a fool to come up here alone; an old fool.

He took tiny breaths, trying to regain control of his body. Gradually he realized Tony had left him. Or maybe he stood over him with the gun poised and ready to fire if Fred moved. Then he'd have everything.

Fred thought of Madison. Of her innocent little face and her trusting nature. He imagined her with Tony, growing up and learning from him. He thought of her, unloved and unwanted except for what Tony could buy, and fury rose like bile in his throat.

He'd be damned if he'd let that parasite get her. He'd die first.

He tried to pull himself up slowly, but his knee wouldn't hold his weight. Curiously no gunshot exploded, no blows landed. Gathering strength, he lifted his head and scanned the shadows. Nothing. Where had he gone?

No sound reached his ears other than the wind in the

trees. He'd never be able to stand on this knee. He'd damaged it too badly. He'd never get back down the mountain for help, and help might never find him up here.

A faint click sounded in his ear. Tony hadn't gone anywhere, but stayed nearby with the gun, just waiting for Fred to make a move.

He laughed, a low, chilling sound. Subhuman. "Don't try it, old man."

Fred looked toward the sound and saw Tony standing over him, the barrel of the gun ominously close to Fred's head.

"What do you think you can do? An old man running in here like Superman to the rescue. I can't believe it." He laughed again, amused by his own joke. "Well, you didn't make it. She's gone and now you're gone."

Fred waited for the blast, but nothing came. He let out his breath slowly.

"You'll never get away with it."

"I already have. Three times. And nobody even suspects me." His eyebrows rose and fell as he talked. Up and down. Fascinating.

Fred rubbed his knee and tried to relieve some of the pressure. "I did."

"Like hell!"

"Why do you think I'm here? I'm not out for an evening stroll. Enos knows where I am—in fact, he's probably out there watching you this very second."

Tony brought the barrel of the gun closer to Fred's temple.

Fred knew he should be afraid. He should be absolutely terrified of this maniac with the gun, but for some reason he felt curiously calm. And he noticed the strangest things. About Tony and the funny way his face moved when he talked. About the gun and the way it wavered slightly as Tony's unsteady hand pointed it at his head.

He rubbed his knee again and looked into Tony's eyes.

Funny how they looked so empty, as if his soul had left his body. Opaque eyes. What would Summer Dey have to say about that?

His knee felt swollen. He'd be in big trouble with Margaret over this. And Joseph. And Jeffrey. They'd probably want to put him in a home.

"Get up!" Tony prodded him with the gun.

"I can't."

"I said get up!" Tony screamed, and the gun wavered a little.

"I'm hurt."

"You stupid old man! Get on your feet! Now!" Rage had control of him. His face twisted and pulled as he shouted, his mouth wide.

With a peculiar sense of peace Fred tried to push himself to his feet. One last chance, he told himself, but his knee would never hold him.

As it buckled, he fell forward, throwing himself toward Tony with every ounce of strength he had left. With a roar of pain he pushed off with both legs, aiming at Tony's midsection, and prepared himself for the shot he'd been expecting all night.

It didn't come. Tony hadn't expected him to do anything. Caught off guard, he lost his balance. His arm flew wide, and with it, the gun, and for the first time Fred knew he had a chance.

Fred brought his arm up, catching Tony in the neck and pressing back with all his strength against his throat. Tony fought, but his blows did little more damage. Fred was fighting for his life.

Hatred twisted Tony's face into a demonic mask. He swore, threw expletives into Fred's face like weapons. He twisted and pushed and kicked, but Fred found strength he'd never tapped before and held on, pushing with all his might until Tony's breath caught and his eyes began to bulge.

Footsteps, heavy rapid footsteps, came from behind. And

shouting. And the sound of something heavy moving through the trees, but Fred would not be distracted.

He had to hold on. He had to prevent this man from killing or hurting anyone else. For Kate. For Madison.

He heard someone shouting his name.

He saw Kate falling over the rim of the ledge again and again, and he wanted to hurt this man for all the damage he'd done. Joan and Brandon and Kate and poor, boring old George.

Someone pulled his arms from behind and shouted at him, "Fred!"

"Fred, let go! Good billy hell, Grady—get his other arm and pull him off before he kills him."

Gradually, through the mists of fury that still swirled around him, he realized that Enos had arrived. Finally. But his arms and legs wouldn't obey his foggy mind. He didn't release the grip he had on Tony, didn't pull his arm back.

When they dragged him off Tony, one on either side, his knee gave out and he staggered. Grady gripped him with one arm around his waist, the other on his arm and held him while Enos checked Tony. Apparently satisfied he was still alive, Enos brought out his handcuffs and locked them around Tony's wrists.

Fred's throat burned too much to speak, but he needed to tell them about Kate. He dragged cool air into his blistered lungs and croaked, "Kate." He couldn't manage anything more.

"Where is she?"

Fred lifted his arm to point toward the edge of the sinkhole and found, to his surprise, that his limbs shook almost uncontrollably.

Ivan hurried to the edge of the quarry. Using a high-powered flashlight, he searched from the ledge. A minute later he disappeared over the side.

Grady watched, his eyes wide, like a puppy on a leash.

"Help me over there so I can sit and get yourself over there to help him."

Grady shook his head, disappointment coloring his features. "That's all right, I'll stay with you."

"I don't want you to stay with me, you young whelp! If my knee wasn't so torn up, I'd kick you over there myself. Just help me get over to that rock, then you get yourself over there and do your job."

Grady didn't need to be told twice. Flashing Fred a look of gratitude, he raced to help.

Tony, rousing himself, struggled against the restraints they had on him. "That old man's crazy, Enos. He attacked me—just came out of nowhere. I want him arrested. He nearly killed me."

Enos firmed up his grip on him and shot him a look of disgust. "Shut up, Tony."

"He killed Kate," Tony raged. "He attacked us both. I think he's your murderer, Enos. He's crazy. I brought her up here because she wanted to see the place. She wanted to see where Brandon died. I was showing her the mine, describing the construction that's scheduled to start in May when he came out of nowhere and attacked us. He pushed her over the side." His voice had reached a high-pitched whine.

"Shut up, Tony. For your own sake, just shut up."

From far below came a shout, too far away to hear clearly. The boys had found something. Fred hoped against hope that they'd found Kate alive, but he didn't dare believe it. This same fall had killed Brandon; how could she survive it?

The minutes ticked by, long, agonizing minutes while they waited for word. The pain in Fred's knee grew steadily worse until it nauseated him.

Finally the shouts grew nearer. Gravel skittered down the eroded side of the sinkhole and at long last, Grady's head appeared. "We found her! She's hurt, but she's alive."

Relief washed over Enos's face and Fred's entire insides. Alive. He had hardly dared to hope.

"Tony Striker," Enos said grimly. "I'm placing you under arrest for the murders of Joan Cavanaugh and Brandon Cavanaugh, for the attempted murder of Kate Talbot, and for assault with a deadly weapon upon the person of George Newman. You have the right to remain silent . . ."

twenty-seven

Fred leaned back against the pillows propped behind him and smiled at the picture of Phoebe in her wedding dress that had graced the corner of his dresser for the past forty-nine years. From behind the protective glass she returned his gaze, and he remembered her just as she had been the day the picture was taken.

He adjusted the leg brace, pulled the quilt up under his chin, and reached for his copy of *Vengeance Trail*. A car door slammed in the driveway followed by the strident notes of Jessica Asay's high-pitched voice—complaining, as usual. Something about an episode of "The Love Boat."

Benjamin poked his head into the room and grinned. "Mrs. Asay's here with Enos, Grandpa. Can you hear her?"

Fred grinned back and nodded.

"Mom's got your breakfast ready. She told me to tell you."

Sixteen-year-old Sarah bumped into Benjamin with the breakfast tray, and Fred leaned back, savoring the aroma. For the third morning in a row Margaret had made him bacon and eggs, toast with butter and jam. And coffee.

Deborah peeked shyly through the open door. "You know what Daddy said this morning, Grandpa? He said you're a hero. He did, didn't he, Sarah?"

Incredible praise coming from Webb.

Jessica Asay's voice grew louder. Somebody must have let her in the house. But as long as they didn't let her in his bedroom, he didn't care.

He buttered his toast and dug into the jam dish. "What time is Kate getting out of the hospital?"

Sarah perched gingerly on the foot of his bed. "They said she'll be here any minute. Mom said she made such a fuss the hospital let her out early."

"Kate? I can't imagine."

The coffee tasted wonderful, earthy and rich—almost as good as it smelled.

Jessica Asay had found the television and tuned in to the closing credits of "The Love Boat."

Enos poked his head through Fred's door. "Need company?"

"I've got the best company a man can ask for right here, but I can always use more."

Enos clapped a hand on Benjamin's shoulder and pulled the boy toward him for a hug. "Guess we can't keep your grandpa down, eh?"

From outside, the rhythmic sound of a snow shovel being plied against the walks signaled Webb's presence. About time he did something useful.

Madison padded into the bedroom on stockinged feet, a tube of lipstick in one hand, the contents of it all over her face. "Where's Kate?"

Sarah shrieked and dived after the child, but Madison could run faster. Deborah chased after them.

Fred closed his eyes and basked in the commotion. This house hadn't felt so full of life since before Phoebe passed away. It was time for things to get back to normal. The noise felt good. The running feet, the television, the telephone— all of it.

"You going to be all right?" Enos asked when the children had gone.

Fred opened his eyes and stared at him long and hard. "I swear, Enos, the next time you ask me that, I'll . . . join up as one of your deputies."

Enos smiled and took his battered old black hat off his

head. "The county attorney stopped by to take a statement from Tony this morning. He still denies everything, even with Kate's testimony."

"He's not stupid."

"I guess not, but I don't know how he thinks he can get off."

"Because he's gotten away with everything he's ever done in his whole life. The guy's a bloodsucker. But I still don't understand why he killed Brandon."

"Best I can figure," Enos said, leaning against the dresser, "Brandon realized Tony killed Joan and made the mistake of letting him know it. Until then, I think Tony just planned to let Brandon divert Madison's money into whatever project Tony dreamed up for Basin Development, and from there he'd make sure it got into his own pockets. Once Brandon figured it out, he had to go, and with Brandon out of the way, Kate controlled Madison's money. He either had to get control of it from her, which he tried to do with that power of attorney, or get rid of her."

"He almost got away with it."

Enos's face crumpled into a scowl. "I was right on his trail."

"Of course you were."

"Another few hours and I would have figured it out—in fact, I would have figured it out a darn sight faster if I hadn't had to waste so much time trying to keep your nose in its place."

Fred pulled himself up rigidly. "You old windbag! If I hadn't pointed you in the right direction in the first place, you'd have written Joan's death off as a suicide and you know it."

"I never suspected it was a suicide. Not for one minute. I knew the minute I laid eyes on her she'd been killed, but I have to work around the law. I can't just go haring off in some cockeyed direction whenever I feel like it."

Fred snorted in derision. Enos glared, but beneath the

scowl his eyes held a twinkle. Their relationship would never be the same. Fred liked it better this way. But he still would have liked him for a son-in-law.

"I drove past the art store on my way over here this morning. Winona's gone."

Fred had expected it. With Joan and Brandon dead, Cutler held no fascination for her any longer. No doubt she had more exciting roads to travel.

"You'll never guess who bought the place from her." Enos smiled mischievously.

"I can't imagine."

"A friend of yours."

"Who?"

"She's busy as a bug in there—got her paintings in the windows and everything."

Enlightenment began to dawn, slowly, and Fred resisted. He had to be wrong. "No."

"She finally got those paintings back that Winona stole from her. When she heard how much they were worth, she sold them all to buy the store."

Fred groaned.

"She's changing the name. Going to call it the Cosmic Tradition. Art gallery and New Age bookstore. Right here in Cutler—imagine that! Oh, she said she wanted you to have this." Enos held up a book from behind his back. *Reincarnation and the Elderly. Where You're Going Next.* "I didn't know you were interested in this stuff."

Fred buried his face in his hands. Margaret poked her head into the room, still checking on him.

"In fact," Enos said, "she said to tell you she has a lot of reading material you'll be interested in. She's going to drop by tomorrow with some other books for you to borrow."

Fred shuddered and looked up to meet Enos's amused eyes.

Margaret grinned broadly. "I saw her at Lacey's this morning, Dad. She wondered if you might be interested in

a job once your leg gets better. She said you'd shown an
interest in the subject last time she spoke with you."

"No."

"It would keep you busy—"

"Absolutely not."

Margaret laughed, then sobered slightly. "You've got
another visitor, Dad."

"Well, don't let anybody else in this room today. I've had
all I can take from jokers like this one here."

"You'll want to see this one."

She stepped back and Kate stood in the doorway looking
like she'd been tossed off the edge of a cliff. One arm hung
in a sling, her face and neck had been scratched and bruised.

"I won't ask how you are," she said softly. "I know how
much you hate that. But I had to say thanks. You saved my
life."

"You're welcome." He studied her a minute until, aware
that he stared, he cleared his throat and asked, "So you're
heading back to San Francisco?"

"Tomorrow morning."

He'd miss her. He'd grown used to her in the two weeks
she'd been with him. Funny how much he'd learned to like
her in such a short time, how much he counted on having
her around. Now she'd leave, and when the hoopla died
down and life returned to normal, what then?

"And Madison?"

She shrugged. "She'll go with me."

"How's that going to work?"

"I haven't got a clue."

"You can do it," he told her and pushed himself up in the
bed. "She needs you, but you need her, too. And she loves
you, though I can't figure out why."

A shadow of her old smile crept onto her face.

"Just remember to love her. Whatever happens, just love
her. Sooner or later it'll come naturally." He paused as Ben
chased Sarah down the hallway with a snowball and

Margaret called after them angrily. "It doesn't get any better than this," he confided.

"I don't know. This would drive me crazy."

Fred chuckled. "Of course it would. It's supposed to. It's one of the ways it all works—don't ask me to explain it."

Stocking feet padded down the hallway, and the child's voice shrieked, "Kate!"

Madison reached up with two chubby arms, and Kate knelt down to meet her, still uncertain. Nobody had washed the lipstick off Madison's face, and Kate pulled back a little as Madison's arms wound themselves around her neck.

She had such a long way to go. How would Madison survive if Kate never relented, even a little?

"You comed back," Madison said in awe. "You *do* like me." Her arms tightened around Kate's neck.

Slowly Kate raised her good arm and brought it around until it barely touched the child's back.

Madison reached up with her ruby-red lips and planted a kiss on Kate's startled cheek. As Fred and Enos watched in silence, Kate's arm tightened, almost imperceptibly around Madison's waist until she held the child against her in an embrace.

Fred looked at Enos and saw the same look of relief he felt. Kate's eyes closed and her face reddened. To Fred's surprise, a tear appeared in the corner of the one eye he could see, then another, until they fell freely and she hugged the child to her almost desperately.

If he could have gotten out of bed, he would have left them together, but he had to sit and watch them and feel the lump grow in his own throat and blink back the burning sensation in his eyes and hope Enos didn't notice.

At the sound of another set of footsteps, determined ones Fred didn't immediately recognize, Kate pulled away and looked at him sheepishly as Fred's oldest son Joseph stormed in.

It had been a year since he'd seen Joseph. Too long. The

last time he'd come for a visit, they'd argued. He'd wanted Fred to come to New Hampshire for a visit, and Fred had refused.

He looked wonderful, tall and thin and handsome— people said he looked just like his father.

Joseph glared at him. "There you are. I couldn't believe it when Margaret called me and told me what you'd been up to. What do you think you're doing?"

Fred shrugged.

"You're lucky you weren't killed. You could have been shot! You could have frozen to death! You could have fallen off a cliff!" He whirled around to Margaret. "I can't believe you let him go off like that."

Margaret didn't say a word.

When had Joseph become such an old stick-in-the-mud? Look at him—suit, tie, button-down shirt.

"This isn't normal behavior for a man your age, Dad. You're sick. I'm sorry, but you're too old to act this way. You ought to have more sense. And you"—he turned on Margaret again—"maybe it's time somebody else kept an eye on him. . . ."

Actually, a visit to New England didn't sound so bad now. Maybe for Thanksgiving or Christmas.

". . . can't just let him wander around like that. He could hurt himself. And look at this breakfast. I thought you were supposed to cut out the cholesterol. . . ."

Of course, he'd probably miss the leaves, and that was a shame, but the holidays with Joseph and Gail and the kids didn't sound so bad. Gail made an excellent Thanksgiving dinner. Fred popped a piece of bacon into his mouth.

". . . I'm taking him home with me for a while. Gail and I have talked it over. . . ."

He wouldn't stay long. A month or two, maybe. He couldn't leave Margaret alone that long. She'd get herself into some kind of trouble without him here to take care of her.

". . . plenty of room. We've got a nice guest room, and

we're close to a senior center, where he could spend some of his time during the day with people his own age. . . ."

On the other hand Douglas had just gone through that messy divorce. He'd sounded upset and lonely the last time Fred talked to him. And he had that nice cabin on the island. It would feel a lot more like home than New Hampshire. Maybe Seattle wouldn't be so bad this time of year.

". . . if you can't control him, you're just going to have to let one of us boys take him. . . ."

Fred met Margaret's amused glance, and they shared a secret smile.